KENDRAI MEEKS

RAVENING

RED CHRONICLES
BOOK 3

Published by: Kendrai Meeks

Text Design by: The Last TK

Edited by: Laura Martone and The Last TK

Cover Design by: MIBL

ISBN-13: 978-1-953073-11-2

To Ursula K. LeGuin,

FOR DEMONSTRATING HOW LITTLE GIRLS LIVING QUIET LIVES IN TINY CORNERS OF THE WORLD, COULD CREATE HUGE WORLDS ALL THEIR OWN, JUST AS LOUDLY AS THEY DAMN WELL PLEASED.

PROLOGUE

With growing scorn, she observed the revelers in the street below. Brünhild Kline detested revels. She abhorred festivity. She disparaged all those who celebrated Mardi Gras without a care for this world or the next.

And yet, she so wanted to be one of them. It could never be, of course. Duty. Duty to herself, to her kind, and to her birthright had kept her grounded and alienated since she was a little girl. The only time she'd forgone the burden laid upon her as a red matron, indulging her heart instead of obeying her head, had laid the foundation for the battle taking shape just over the horizon. The cynical voice deep within her said this was one war her stoicism and command could not win. Brünhild persisted. She would win, *must* win. It was her *duty*.

A string of plastic beads landed by her feet where she perched on the balcony just as this thought crossed her mind, just as her *indulgence* opened the door to the suite in the background.

A metallic clack echoed off the thin, pasteboard walls covered in faded yellow wallpaper. Brünhild kept her eyes on the street below; she did not require the benefit of vision to sense his movements. His presence had always registered on a visceral level; the first time they'd met, it had been what drew her to him. Over the years they'd spent together, she'd become numb to the sensation. But now, after eight months of separation, it pricked at her, like a tantalizing form of foreplay.

Her knuckles became pearls on the railing of the balcony.

"I wasn't sure you would come."

Pietro's hands ran over her hips, his grip firm as he pulled her back into his frame and lowered his mouth to the junction of her neck and shoulder. Heat crawled under her skin, electrifying her senses.

"Could I deny you?" he mumbled against her skin.

No, he couldn't. The fact both thrilled and saddened her.

Brünhild closed her eyes against traitorous thoughts. "After what I did to you, I'm not sure how you can even bring yourself to speak to me."

He nipped his way up to her earlobe. "I understand why you banished me."

"I didn't banish *you*."

She yielded to Pietro's attempts to pull her away from the line of sight of the drunken masses below. An amorous couple on a balcony in the midst of this celebration wouldn't get a second look, but if their eyes glowed silver in the haze of night, avoiding attention might prove difficult. She only wanted *his* attention.

Her breath caught as his hands worked at the belt buckle. "The red matron banished a member of her clan who had openly defied her."

"I know."

"And yet, you still desire me."

It couldn't be a question. There was no doubt of it. Brünhild merely stated an intellectual observation.

"Blame it on my Latin blood if you must. You knew that when I chose you, you would be the only for me. It is an eternal fact." Hot breath over her eyes whispered the words that had always made her knees go weak.

And Brünhild Kline did *not* have weak knees.

"I am your sacrifice."

For the first time since Pietro had entered, a pang of guilt licked at Brünhild's resolve. She loved her husband; she had always loved her husband. But when they had decided to be together, the red matron made it clear that her first priority would always be to her clan. Pietro was already so gone on her by then, he'd have agreed to anything to be with her. Little had she known the depth to which his self-sacrifice would be forced to plunge.

"It must be torturous to you, to be…" Brünhild bit her bottom lip as her husband managed to pull her shirt off over her head. "…separated."

Bare from the waist up, she turned in his arms, ran her hands over his shoulders, and laced her fingers behind his neck. She'd never known of eyes so black, and when the silver hue overcast them, Brünhild felt no full moon could ever be more beautiful than her husband's hungry gaze.

"Each breath is death." The kiss was light, foreshadowing the rapture to come. "Reanimate me, *mi amor. Sálvame.*"

Later, as they lay in the bed, spent and euphoric, the hum and squeal of the streets unfettered by the late hour, Brünhild sensed that Pietro wouldn't remain mute on the elephant in the room much longer. At last, he invited it into the open.

"It would have been fine, if she'd been a yellow."

"Perhaps."

Pietro hitched himself up on one elbow, running the finger of his free hand over her flushed cheek. "Then why did you stop it? Do you doubt Consuela's valor?"

"Not in the least. Your cousin is a righteous hood, and she honors the yellow bloodline with her leadership. But our daughter... I cannot risk putting her under anyone else's command. Gerwalta's power will be too great, and her blood, too much of a temptation."

"Then why leave her defenseless?" Pietro queried, the smile chased from his face. "Why relinquish her powers? Is she in any less danger because she's a huey?"

Brünhild shook her head. "I *didn't* relinquish her."

From elbow to palms, Pietro jolted up, his unkempt, gray-streaked black locks flipping. "But I saw you do it. I *heard* you speak the words."

She rolled over, her gaze falling softly over memory. "There is no such thing as being relinquished. It's an old hood's tale, one we mothers tell our children to scare them into submission. I did nothing more than hit her with silver flame. It would have shocked her, temporarily damaged her, but no matron can take her power away. She believed it, and the silver flame added to the perception. The mind is a powerful thing, Pietro. Gerwalta's, more powerful than most."

No need to look at Pietro to sense his confusion. She could feel a vague sense of it tingling in the air around her. "You used silver flame on our daughter, when we both know that—"

"We know nothing," Brünhild interrupted as she slipped from the bed and grabbed her clothes from the floor. "We can't. Gerwalta isn't you, and she isn't me. There hasn't been a child like her born for centuries. Neither you nor I have any idea what the effect will be."

"There was an effect," Pietro countered. "Cody says she is relinquished. The wolves can't sense her anymore, nor she them."

Brünhild frowned; whether it was because her banished husband had just admitted to staying in contact with her custodial pack, or because he knew more about the state of their daughter than she did, she couldn't say. "The longer it takes her mind and her body to realize she's not, the better. Perhaps the Ravens will not be so eager to get their fangs on her if they believe her a huey."

"We should have told her about them long ago. Ignorance is never an excuse, but we've made it her only choice." The matron's groom shook his head. "It's already been months. How much longer can we hope for the effects of the silver flame to last?"

Through a squinted gaze, she scrutinized his expression. "Not too much longer. Besides, it could be a benefit to her for the time being, being perceived as weak. A dull blade inspires less terror, though its *potential* to kill is no less."

"Then we must hope her edges sharpen soon."

The red matron spun, her dulled pupils growing silver. "Why?"

Pietro stood, ambivalent to his nudity. Unlike her, he felt just as strong in his own skin as when he donned his hood. "They are planning on going after the Ravens."

"When?"

"After graduation. And that *boludo* wolf is going with them."

Brünhild wondered if her husband's dislike of Tobias Somfield was simply because the latter was a werewolf, or because Tobias was English. Argentines could hold a grudge.

"Good."

Any heat remaining between them dissipated with the spike in Pietro's anger. "Good? How can you possibly think our daughter spending time with that mutt is good?"

She crossed to him and planted a kiss on his pursed lips. "Because then they must come back within three months, mustn't they? Otherwise, the wolf will go moon mad. And in the meantime, Markus will shadow them."

"Markus?" Pietro repeated, as though it were a word in a foreign tongue whose pronunciation was uncertain. "You want to send Markus to Istanbul?"

One perfectly drawn eyebrow arched. "Is there something wrong with that? You know he's had some fascination with the Dracule since he was a child. He is young, but he is a fine and righteous hood."

"Yes, but he is…" Pietro smirked as his hands pantomimed whatever words could or would not come from his mouth.

"I am aware of my nephew's proclivities. It is irrelevant. He is the right man for this situation. Besides, he is more vested in her safety than any other under my command."

Her husband flinched at the implication. Banished, Pietro could offer no official duty as a member of the House of Red, even if only by marriage. Taken in by his cousin, a yellow matron, he also could not elect to make the journey himself. After the standoff with Brünhild, Consuela's readiness to upset the indomitable red matron so soon was small.

"You still hold hope that Markus and Geri will someday be joined." He side-eyed his wife. "I fear that's a stock which holds no cattle. It's against both their natures."

"What do their natures matter?" Brünhild pulled on her second boot, making the leather creak. "It was against my nature to marry you, but I did."

"And you regret every day of it," Pietro said flatly.

This was one thing of which she wanted Pietro to be certain. "I have never regretted who we are, Pietro. I've only regretted who life forced me to be, and what it cost us all."

ONE

"GODDAMN IT, GERI! DO WE LIVE WITH A YETI?"

A hot iron pressed to my feet would not have woken me faster. I found my silver blade in hand and held ready for attack. Luckily, reality caught up just in time.

Any other person might flinch at having their roommate brandish a knife. At the very least, they might give said roommate TEN FREAKING MORE MINUTES TO SLEEP IN ON THE ONLY DAY OF THE WEEK THEY COULD. Amy, however, had danced this dance before.

"Put your butter knife away. Like I said, I'm a New Yorker. It ain't a gun, I ain't gonna run."

The silver blade found its way back into the sheath hidden under the pillow. "And this is why werewolves make better roommates."

"What the hell does that mean?"

"Nothing." The pillow's warmth had already started to leach away. "It's Sunday, Amy. Why, in the name of Godric's Hollow, are you waking me up before nine?"

"Because our bathroom sink looks like the floor of a dog-grooming parlor, and your boyfriend—"

"For the five thousandth time, Tobias is *not* my boyfriend."

"Since he's your shack-up honey, then, I'm laying the ability of our bathroom to be braided at your feet."

Chances of getting back to sleep: zero.

Chances of me being required to decontaminate the bath: higher than James Franco at a Snoop Dog concert.

I rolled out of bed, pushing sleep from my eyes and eking resolve into my determination. "And for the *six thousandth* time, I'm not sleeping with Tobias."

"Methinks the lady doth protest too much."

"Fine, we are *technically* sleeping together, as in we slumber in the same room. Rarely, when we're both home and sleeping at the same time. And FYI: *He* makes his bed on the floor."

In a discount dog bed I'd brought home as a practical joke and which he actually decided he liked.

The blonde cocked a hip and twirled a braid around her finger. "Send him to my room, then. I mean, really… Minus the fact that his personal hygiene practices are seriously deficient, and that he has some sort of obsession with dumplings that I'll just never understand, why can't the two of you get together? I know his wife died, but that was, like, a year ago. Even Puritans would roll their eyes at you."

Cast the girl in one university production of *The Crucible*, and suddenly she thought she had a PhD in American history.

How could you explain to your huey roommate that the man who had been sleeping in your room since the beginning of the school year was a widower werewolf who would never love again, and that she stood as much chance of a hook-up with him as grapefruit taking on a semitruck? You didn't. You just rolled your eyes, sighed, and repeated your boilerplate response.

"Tobias and I are only friends. It's never going to happen between us, and most importantly, it's never going to happen between the two of you either. So just let it go."

Just as I turned to the coat closet to grab the bucket full of cleaning supplies, the front door opened and the werewolf with burning ears came in.

He was suspiciously unshaven.

"Ladies." Tobias pushed a cardboard tray holding two cups of coffee toward us. I had never thought that werewolves were psychic, but could there be any doubt he'd foreseen Amy's anger? "Mocha for Geri, soy milk latte with two pumps of mango syrup for Amy."

Even a werewolf would flinch when a huffy, blonde New Yorker growled.

Amy snatched the coffee away in a fit. She pointed a finger in Tobias's chest with her free hand. "This doesn't excuse anything."

And with that, she went in her room and slammed the door.

Tobias's confusion drew lines in his forehead. "What was that about?"

A methodical sip of mocha with my eyes open and staring over the rim of the cup at the werewolf proceeded my answer. "Did you shave last night before you left for work?"

"Yes, but I…" Memory called up guilt and invited it to the party. "Shite, I didn't clean out the sink."

Shoving the basket of cleaning supplies into his arms, causing him to drop the empty tray, I nodded. "*Yet*, Tobias. You mean you haven't cleaned out the sink *yet*."

A werewolf could pull off an amazing amount of reticence once you got to know them. Without further prompting, Tobias snatched the fallen coffee caddy from the floor, went to the bathroom, and began to excavate.

"Quickly, please!" I called at the door. "I just got up a minute ago, and nature is calling on speed dial."

He paused to look at me back over his shoulder. "Do you think sometimes that there's reasons hoods and wolves aren't supposed to be bosom buddies? I don't want to know about your toilet habits. We'll never be that close."

"This from the man who yesterday told me and Amy not to open Netflix until he got out of the pisser."

"That's different."

"How?"

He shrugged as the last bit of hair-flecked soap scum transferred onto the sponge. "Because I'm a guy."

"And THIS is one of the reasons why hoods are matriarchal, because we clearly are the better sex."

When I slipped back out of the bathroom a few minutes later, he took up the conversation right where it had left off.

"Speaking of sex…" Tobias grinned. "Guess who's coming back on a midnight flight?"

Any ire within me faded in the wake of such a delicious tease. "He's coming tonight?"

"That part will be up to you, won't it?" Looking all smug and superior, Tobias nodded as he deposited the bucket back in the coat closet. "Got the word from Inga's assistant last night. No idea if they found out anything, though. I don't think Clark is that in the loop on his boss's personal life."

The reminder that Inga Rosethorn was the center of WWL gossip as having a boy-toy lover, i.e., my boyfriend, Caleb Helsing, and that she regularly whisked him away to exotic, foreign locales, burned in my gut. Even though I knew the rumors were nothing, and that Caleb himself admitted that, for once, he didn't enjoy his sex-god reputation, the fact that that woman put her fangs on him regularly to drink his blood and keep herself alive still smarted.

"It's about freaking time. They were only supposed to be gone for ten days. I want to know what the hell they were doing for a whole month."

"I can draw you a chart of the mechanics, if your mother never gave you the talk."

My fingers pinged his rock-hard chest. "They are not sleeping together."

"Why shouldn't they be? After all, you and Caleb aren't."

"Oh, I see. 'Toilet habits' you want nothing to do with, but my sex life is open grounds for analysis."

"You don't have a sex life, Geri. You have to actually have sex to have a sex life."

I crossed my arms in the perfect act of childish petulance. I could tell the werewolf that Caleb and I had actually decided we'd make the beast with two backs when he came back to town, and that that, in part, was why his being gone so much longer than anticipated was so annoying, but why should I? "And just what makes you think we're *not* sleeping together?"

"Because you don't smell any different."

"I'm not going to believe for a second that makes any sense. Got any other theories?"

I almost dropped my coffee when Tobias put his arms around me and pulled me to him. Within moments, my body went into high alert. My breath hitched when Tobias lowered his mouth to mine, just inches away from kissing me. He might be an ass sometimes, but he was, in fact, a very sexy ass (with a very sexy ass) who loved to tease me with his looks. With his shoulder-length brown hair tied behind his head, his biker-inspired stubble, and a body that set off the tingles, the werewolf's human form could make a nun give up her vows.

A knowing smirk pulled taut the corners of his mouth. "Once you've been with him, I won't be able to do this to you."

I tried to keep myself in control, even as little demon voices called out inside me. *Kiss him. Take him. Be with him.*

"I'm not a wolf, Tobias. I won't bond with him that way. I won't have what you and Kara had."

The reminder of his slain mate's name loosened a bit of his hold on me. Still, his hands stayed on my waist as he tried to shake off the sadness. "If he doesn't at least make you feel like you should, then you shouldn't be with him to begin with."

Just at that moment, Amy's door opened as she emerged with a backpack slung over her shoulder. As soon as she caught sight of us, instead of going all squeaky with delight at our proximity, she just rolled her eyes and huffed.

"Oh, my god, will you guys just fuck already and get it over with? This will-they-won't-they thing is getting really tedious." Without giving me a chance to respond, Amy pushed a plain white envelope into my face. "Here."

I broke away from the werewolf to take it. "What is this?"

"Your tickets."

"Tickets?" Tobias said, moving to the fridge to grab a pint of milk to chug. We'd given up on coaxing him into using a glass months ago. "Tickets for what?"

"For my play," Amy said. "Remember? My senior performance for my drama minor? You two said you'd come cheer me on."

Nervous chuckles filled the room as Tobias and I exchanged manufactured smiles. "Oh! That's tonight? I must have forgot to put it on my calendar. But, yeah, looking forward to it."

"I'm not, but I'll be there." Tobias winced when I elbowed him in the side. He quickly got the hint and corrected his rudeness. "I mean, I don't like being in tight, packed crowds. Of course, I'll be there, Amy. It's the least I can do to thank you for letting me move in."

Amy admonished him with a glare. "The very least. Especially since I didn't *let* you move in. In fact, I remember the promise being 'it's only for a few weeks until he finds a new place.' Curtain time is seven-thirty. I have to go. We're sneaking in one more dress rehearsal before show time. See you tonight."

The second the apartment door closed, Tobias spun on me.

"Okay, two things. One, please tell Amy about Caleb so she stops trying to make you and me happen. And two: please, please, don't make me go to this."

"I can't tell Amy about Caleb. Officially, Caleb doesn't exist, remember? He's contraband. And two, I'm not making you go. I'm going to support my friend."

His knuckles blanched as his hands became fists at his side. "And de facto, that means you're making me go."

"It wasn't my decision for your alpha to order you to ensure I never went outside without a supernatural escort at night. Believe me, having you walk me to Caleb's apartment, then waiting for me outside isn't my idea of convenient."

"Well, at least we can come together on that," he huffed. Tobias leaned against the wall, disguising a yawn with the back of his hand.

"Go to sleep. *Comfortably.*"

He raised an eyebrow. "I thought you told me no more sleeping in my wolf since that time Amy almost walked in on me?"

I waved a dismissive hand. "She'll be at the theater the rest of the day. I'm just going to take a run and spend the day studying. Only have one more final exam and then I'm free."

"You're an ex-hood who's likely on the kill list of a fifteenth-century Transylvanian vampire prince. Free is the last thing I'd call it."

"Dr. Taylor's threat to my long-term well being seems more imminent at the moment. I'll grab my things from the bedroom so I don't have to come in and disturb you later."

"Actually, then, that sounds like a right good thing." Tobias's hands went to the row of buttons running down his shirt, starting at the top, opening a pathway my eyes longed to tread. Suddenly, he paused, meeting my stare. "I thought 'all the better to eat you with' was my line."

I shook my head and stuttered through embarrassment. "Sorry. I just…"

A catch of sorrow crept into his voice. "Yeah, I know. You miss your boyfriend. But maybe hold that heavy-lidded-eyes-and-parted-lips thing for Caleb. He'll appreciate it more. Now, weren't you going to take a run?"

I clapped my hands and rushed into my bedroom to ferret out two sets of clothes. "Yes! I definitely need to take a run."

And then, maybe, a cold shower.

TWO

                                        Where are you?

Walking.

                    "Walking" is a verb. The question
                    I asked can only be answered by a
                                        NOUN.

Bloody Chicago.

                    Did you have to use that word? You
                    do know I have a legendary clutch
                    of vampires who want to kill me,
                                                right?

Keep it up, and there'll be a
werewolf too.

                    Just get here already. Or should I
                    wander the streets unprotected and
                                        look for you?

"Don't you fecking dare, Geri."

Mesmerized. I was freaking mesmerized. The werewolf who had just walked into the theater lobby had two fashion modes: security uniform for when he was at work at WWL, or blue jeans and tees when he wasn't. Three, if you included fur as a mode. What Tobias did not do, or at least had not done in the time I knew him, was formal.

Where he got the three-piece suit from, I couldn't begin to imagine. The things I actually *could* begin to imagine, however, were not appropriate for a woman with a boyfriend. The man defined the term "rugged hot." His ever-present stubble combined with the dark navy of his slacks and jacket to present a rock-star-at-the-Grammys feel.

The illusion of him as a confident, easygoing playboy melted away, however, as Tobias observed the packed theater lobby. Werewolves were creatures who favored wide open spaces or forests. Crowds distressed them. Suddenly, I realized how much I was asking Tobias by being here. His heavy breathing wasn't from rushing over; it was born of anxiety.

I wrapped my hand around his and flinched when his grip tightened. "Just a bunch of hueys. No threats. Focus on me."

"I'd focus on you better if you had dressed up like I did."

"Tobias, no one is dressed up like you." I pulled him towards the entry, digging the tickets out of my pocket.

"I've never been to an actual theatrical performance before. This is how everyone dresses for the annual Royal Variety Performance they have on the telly back home each year."

"Well, on the northside of Chicago at the WCU Arts Complex, jeans are just fine. Not that any woman here between the age of eighteen and eighty is going to complain, mind. But where did you get the getup?"

"I called Igor to ask where I could get a suit on short notice. Twenty minutes later, there was a tailor at our door. Seems like being rich lets you do things like make all manner of manservants magically appear. We should definitely try being rich sometime."

The usher guided us to our seats in the third row, stage left, right on the aisle. Hopefully having access to an escape route would ease Tobias's nerves somewhat.

"If I were still a hood, I could wield silver, and make us very, very rich. Not as rich as Igor, I'm willing to bet, but comfortably cozy."

With a newfound revelation, his head swiveled in my direction as he settled into his seat. "Bullocks, I've never thought of that. Why aren't all hoods rich, then?"

"Discipline. Values," I answered. "We can't *make* silver, so what we do have, we hoard. Besides, you can't exactly toss a few ducats up on the counter to pay for things, can you?"

Other theatergoers milled around. As expected, women eye-screwed Tobias as they walked by. It was nothing new. Women were drawn to the wolf, and I frequently got acidic glares from those who thought I was touting hot property out of my price range. Normally, I'd just ignore the fact, but today, when he was already nerve-wracked from being enclosed on all sides by hueys who liked Arthur Miller, chancing anything setting off Tobias's protective instincts seemed like a bad idea.

I unlaced our fingers and drew back my hand, only to have him snatch it back and wrap the back of my hand in both his paws.

"Please." He stroked my knuckles like he was petting a cat's ears. "If it's okay?"

"It's okay." I leaned into him, easing the strain on my arm on the armrest. "Only you're going to have to put up with my head on your shoulder or my hand's going to go numb."

"You say that like it's a bad thing."

"A numb hand is a terrible thing."

He coughed a laugh as the house lights started to lower. "Always ready with a quip, aren't we?" Before I knew what was happening, and done before I believed it, Tobias turned and kissed my forehead.

The next hour and a half was the longest of my life. He never let go of my hand, and I never picked up my head. That was, at least, until the end of the third act.

I couldn't recall if Amy had shared with me many details of the play in which she was starring. For example, I didn't remember hearing her say she was, in fact, *the* star. Her ability to pull off the part of the deceptive, selfish, manipulative Abigail Williams astounded me. The character Amy played was the antithesis of her own. I wondered if her ability to render the role so believable was just her doing the opposite of what she herself would do. Except for the part where she wanted to sleep with John Proctor so bad. *That* was full-on Amy Popowitz.

Tobias leaned down to me, his voice barely a whisper. "I've seen the film version of this at least ten times. I don't remember fog."

I shrugged. We'd read it in high school in our stilted teenage awkwardness, but I couldn't stand Winona Ryder in anything. "Everything's more dramatic with a fog machine."

As the billowy clouds filled the stage, however, the growing worry on the faces of the acting company suggested the fog was assuming an unwritten walk-on role. All about the stage, college kids dressed up as Puritans looked on with utter bafflement as the low-pressure system entering stage left stole the scene.

Amy shook away her confusion, trying to recover her character and get the cast to do the same. "Oh, Mary, this is a black art to change your shape. No, I cannot, I cannot stop my mouth; it's God's work I do…"

My roomie's hands went to her throat as another of the cast members shouted out her complicated line, "Abby, I'm here!", followed by a guy I knew to be a freshman wearing a gray wig adding, "They're pretending, Mr. Danforth!"

Amy fanned herself, the fog thickest around her. "Oh, please, Mary— Don't… Don't…"

When Tobias yanked back his hand and stood, my first impulse was to bemoan the loss of my headrest. A moment later, the actors themselves began to scurry around the stage. The fog cleared for just a moment, and what the fuss was punched me in the stomach. There, nearly doubled over, stood Amy, her hands on her throat, her face red, the other members of the cast attempting to pull away the white collar of her costume as she gasped and coughed.

"Tobias?"

He didn't look at me. He didn't hesitate. One moment he was beside me, and the next, he had bounded up on the stage and had Amy in his arms, rescuing her from hitting the ground in the nick of time.

"Call an ambulance!" he bellowed, and even as he moved, the fog moved with him.

The fog moved *with him*.

"Oh, my god. Amy!"

The werewolf leapt off the stage just as the director ran on, his eyes tracking Abby Williams.

"My star! My ingénue!"

The crowd gathered in, making my stomach tighten. Tobias had been nervous in a group of this size in tight quarters; what was he going to do when he thought they might be intending to harm her? Was he going to wolf out right here and blow our cover? Would the yellow matron who controlled this territory send one of her righteous, or would Consuela come in person to terminate my friend? More importantly, what in the hell was wrong with Amy?

A man on a cell nearby put a hand on my shoulder. "The paramedics are on their way. You know her?"

I nodded. "She's my roommate."

The man acknowledged me with a jerk of his head and pressed the cell back to his ear. "Okay, I'll ask her. The dispatcher wants to know if she has any allergies."

"She's allergic to cats."

"And what medical conditions. Does she have any of those?"

"It's not a medical condition!" I dropped to my knees and tried to do the impossible. My hands strained the smoke, but I couldn't find anything tangible. The vampire who was doing this had no interest in being caught. "Leave her alone, asshole!"

Just as Amy's face went from red to purple, Tobias sucked down air so deeply, he had to arch his back to contain it. As he exhaled with all his might, the fog blew away, but not before an airy voice whispered in my ear.

You have been warned. Stay away.

And then, the vampire was gone.

THREE

"This is all my fault."

Tobias played with a strand of my hair that had come loose from my braid and fallen across my eyes. My head moved in time with the cycles of his breath. "No, it's not."

I sat up and glared at him. "So it's pure coincidence that my best friend was just attacked by a vampire in front of a large crowd?"

"Of course, it isn't coincidence, but that doesn't mean it's your fault. Don't own their shame, Geri."

I'd been arguing the point with him in the hospital waiting room for the better part of two hours. He wasn't going to budge, and neither was I. A quick sweep of the waiting room confirmed that, other than a shabby, bearded man wrapped in three layers of flannel snoozing on a pleather-wrapped loveseat, we were alone in the sterile, copacetic space. Other than the faces on some thirty-odd magazines spread out over every flat surface, no one was around to hear us.

"They know about us," I concluded, changing lanes. "The Ravens know we're coming for them. Now that graduation is near and we're about to leave for Istanbul, they're sending off warning shots."

"Seems that way."

The flat tone of Tobias's response made my head swivel. "Doesn't that bother you?"

"No, I think it's a good sign." My dumbfounded expression forced him to continue. "Of course, I'm pissed they came after Amy, but they wouldn't send a warning to us if they didn't see us as some sort of threat. Yes, Geri, they know we're coming. And now, we know they're scared."

"You know, this kind of shit is originally why I left home to come to Chicago. All I wanted was to be normal, *not* to have anything like threatening vampires or crazy wolves—no offense—hounding me. But instead of getting out of the supe world, I've only succeeded in sucking Amy into it." The memory of seeing my roomie fainting, turning unnatural colors as the life leaked from her, reverberated in my mind, sharpening my anger. "I'm going to kill Vlad myself."

Tobias grinned and pulled me back to his chest, kissing my forehead and encircling me with his arms. "That's my girl."

A rush of warmth flowed through me, and for a moment, it was almost like I'd recaptured my hood senses. My eyes tilted up to Tobias's; his beard didn't hide his smile. Was he feeling it too? The glow of it overpowered my senses. I opened my mouth to speak when a bell rang, followed a moment later by the elevator doors at the far end of the lobby opening.

I was out of my seat the moment he appeared. Igor, grinning in amusement, sidestepped Caleb and I as we devolved into hormonal creatures, more octopi than humanoid. Even if it was a hospital, truth was truth: I hadn't seen the guy in a month.

"Thank god you're okay." The slayer covered my face in kisses as I wrapped my arms about him. "You are okay, aren't you?" Another kiss on the cheek, another on the nose, all as I bobbed my head to answer his question. "I was so worried when you called. Igor picked us up and brought me straight here. Damn it, I missed you, Ger-

Bear."

The woes of the world took a respite when his mouth finally lowered to mine. Caleb's kiss was like the man who gave it: full of sunlight and warmth, and as likely to set me afire. I allowed myself three seconds of dismissing everything that existed besides him and me. When Igor started to get the rundown from Tobias, however, the time and place slapped me back into the moment.

"It was one I hadn't smelled before," the werewolf was saying to the patron of the Dracule line. "Musky, spicy, like a shop that sells incense."

"And the accent?" Igor asked, his eyes unfixed as he sorted through his memories.

Tobias shook his head. "I didn't hear it. Only Geri did."

That was news to me. Caleb and I uncoiled as I walked toward the vampire and the wolf. "What do you mean, you didn't hear it?" I asked. "Your hearing is, like, ten times better than mine, and it was so loud."

Igor repeated my previous scan of the room. He must have considered the other occupant as little a threat as I did. "A smoked vampire can finger into your ear. It can seem like he's talking right into your brain. Even a werewolf would have difficulty overhearing. Did the voice appear to be male or female?"

"Male," I grumbled. "I didn't recognize the accent. Then again, the only ones I'm fully aware of are Yooper, Argentinian, and British."

"English." Even under present circumstances, the wolf would still correct me on that. "Igor, any ideas?"

The vampire bit his bottom lip. "It's not enough to go on. I might be able to get more clues when I talk to Amy."

If I had hackles, they'd be raised. "Why do you need to talk to Amy?"

His deadpan expression was tinged with pity. "To learn what she experienced, and then to erase her memory, of course."

Instinct drove me to step up and block Igor's path—even though he made no movement toward the patient area. "I don't *want* her memory erased."

Igor chuckled. "Geri, please. We can't have an innocent huey running around with the recollection of being fogged by a vampire. At best, other humans think she's crazy. At worst, she develops PTSD from her near murder. Think how traumatic this must be for Amy. Don't you want her to never have to deal with that again?"

The truth lingered in those words. I knew it, and I couldn't deny it. Having lived my life as a huey for the better part of a year, however, gave me a little more sympathy for their powerlessness when faced with a supernatural threat.

"This wasn't a random attack. The Ravens did this, and unless we're willing to capitulate, I don't see why they'd consider Amy any less of a target if we go forward with our plan to track them down. Once we leave for Istanbul, Amy's going to be on her own. The only thing that will possibly protect her from another attack is her instinct to be afraid. You're not going to do anything that dampens that at all. Her life may depend on it."

"But—"

I cut off the vampire's argument with the tip of my silver blade pushed to his throat. Just because I was a huey didn't mean I'd stopped being prepared. The only thing sharper than it I could wield was my glare, which I did.

"It's not negotiable."

"Understood." Nonplussed, Igor stepped back. My blade couldn't inflict any mortal wound on him, but it wouldn't exactly tickle. "In that case, it's on you to tell her something that lets her process this. What, prithee, do you think you can say to her?"

Tobias, who'd slunk back to the least comfortable chairs ever, spoke up. "You could tell her the truth."

The ballsiness of the statement made all three of us turn to see if he'd grown a second head.

The werewolf shrugged. "Igor's right; her memory should be wiped. But if you're not going to do that, then…"

"*Et tu*, Brute?"

Tobias grimaced. "I don't speak Greek, hood."

"It's Latin," Caleb corrected with no little amount of smugness. He did so enjoy any opportunity to outshine Tobias. Which, given his slick sophistication, was frequent. "I agree with Geri. Fear and braveness are powerful defenses when paired. The question is *what* to tell Amy, not what to make her forget. It should be something powerful, but not traumatizing."

"She just was traumatized. Or what would you call a huey being—"

Tobias cut himself off as his eyes scanned the room and focused on the corridor which led to the exam room. A moment later, Igor assumed the same stance, then Caleb. What they could hear I now relied on huey-powered eyes to confirm. A russet-skinned doctor, equipped with a stethoscope and a clipboard, studied each of us in turn.

"I'm Miss Popowitz's doctor. Are any of you a family member?"

Igor stepped forward, and even without being able to see his face, I'd grown to recognize the shift in the air that occurred whenever he took someone under thrall.

"We're all family members," the vampire said, pointing at first himself, then each of us in turn. "I'm her father, that's her sister and brother, and her sister's boyfriend."

The doctor twitched, his mind fighting Igor's influence. Finally, after several tense moments in which I was beginning to mock up a case of the whinnies to get past administrative red tape, he coughed. "Yes, of course. Well, we just wanted to let you know, she's fine. We're still not certain what happened. Our leading guess right now is there was a malfunctioning fog machine that hadn't been cleaned out in a while. If untended, those things can become little breeding grounds for molds and bacteria. We're still waiting for a few more routine tests to come back, but she should be ready to go home shortly. As a precaution, she shouldn't be home alone tonight, just in case there's something we missed. Will any of you be staying with her?"

I stepped forward. "Yes, of course, I will."

Caleb's shoulders fell. He didn't hide the frustration he felt. No doubt he, like me, had anticipated tonight being a milestone in our relationship. What was to be done, though?

Meeting his eyes, I mouthed to him "tomorrow night."

The doctor acknowledged me with a nod. "Good. Just be sure she gets a good night's rest, and don't hesitate to give us a call or come back in if she has any problems tonight."

FOUR

Back home a few hours later, Amy hit the *end* button just after three AM. I'd never met her parents; George and Katrina Popowitz didn't care for Chicago, and despite repeated efforts, I'd never succumbed to Amy's attempts to drag me to New York City. Nevertheless, it spoke to their credit that they took a call from their daughter in the middle of the night and that they had to be convinced three times in the ten-minute conversation not to hop a plane and come force her into passive convalescence.

"I guess I'll head to bed, then." Amy smiled and reached for me. Or at least, I thought she was reaching for me. When her hand settled on Tobias, however, I wasn't the only one who felt the awkwardness about us sharpen. "Thank you, but next time I'm about to pass out on stage and you sweep in to save the day, I insist… Don't hesitate to perform CPR. Mouth-to-mouth saves lives every day."

Tobias grinned, a gleaming set of teeth setting my own irrationally on edge. "Glad to see you're okay."

As Amy's cheeks blushed, and she turned way too coquettish to be talking with a grieving werewolf, my concern for her health took a nosedive. Amy let out a little yelp when I pushed her toward her room. "Your doctor said you needed rest. Go rest."

"But you guys seem wide awake, maybe we can just stay up and hang out?"

I clicked my tongue. "When you're the one with the PhD in

medicine that says that, we'll do it. Good night, Amy."

Tobias admonished me when I'd shut her door.

"What?"

Annoyance colored his words. "Let the poppet have a little comfort."

"Oh, my god. You have never sounded more British than you do right now."

"I'm not…"

"British." I dismissed him with a wave of my hand as we both made our way into my bedroom. "Yeah, I know. All I'm saying is, I know Amy's I'm-coming-on-to-you script. You're too sweet to shoot her down, so I did it for you."

"Just because I can never love again doesn't mean I don't like to be flirted with." Tobias closed the door and locked it—a precautionary normalcy since the time Amy had nearly walked in on him wearing his wolf. "This wouldn't be an issue if she understood *why* I could never be with her."

I paused at the closet, a hanger in hand as I took off my sweater. "I thought we discussed that back at the hospital."

"I said one thing, you said something different. That's not a discussion, it's an opening statement." His finger went to work trying to loosen his tie, but all the effort resulted in was a tighter knot. "Bollocks! Do you see now why I hate wearing monkey suits?"

He huffed and puffed and ripped the tie into shreds.

No doubt about it. If Tobias's suit was going to survive to see another night—and it should, because every woman benefited from the vision—I'd have to be the one to rescue it from his wolfie ways.

I waved him to me. "Oh my god, just come here."

As the puppy obeyed my command, I continued, "Don't get me wrong, I love Amy. I never thought I could be real friends with a huey. Even before I was one, Amy proved me wrong, though. But to bring her into our world… I'm not sure Miss I-got-it-at-Saks-and-not-on-sale can handle that. There's a reason we keep hueys in the dark. Believe me, I know all those ones at WWL who are privy are going to regret it someday."

"And what I'm saying is that, as of tonight, Amy *already is in* our world." He stilled my hands as I undid the last button of his dress shirt and pushed it aside, taking my eyes off the bottom of his undershirt and back to his eyes. "Geri, she was attacked by a vampire and we didn't hesitate to rush in to protect her. If we had ignored her, so would they from now on. Our compassion for her has condemned her; they'll come for her again if they think it's likely to rattle us. She needs to be prepared. She has to know, for her own sake."

The truth of his words struck guilt deep within. I pulled away. "It's like being pregnant—she can't just know a little. She's in all the way or out."

"At least on the inside, we can protect her. Help her protect herself." Tobias shimmied off the shirt and pulled the undershirt over his head. "I'm sure Inga could assign her security until we deal with the Ravens. If we're lucky, her guard will be some sexy, buff vamp who's really into smart and loyal blondes."

"Tobias Somfield, we are *not* fixing Amy up with a vampire!" Realizing the volume I'd reached, I threw a hand over my mouth.

Tobias turned his head, angling his ear. "I think she's asleep.

Speaking of which…" He went to work on his belt, and I suddenly found I needed to be very busily reorganizing my drawers. "You seem spirited tonight. Reclaiming some of your nocturnal habits?"

"Adrenaline, I guess. Plus, I drank a lot of coffee before I left for the theater."

"Why, did you want to be—" His words dropped off as a rustle of cloth suggested his pants had done the same. "Oh, that's right. Caleb."

I didn't know why I was admitting it to him. I shouldn't be. What business of Tobias's was my love life? "We had a big night planned."

"And I would have, what, stood guard while you guys finally got busy? Knitted and read magazines?"

"I hear there's a new issue of *Fangs & Fur Monthly*." My attempt at humor died on his grimace. "I don't know. I guess I assumed you'd just hang out in the lobby or the employee gym, like you always do. But let me point out again, not my fault. Blame the fact that you're my after-hours security detail on Cody."

Tobias coughed a laugh. "Oh, believe me, I blame a lot of things on Cody," he mumbled. "I got a sheet wrapped around myself, Geri, so you can stop pretending to be looking for the perfect pair of socks. God, you've become so proper. As if you haven't seen naked wolves all your life."

I had. Of course, I had. But Tobias wasn't just another wolf. He was Tobias, the werewolf who slept on my floor, curled up in a ball of fur, and occasionally, when I was about during the day, in my bed, naked as the day was long.

And long seemed the operative word in that analogy.

"Since when is modesty something to be ashamed of?"

"Since it's not your nature. I don't care if you're technically a huey now; you're still culturally a hood. And as a hood in the way that counts, you should understand that what I'm saying is right. Amy needs to know. Unless you want to—and I use this phrase only as a metaphor—throw her to the wolves. And by wolves, I mean Ravens. And by Ravens, I mean the evil pack of vampires who've already killed at least two of the people I love and, likely, one of yours."

Damn him and his ability to manipulate my emotions. "Fine, you're right." But if he thought I was the only one in for a penny, Tobias was about to get smacked in the head by the whole pound. "And if she's going to be in the know, she should probably come to Istanbul with us."

A shell-shocked werewolf in his huey form clutching a bed sheet proved to be an amusing sight. "What?"

I crawled into bed, despite the fact that I was still wearing most of my street clothes, minus my jacket, shoes, and socks. "What good is it to tell her and then just leave her behind? We should offer to let her come. Let the Ravens see I protect my own, and at the same time, we can get her trained up a bit while we're there. After all, you and the others will be sleeping all day long. It'd be nice to have someone spend the daylight hours with."

"Daylight hours? Trained up a bit?" Tobias repeated as he turned his back and dropped the sheet to the floor.

I didn't look.

For too long.

He continued as he nudged around the pile of blankets atop the dog bed into an agreeable form. "What exactly are we going to train

Manhattan Barbie to do?"

"To fight. Or at the very least, to defend herself. I can teach her how to handle a blade, you can teach her some wrestling, and I'm sure Caleb can teach her some martial arts. He's actually quite good at Krav Maga."

"I don't see how learning to play video games is going to protect Amy," Tobias said through a yawn. "Unless the Ravens are going to take the battle into *World of Warcraft*, probably not much good for Amy to master either."

"It's *not* a video game. It's a type of hybrid boxing-judo-other-stuff thing. And don't pass her off so easily. The woman didn't flinch this morning when I pulled a knife on her."

"Did she try to wake you up early again?"

"She's got spirit," I said, ignoring his quip. "With a bit of patience and motivation, she could hold her own."

"Not if she can pay someone to hold it for her."

"Look, it was your idea to tell her anything. I'm just saying, that's going to have consequences. *These* are the consequences. Are you going to help, or should we reconsider having Igor toss her memory around?"

I reached over to the wall and flicked off the light, but his voice still reached through the darkness.

"Seeing as I can't stomach the alternative, yes. But if you think she's convinced you and I should be a thing now, just wait until she knows I'm a wolf and you're a hood. *Were* a hood. You know what I mean."

"Why would that make a difference?"

"Because it's Amy. Doomed relationships are her superpower."

FIVE

I'd grown up in the supernatural world. Never had there been a time when I'd been in the dark, and never had there been a time that I thought it was my place to bring people into the light. It wasn't that no hueys knew of the supe world, as the several dozen vampire-aware hueys at WWL attested. It was that hoods (and wolves, frankly) by nature didn't trust outsiders. In my twenty-two years, I could think of only one I knew who was intimately integrated into our society, and she to the point of immersion: the gatekeeper of Schloss Wolfsretter, the reds' ancestral estate, deep in the Black Forest.

Hueys were so not my area of strength.

"So, Amy…"

She looked up expectantly from the couch, balancing a ballpoint pen on the palm of her hand.

Okay, so now what? "What was it you said you were doing after graduation?"

Her head cocked to the side. I'd gone from zero to what-the-hell in one-point-two seconds.

"What? Oh, going home, I guess. I'll probably go to grad school in a year or two, but I just want to take some time and live a little, you know?"

"Oh, I know. I'd like to live too. Ideally, of course."

"What?"

Heat pricked in my cheeks as I tried to overcome the oddness. "I mean, I'd like to have an adventure. I'm not in a rush to go home. I'd like to wait for all that stuff with my parents to blow over."

Amy set the pen and notebook down, her eyes softening. "Still on the outs, are they?"

"In a way. They're not talking to each other, and neither of them is talking to me." I took a seat on the armchair next to the couch. "Anyway, I was thinking, would you be interested in going on a trip with me? I mean, it's not just with me."

Her eagle eyes narrowed in my direction. "Is Tobias going on this trip too?"

"Yup. Also Inga Rosethorn and Prof. Karmarov."

Any amusement she wore melted away. "The creepy boss lady from your internship and the creepier biochem prof who has his weird lab at school?"

"They are not creepy!"

"They are the definition of creepy," Amy insisted. "I looked up that Inga woman after she offered the job to Tobias. There's nothing on her anywhere online. How does an executive from a big corporation like that stay off the web? More importantly, why? Why? Because she's up to freaky shit, is why."

"Or just likes her privacy."

She continued, undeterred. "And I took one of Karmarov's classes my sophomore year. There's just something about that guy that gives me the heebie-jeebies. You and Tobias are going on a trip with them? Is that what's really going on between you? There's some kind of weird cult thing or something, one that makes two people who are obviously attracted to each other sleep in the same room but resist temptation?"

"As I keep telling you, there's nothing going on between Tobias and me, and there never will be." Oh, shit. This was my break, wasn't it? I scooted to the edge of the cushion. "Actually, there's another person coming on the trip too. His name is Caleb."

Now I had her hooked again. "Caleb? That's a sexy name. Is he cute? Is he *available*?"

"Yes, he's cute. But no, he's not available. He's actually… my boyfriend."

The pen flew as Amy sat bolt upright. "No. Fucking. Way."

"Yes, way." I quelled my tongue which wanted to add, *though not so much fucking. At least, not yet.*

"I can't believe it! Yes!" The woman actually squealed and clapped. "I have so many questions, I don't know where to start. Is he cute? Is he a good kisser? Does he dance? Hell, do *you* dance? Does he ever wonder why he's never been to your house? Has he been here? Have you been sneaking him in for quickies when I've been gone? What about the whole Tobias situation? How does that all work? Have you guys talked at all about a three-way?"

"Amy!"

Her eyes went wide. "What?"

"No, no three-way—and we will never discuss that possibility again." Now that the cat was out of the bag, I guess I had to outline the whole thing from the beginning. "Caleb and I met last summer during my internship. He lives in the same building WWL is located in.”

“Oh, penthouse view. He must be rich then.”

I scanned my memory. “To tell you the truth, I’m not sure if he has any money. He’s… *friends* with Inga Rosethorn. I don’t think he’s exactly getting charged market rent rates.”

Amy chewed on that a moment. “Influence is almost as good as money. So, how is he in bed?”

I gulped. “Um…”

A switch went off in Amy’s brain. Her beaming pride became withering scorn with a scrunched-up forehead and a tilt of her chin. “How long have you two been together?”

I counted out on my fingers. “Officially? I guess about eight months, although he travels a lot. And, of course, Tobias and I head back to Michigan all the time, as you know.”

“Eight months, and you haven’t slept with him yet?” Amy cleared her throat, laced her fingers, and set her hands on her lap. “So he’s as much of a prude as you are.”

“Caleb is the polar opposite of a prude!” I exclaimed. Wait, was I *bragging* about my boyfriend’s licentious leanings? “The situation just hasn’t… if you’ll forgive the pun, *arisen*.”

She put a hand to her forehead and sighed. “Of course, it hasn’t arisen. You won’t let it. Ever since I got back from New York last fall, you don’t leave the house unless Tobias is with you. And also, you’ve kept this Caleb guy secret from me for, what I’m sure, are good reasons, but that makes sneaking him in on a night Tobias works impossible.”

I held up my two index fingers. “Actually, can we pause there and drill down a bit? That's what I wanted to talk to you about: why I kept him a secret. You see, Caleb comes from an old family with a lot of enemies."

But Amy was not hearing it. "Yeah, we'll get back to that later, but I would be remiss as your best friend if I didn't stage an intervention, and to do that, I need you focused on the problem: Tobias."

"So Tobias is a *problem* now?" If I had hackles, they'd be raised. Again. "You've been suggesting that the solution to everything wrong in my life—and possibly a way to bring about world peace—is to sleep with him."

"That's before I knew you were dating a member of the Mafia."

"What in the hell makes you think Caleb is in the Mafia?"

"You just said it yourself: old family, lots of enemies. Wait." Amy bit her finger. "Is Tobias some sort of bodyguard that Caleb arranged? That would actually make sense."

"No, Tobias is not a bodyguard. Well, actually he is, but *Caleb* isn't the one who sent him."

"Feds?" Amy asked. "Or what are they called in England? MI6? Is Tobias some sort of British agent, using you to get to Caleb's family?"

I pressed my fingers to my temple. "This is not going how I pictured it."

Again, my roomie steamrolled forward. "'Cause if that's not what's going on, then you really need to get him out of your life. Oh, sweetie, don't get me wrong. I'm not saying anything bad about Tobias. I like him a lot, even if his living here has exploded our Drano budget. It's not your fault, you're too close to the situation to see it clearly. But him living here is clearly cockblocking your love life—

both emotionally and physically."

When had trying to tell Amy about the supernatural world become a discussion about my love life? "This isn't what I wanted to talk about."

"But it's what you need to hear. Listen, Geri—" She reached out and rubbed my arm. "Ever since you came to me two years ago, brokenhearted and ignorant because of your small-town upbringing, it has been my mission to ensure that you fully seize the opportunities your life holds. I got excited for a while when you were seeing the Jess guy, but he turned out to be a flake."

"Actually, he turned out to be using me to get to Tobias."

"Ah, so that's what happened." Understanding brightened her eyes. "Point is, this is what I wanted for you all along. You've been with this guy for months. Obviously, you have feelings for him. And if he's not a prude like you, and he's still hanging around this whole time, it's got to be because he feels something pretty damned compelling for you too. Don't blow this. Tobias has lived here for almost a year now. I know he still misses his wife, but like I said: a year. He should be able to fend for himself now. You can still be friends, I'm not saying you shouldn't be. But please, be a big girl and do what's right: move Tobias out of your bedroom, so you can get Caleb into it. Even if Tobias is only a friend, trust me, it's like with dogs. They mark their territory. Tobias is marking you, and that's why things with Caleb are so dull."

"Amy, please. I really need to talk to you, and it's not about Caleb or Tobias. Well, okay, that's not true. It's all about Caleb and Tobias. And me. And other people too."

"If you're about to tell me you're in some kind of cult, then I have to admit, I already had a suspicion."

My train of thought plunged off a bridge. "Why would you think we're in a cult?"

"I don't know… Your tendency for being nocturnal? The way you usually disappear on full moons, and even if you are around, you act like you're all hyped up on something, the way you put silver trinkets all over the house when you first moved in, your weird obsession with Thai dumplings…"

"Lots of people like Thai dumplings. It doesn't mean they're in a cult!" My hair fanned out from my face as I blew out my frustration. "I was trying to tiptoe you into this, but looks like I just have to lay it all out. Tobias is a werewolf, my boyfriend is a vampire slayer, and even though it's confusing, Inga Rosethorn and Igor are both vampires. Not only that, but I used to be what in German is called a *wolfsretter*, but most people just call us hoods now. I'm actually an indirect descendant of Little Red Riding Hood, and no, not the Disney version of Little Red. In fact, I'm even named after her, which isn't all it's cracked up to be, since in my world, she's just about the evilest hood who ever existed. Which is ridiculous, because actually *my mother* is the evilest. And, oh yes, my mom… Last summer, she performed a rite of denial which ripped all my powers away, so that now I'm basically just as huey as you are, but with a lot of combat training. Oh, and FYI: that's what you are to us, a huey. We call humans *huey*."

By the time I finished my screed, I'd worked up both my heartbeat and my lungs. Perched on the edge of the armchair, I watched a wide-eyed Amy glare at me. Finally, after a few silent moments, she blinked, stood, and patted me on the shoulder.

"I'm only going to say this once, Geri, but it's said with love. You're too good a person to ruin your life with drugs."

And with that, she slipped into her room.

SIX

"She thought you were high?"

Across the table, seated far from the other patrons of the Italian restaurant near WWL, I couldn't tell if Caleb was horrified or about to break out laughing.

I shook my head, quelling the temptation to cackle. "Ridiculous, isn't it?"

"Depends." Caleb drew a bread stick to his mouth. "Are you?"

"On drugs?"

"Yeah."

I squirmed in my seat, doing my damnedest not to slither out of the black tube sock substituting as a dress in the process. The moment Amy found out I was going out on a date with the boyfriend of whom she'd only recently become aware and with whom, after eight months, I had not yet slept, she had blocked the door and refused to let me leave in anything less. Or, more aptly put, anything more.

"I took some aspirin a week ago when Tobias threw me down too hard in the gym."

The ire of Caleb's inner caveman swelled. "He what?"

"It was nothing." I took a quick sip of the sparkling grape juice. "The fact that I'm not still a hood doesn't mean a thing to the

Ravens. I train. Tobias helps. He doesn't go easy on me just because I'm not supernatural anymore… at my request. Sometimes, I get a little bruised."

"Well, that stops now. If anyone's going to slam you on your back too hard, it's going to be me."

"Speaking of which…" The flute balanced on the edge of my lip, a dramatic pause for a dramatic effect. "How's Inga?"

The slayer worked his jaw. "Inga and I do not have a thing going on. Yes, she likes drinking my blood—perhaps a little too much—but my neck is where anything physical between us begins and ends."

I did like to tease. "And the trip? Was it successful?"

I waited through his slow, steady chew of the steak he'd shoved in his mouth. "Only confirmed what we already suspected. The Ravens are in Istanbul; the question is where. It's a big city, you know. Almost fifteen million people, two thousand square kilometers of land covered in buildings folding in over themselves. Finding them will be no easy task, nor a quick one. You sure you want Tobias going along? Unless I misunderstood, a werewolf has to be with his pack on a full moon at least every three months to keep from going insane. Finding the Ravens' clutch could take years, and that's assuming we don't tip them off and they go scurrying."

Amy's comments replayed in my inner ear. It wasn't the first time Caleb had said something that suggested putting some distance between the werewolf and myself, but this wasn't the time.

"Tobias actually has a bigger dog in this fight than I do, if you'll forgive the pun," I said. "I kind of just stumbled into this whole Ravens-werewolf thing. No one is sure if Cody's dad's death had anything to do with it or if it was just coincidence. But we know for sure that Tobias's mate and brother died because of the Ravens' quest for eternal life."

He cocked his head to the side. "And what about what your mother said last summer?"

"About the Ravens finding me?" I shrugged. "My mom has enemies all over the world, of every species. Besides, you heard what Inga said. She only *suggested* my mom kill me when I visited her as a kid because she was scared my wolf-luring ability would be too useful to them. As usual, I think my mom's real fear was having a situation where she wasn't the one totally in control of me."

"Speaking of control…" He leaned over the table, his voice drifting into a husky register. "I'm having a difficult time with mine."

The corners of my mouth twitched. "Good thing we're so close to your place then."

In retrospect, the fact that we shared the elevator with Caleb's WWL-assigned bodyguard was probably the only reason I didn't lose my virginity on the ride up. The moment the slayer closed the door to his apartment, however, the game was afoot.

His hands hovered over the curves of my body, as though it were a glass figure he'd break. "Damn, whose idea was this dress and where do I send the thank you card?"

I stepped back toward the couch, kicking off my heels. Pink-tinted walls, more glass than frame, ringed my silhouette in city light. "Amy insisted."

"Makes me wish you told her about us a long time ago." Caleb's grin spoke a silent promise as he, too, shook off his shoes and let his suit jacket fall to the floor.

"You saying you don't like the way I dress?"

My feigned offense had him stupefied. "What? No. Damn it, no. I didn't mean—"

His words died on my tongue as Caleb came close enough for me to grab by the tie. I worked my mouth against his, hoping he understood tonight wouldn't end the way the others had. Tonight, this was going down.

When he pulled away, breathless and flush, I giggled. "I was just teasing."

His hands anchored on mine, pulling me to him at the hip. "I hope not."

Amy's dress didn't last long, but neither did Caleb's suit. After a few minutes spent becoming more naked and less clothed on the living room couch, Caleb cupped my backside as he pulled me up. I threw my legs around his hips, locking my ankles behind, never letting his lips leave mine. In the bedroom, silk sheets, chilled from the night air flowing into the room through a vent, made me shudder as he laid me on the bed.

Caleb stood at the edge of his bed, his heroic briefs putting up the only other remaining barrier between him and my innocence. "What's the shiver for? You afraid?"

"No, the sheets are cold."

He grinned as he leaned forward and hooked a finger on the waistband of my underwear. "We'll have to make sure we heat them up pronto, then, won't we?"

This was it. This was finally going to happen. I dug my heels into the edge of the mattress as I lifted my backside, helping Caleb's effort. The garment dropped off the end of his finger and out of sight, after which he sent his own briefs to keep them company. When I settled back, Caleb followed my arc, crawling over me as I scooted up the mattress. His lips met mine. His hips shifted. Heat raged.

And yielded as ice took my body.

Caleb froze over me, one hand beside my head, the other hooked under one knee in an attempt to pull it over his shoulder. "Geri?"

It wasn't the sheets that were cold; everything was. The air, my body, my desire. In a snap, all the warmth of the world fled. Even the feel of Caleb's touch blistered beneath my skin.

He let my leg fall. "It happened again, didn't it?"

"Can't." It was the only word that I could utter, though five thousand more were battling in the back of my throat, wanting to charge across my tongue.

He stared at me, awestruck. "Can't what?"

"This." I scooched back, working my back up the headboard and covering myself with the sheet. "Oh my god, Caleb, I'm sorry. I don't know why it happens."

Caleb pushed himself off the mattress, cursing under his breath. "We were so close."

"I know. Damn it, I hate this. I want to be able to do this."

When he came back into view, he wore a silk robe that complemented the gray slate shade of his bedding. "You say that, but you never do anything to change it."

Defensiveness shot through me. "And what, exactly, do you think I can do? Go to a doctor? What would I say? That I'm unable to get too hot and heavy with anyone since my mother stripped me of my powers?"

"Of course not, I just…" Groaning, his hands mussed his ebony hair, setting bits of it pointing in a hundred directions. "What about Igor? He might be able to figure something out."

"I can't go to Dracula to discuss sexual dysfunction. It's just too weird."

Caleb fell back on the bed, and by the rise in his robe at a suggestive place, I could see he was still open to engaging in bedroom politics. "We've got to do something, Geri, or we're never going to have sex." He chewed on his thoughts for a few moments before adding, "You don't suppose it's something psychological, do you?"

"You're saying I can't have sex with you because I'm crazy?"

He tried to bring levity to the situation…

"I've always thought a girl would have to be crazy not to want to screw me. You're just providing empirical proof."

…and failed.

"I'm not crazy," I assured him. "I want this. I want *you*. It's just… I don't know, maybe you're right. Ever since I was a little girl, I've been lectured on the importance of having the right kind of mate. *Hoods beget hoods* was one of my mother's slogans. Maybe it sunk in deeper than I thought. Maybe all the years spent blocking myself with Cody trained my body to cut itself off at a certain point. Maybe it's something else altogether. Some sort of nascent hood, biological cockblock."

He ran a hand over his face, laughing into his palm. "Only you're not a hood. Not anymore."

Feeling like shit wouldn't help this situation at all, but it seemed to be the only thing I was capable of at the moment. I shimmied under the sheet, settling down on my side, facing away from Caleb.

"I'm not much of anything, am I?"

A moment later, the silky robe became the only barrier between Caleb's body and mine as he threw an arm over me and nuzzled his nose under my ear.

"You're so much of so many things," he said, kissing my cheek. "We'll get there, I promise. And when we do, it'll be worth the wait."

"Yeah, well, it's a long time coming."

"Touché." His fingertips brushed down my arm, over my hip, and past my navel. "But at least we already know that, even if we can't seal the deal, I can still fill the inkwell."

I rolled back over, flattening my back on the mattress as his head disappeared beneath the sheet. "Your metaphors suck."

"Luckily, so do I."

SEVEN

My body was a lost connection of tissues and bone, held together more by theory than fact. Why was Caleb so focused on us having actual sex? We were doing a damned good job making each other happy without it, so much so I was convinced actual intercourse was going to be a letdown.

All I wanted to do was sleep. This was my last week of Chicago living and, while I didn't feel any particular affection for the city itself, the freedom and sense of self-determination I'd found in it seemed anchored to the top of the Sears Tower. Later in the day, I'd start packing: some things into boxes to go to a storage locker Inga had arranged for, some things into suitcases bound for Istanbul. In two days, Tobias and I would head back to Paradise one more time so he could run with the pack for the full moon. It would set off a three-month timer, near the end of which we still knew, sadly from experience, that Tobias would start to deteriorate mentally. A few days before the third full moon, he'd need to come back to Paradise, or suffer eternal lunacity.

Though, judging by what I found him doing on the couch when I crawled in just after sunrise, he might have done so already. Tell the guy he could go home and I'd wait until daylight to return safely alone, and he did weird things with his newfound time.

"This is how you took advantage of your night off? Watching

foreign *Sesame Street*?"

The wolf turned away from his phone perched on his knees, whereon a purple puppet that looked like the result of crossbreeding Cookie Monster with a cow prattled on about god-only-knew-what in some weird language.

"You look like a mummy in that dress." His tongue stilled as he closed his eyes and inhaled. "And it didn't even work. Struck out again, huh?"

My spine went rigid. "My sex life is none of your business."

"True. Also, I don't give a damn." Tobias chuckled as he hoisted a bowl of cereal he was holding up to his mouth and took down a spoonful, after which he pointed vaguely to the screen. "I've been trying to pick up some Turkish for the last few weeks. Kid shows are easiest for learning; they tend to repeat phrases over and over and keep the vocabulary simple."

I plopped down on the couch, scooting close to him so I could see the screen. "Inga, Igor, and Caleb all speak it already, and it's a very international city. I don't think we're going to have much use for it."

"Well, call me a wolf, but I don't like to be dependent on anyone except my pack."

"And me."

"You wish."

We both laughed under our breath, watching the puppet on the screen go through the motions of preparing breakfast. If the program was to be believed, in Istanbul, I'd start the day with cheese, olives, honey, and bread.

"I hope there's more meat than what that's suggesting."

"Don't worry. Another of the shows I've been watching is a restaurant review program. There's no shortage of meat. *Et*, they call it. Or, if you prefer, *kuzu*."

"What's *kuzu*?"

He turned to me, a grin on his face. "Lamb. Succulent, moist, tender lamb."

"Oh, I do like lamb."

"Yes, you do. Fluffy, furry, little well-roasted lambs. Juicy as rain."

I tried to ignore the way his eyes lingered on my lips, then internally scolded myself for seeing things that weren't there. *Caleb failed to win your castle, and now you're looking for weaknesses from lesser fortresses.* Tobias couldn't be attracted to me; it was physically impossible. But me? Yeah, he'd pegged my primal draw to him the first time I'd chased him down, knocked him to the ground, and straddled him. Plus, given my history with Cody, that I could feel such attraction to a wolf despite my genetics wasn't theory, it was proven fact.

"What about pork? Have you learned to say that?"

My question broke the tension as Tobias threw back his head and laughed.

"What?"

"It's a Muslim country, Geri."

"Yeah, so?"

"Yeah, so…" He reached out and mussed my hair and, in that simple move, restored our sibling dynamic. "Sorry, love. No pork."

"Not even sausage?"

"Not a single link."

"Okay, I'm rethinking this whole going-after-the-Ravens thing. I didn't realize I'd have to sacrifice bacon as part of the process."

He stretched to the table to set down his phone and his empty cereal bowl. "I'm sure we'll find acceptable substitutes." With that, he stood and pulled me to my feet. "You look like you're about to fall over dead. Let's get you into bed."

"Maybe the second time will be the charm."

Once, when I was still a hood, I felt on a visceral level the moment a wolf came within a certain perimeter. Amy, though a huey, had a similar talent, only her body alerted whenever a sexy man between the ages of twenty and forty said anything that included the words "you" and "bed." Her bedroom door almost cracked down the middle from the force of her throw. Despite the early hour, my roommate looked at me, to Tobias's hand in mine, and then back at me.

She took on her best chiding mother hen tone. "Didn't we talk about this yesterday?"

Tobias leaned back, stretching, yawning so wide he yelped a little. "What is she talking about?"

"I'm talking about your presence and the not-coincidental lack of advancement in Geri's love life, mister."

My chest rose and fell. "If it's any consolation, we got to oral tonight."

The wolf let go my hand and put his hands over his ears. "Blimey, Geri, no. It's none of *my* business, but you just wallop Amy with that kind of disclosure without so much as a prod?"

"I have best friend rights," Amy retorted. "And good. But remember what I said when I sent you to him wearing that?" She pointed at what little bit of a dress I was wearing. "It was supposed to be *the* night. Why am I finding you curled up on the couch with Lord Grows-a-beard-a-day when you're supposed to be waking up in Caleb's bed?"

"Amy, I love you. I really do, but I don't understand why you've appointed yourself as my personal intimacy manager."

The blonde curled her fists and shook. "Because I want you to be happy!"

The moment Amy stepped over the line from cute-but-awkward concern to whiny-bordering-on-rude insistence, Tobias put himself between us.

A move which Amy appreciated none too well. "You!" Her right hand pelted Tobias's chest, a drop of rain in the river of his physique. "Don't you see that she's too hung up on you to give this Caleb guy a chance? I get that you lost your wife, and believe me, I'm very sorry for you. Really, I am. But you can't keep interrupting her chance at happiness like this. It's not fair to Geri."

"You think I'm here because I want to be?" Tobias crossed his arms and belly-laughed. "If only you knew what's really going on here."

"What, you mean your werewolf-little red thing?"

Wide-eyed, Tobias's head swiveled in my direction. "You told her?"

"Isn't that what we agreed to do?"

"Yeah, but I didn't know you actually told her." Tobias turned back to Amy, his hands squeezing her upper arms. "You have no idea how much of a relief that is. Bet it came as quite a shock, huh?"

My roomie blinked thrice in rapid succession. "You don't think I actually believe that, do you? Come on, just be honest. You're in love with Geri, but you're too guilty about falling for someone else so soon after your wife died to admit it, and too scared about being alone to deny it. How is she ever going to have a relationship with Caleb when she's got all that waiting for her at home? Either make a play for her, or get yourself out of the game!"

But Tobias proved uninterested in Amy's early-morning therapy sessions. Instead, he went about pulling his undershirt off his head. "Guess this means I don't have to worry about not doing this in front of you anymore, then."

In the three seconds that it took Amy's eyes to catalog Tobias's bare chest, him to undo the fly of his jeans, and his form to shift from two legs to four, Amy's skin went from cardinal to cadaver. It was one thing to be told your third roommate was a werewolf. It was another thing entirely to watch him prove it.

I swooped his jeans and T-shirt off the floor as I followed Tobias towards the bedroom. "We didn't get to this yesterday, Amy, but it should go without saying: this is a secret. Now I trust you'll have questions, and we'll be happy to answer them after I get some sleep, but I'm beat. Good night. Or well, you know, good morning."

EIGHT

"Silver bullets?"

"True. *Kinda.* Any silver, actually, but it's only deadly if it hits the heart or the brain. Otherwise, it just burns like a son of a bitch. It can scar if left on the skin for a long time, though."

"Do vampires really change into bats?"

"Nope. They can alter into some kind of gaseous state, though. Just don't ask me to explain how it's possible. No one really knows, not even the vampires."

"Are they really immortal?"

Tobias and I exchanged a look across the front seat, understanding passing between us. The werewolf balanced his left arm on the window ledge and a lie upon his lips. "That part's mostly true, but anything that can live, can die."

We'd made a pact before leaving for Paradise this morning: now that Amy was in on our secret, we'd answer any question she had, *unless* the answer was one a supe wouldn't normally know. Hoods and wolves, who more or less lived as long as hueys, were blind to the truth about a vampire's post-conversion life span being only five hundred years or so. From what Caleb had said, they preferred that knowledge to remain guarded.

After the first half of the trip to Paradise being filled with the inane questions we'd have expected, my roomie dug up left field to toss some inquiries at us.

Does a vampire have to drink human blood, or is animal blood okay?

Would it get drunk if it sucked from someone who was already drunk?

Where does a hood's hood come from? Is it magic? Magic really exists?

If a hood and a slayer had a baby, what abilities would it have?

That last one made me squirm, and my discomfort made Tobias grin.

Amy picked up on it. Always observant. "What? What'd I say?"

When I didn't answer, Tobias did. "Geri's boyfriend is a slayer. My guess is you tapped into a nerve a little too close to her heart on that one."

"Oh, my god." A gasping Amy wore a grin that could power an incandescent bulb. "You have a superhero boyfriend? And you're not hitting that every night? I mean, all that power, and you're just—"

"Like I said, we're getting there," I said, cutting her off. "Besides, other than being superfast, being able to throw little balls of sunlight, and being ever-so-slightly stronger, slayers' *other* skills aren't inherently greater than a huey's. One thing I can tell you right now, Amy: you have to overcome all the brainwashing Hollywood has done on you. Supes aren't de facto attractive, porn-worthy sex gods. That's just not how it works."

"Speak for yourself, Geri," Tobias piped up, taking the exit off the main road that led to the packlands. "I am amazingly talented in the sexual arts."

As Amy cackled in the backseat, slapping her hands, heat crawled over my skin, though whether from embarrassment, anger, or some other emotion, I didn't want to know.

"Kara must have really appreciated that," I mumbled, and then hightailed our conversation out of any topic that could make me imagine Tobias in the act of anything. "Supes aren't superheroes, Amy. Remember that. In fact, some are the opposite of heroic."

The Paradise Pack numbered a few dozen adult wolves, spread out over sixteen different primary bloodlines between whom family trees interweaved. To describe the packlands as a compound wasn't quite accurate; without any fences—which would have been an abomination in any wolf's eyes—the twenty-three homes built at odd intervals around a central clearing weren't technically more than a neighborhood. Other than being completely surrounded by and punctuated with pine trees, the style was distinctly European village in formation. Only, instead of a chapel at its center lay a multipurpose meeting house hewn of local timber, big enough to fit a crowd twice the pack's size. When they'd settled in Paradise a century ago, the alpha at the time said it was too small. How times and culture had changed.

Amy wore tension like a second shirt. Moving with the grace of a stick bug, she crawled out of the backseat of Tobias's hand-me-down extended cab pickup, the vehicle kept to her back like a rampart. In some ways, I had to admire the tactical prowess with which my big city roomie maneuvered. *Safe ground behind, a means of escape in sight, moving forward with awareness of what lies beyond.* My mother would be proud. But, as we were in friendly territory, and as every werewolf within a fifty-yard line of sight of our car had stopped to survey the interloper, the signals of *I'll-kill-you-or-die-trying* she was giving off didn't bode well.

I slipped to her side, weaving her hand in mine. "Wolves can smell fear, Amy."

She shook her head. "I made sure to put on lots of perfume."

Even Tobias grinned at that.

Ahead, the crowd turned when a tall, solidly-built woman dressed in white broke through the crowd. Amy's grip threatened to push all the blood from my hands.

"Is that who I think it is?"

No need to answer. Within moments of a visual confirmation, Kim, wearing a wedding gown worthy of a princess but barefoot, peeled away from the pack and was bolting in our direction, arms held wide.

"Hi, Kim!"

A dull thud made me turn my head. Amy's back pressed against the Chevy, her hand searching behind her for the door.

"Amy, what are you doing?"

"She's a wolf!" Her hand found the handle and lifted just as Tobias palmed the door, keeping it from opening.

"Have you gone bloody mad?" the wolf demanded. "Why does that matter?"

"It doesn't. It's just… She's so…"

As did a wolf recognize the weakest animal, so Kim went for Amy first, pulling her up into her arms, yanking her off the ground, and spinning her around.

Crimson strains stretched across Amy's face. "STRONG."

After Kim had finished immobilizing my roommate, she took me and Tobias in turn.

"I'm so glad you were able to make it." Kim's grin could light up the Sears Tower.

"We're happy to be here, and very, very happy Cody agreed to let Amy come along." I pulled my bag out of the front seat of the truck. "Congratulations on your mating. I hear he's quite your equal, but I doubt that's possible."

Kim blew out a raspberry. "I still beat him at arm wrestling two out of three, and even that third time, I'm usually throwing it. Amy, I hear you're in the know now?"

"Seems that way." Amy swatted away the question and the mosquitoes buzzing around her head. "To tell the truth, finding out Tobias was a werewolf was shocking. Finding out you are kinda makes sense."

My insides squirmed as the jab meant for Kim washed over me. Tobias took a step closer. Whether he was doing it because he thought he might have to defend Kim or defend Amy, I couldn't say.

But Kim just threw her head back and howled. "Knew you were an observant one from the start, Popowitz. Kinda had me wondering how you didn't figure it out earlier, frankly. No harm done. Come, meet my mate, and I know Cody and Lisa are eager to see you too."

Lisa spotted us first, even as she bounced the baby on her knee. She stood, and automatically, the awkwardness bloomed between us.

"Geri, Tobias, so good to see you." She shifted her weight to examine my cowering roommate behind me. "You must be Amy. I'm so glad you could make it for Kim's wedding. She's told us so much about you."

"I didn't mean to be such a bitch to her. If I had known she was a werewolf…" Amy's words died on her tongue. "Oh, god, is that still an insult here, *bitch*? Because wolves are a type of canine and a female canine is a bitch, and I didn't mean—"

"Kim," Lisa interjected, cutting off the babbling blonde, "has a strong personality. A strong *everything*, really. I can only imagine that stuffed in a city apartment, she was in a concentrated form. But she's only ever said kind things about you, Amy, so I don't think you have anything to worry about."

Cody's mate had become quite the diplomat, as further evidenced when she turned to me.

"Cody says you're graduating next week. Congratulations, I know he's very proud."

Don't be a bitch. "Thank you, Lisa. Wow, Jenny's grown like a weed since we were here just two months ago." I reached out to twirl a tiny curl of the baby's hair on the end of my finger, admonishing the jealousy on a low boil in my soul whenever I had to talk with the she-alpha. "Before you know it, she'll be tearing all around these woods each full moon, giving my mother fits."

The air stifled despite the pleasant lake breeze that snuck from the shore into the woods.

Tobias cleared his throat and put an arm around Amy. "Come on, Barbie. Let me introduce you to the infamous Cody Ryland."

As he began to pull her away, Amy leaned into him, still unaccustomed to a wolf's enhanced hearing. "*That's* who he left Geri for? Not hard to believe. She's a knockout."

Lisa closed her eyes and grinned. When she opened them again, the mask of indifference was gone. "I know this is awkward, but is it ever going to be not that way? You're still a big part of Cody's life, Geri, but so am I. We have to get past this."

"There's nothing to get past. Neither of us did anything wrong. It's just…"

"You still love him," she interceded. I didn't insult her by denying it. "But you know he's bonded to me now. Why do you keep torturing yourself like this?"

I looked around. Luckily, the music of a four-piece band in the corner helped to lay down enough background noise that none of the other wolves had heard. At a table about twenty feet away, however, Tobias and Cody sat side by side, Amy opposite of them with her back to me. The two wolves watched me and the alpha's mate through suspicious gazes.

I reached out again and tickled Jenny, making the pup squeal with laughter, playing off our conversation as standard pleasantries. What could I tell her? That ever since my mother rejected me from my clan, the pack was the only family I had? That even though I'd been dating Caleb for the better part of a year, I still hadn't felt one-tenth the emotional bond with him that I had with Cody? That I was afraid Cody only let me continue to visit the pack because of the guilt he felt from what had happened between us, and that I was scared he'd turn me away as soon as he knew I'd fallen for someone else? I couldn't even admit half of this to myself, let alone to her.

"I'm trying, Lisa. I swear, I am. But hearts don't listen to reason, not even for a hood."

"The day a hood listens to reason, I'll throw a parade." She played off the comment with a smile that exploded onto her face, and as quickly faded away. "I understand what you're going through, Geri. I know you think I don't, but you don't know me that well. I'm just begging you, please, today, try to squash it more than usual." She looked to her mate, love beaming in her eyes. "Don't make him do something he's going to regret."

"What does that mean?"

Lisa shook her head. "Nothing. Something stupid. Forget I said it. You better go. Get business out of the way so we can all stuff ourselves with cake before sunset."

"One of the Ravens, Timur, has been spotted in the city in the past few weeks. Igor and Inga say they move in pairs, and rarely ever all in the same location. Wherever you find one, though, there's guaranteed to be another nearby. More than likely, it's Vlad."

Cody stared blankly, letting the intel sink in. When we'd first told him of our plan to chase down the vampire that may have had a hand in killing his father, he'd been gung-ho for the idea. Since, the more he learned about the rumors surrounding Igor's wayward offspring, the more his fervor cooled. Where we'd been certain last fall that he'd have no problem giving Tobias leave to make the trip, now doubt lingered.

He fidgeted with a tattered tablecloth stretched over a decades-old folding table. "What's to stop them from killing you the second you arrive?"

I scooted to the edge of my seat. "Igor says Vlad modeled his clutch after the Ottoman court of his era. He thinks of himself as some sort of vampiric sultan, I guess. He'll kill when he has to, but he prefers politics first."

"Inga and Igor can't kill him," Tobias took up. "To do that would be to kill themselves. Igor thinks he won't consider a single werewolf and a relinquished hood a threat."

Cody's face soured. "That's because you're not."

Tobias's hand took mine under the table, squeezing, silencing my automated retort, before letting it go. "Don't forget, we'll have Caleb too, an actual slayer. Once we ferret out the Ravens' location and their behaviors, it's just a matter of divide and conquer."

"One young slayer against at least two vampires born of the most infamous lineage ever, with a member of my pack and one of my best friends forming shallow ranks. Still don't like those odds, Tobias."

"That's because you haven't seen what Caleb can do," I said. "He isn't just any slayer; he's a Van Helsing. One infamous line against that of another, and vengeance for Tobias's mate? Vlad won't stand a chance."

"Yeah, well, you're dating the guy, so your assessment ain't exactly without bias, is it?" Cody turned on Tobias. "What do you think? Is this slayer going to be able to stand up to the Ravens?"

Tobias steepled his hands, leaning into their support. "I don't worry about Caleb taking on Vlad. I'll be more surprised if he ever learns to stand up to Geri."

I reached out, running my fingers over Cody's, drawing his attention from the frayed checkerboard pattern to my face. A nostalgic tingle ran up my arm, an electric buzz I had once thought was because I was a hood and he was a wolf, but now I suspected was more because he was a boy and I was a girl who loved him. "Cody, please. Tobias has a right to avenge his lost ones. Give him permission to come."

The alpha grinned, turning my hand over and cupping it with his. "If I said he couldn't go with you, would it stop you?"

Tobias chuffed. "If you think saying *no* works with Geri, you clearly don't know her as well as I do."

Cody's eyes pivoted to his packmate. After a moment, without letting my hand go, he rose and pulled me up to my feet. "Let's dance, Little Red."

"Wha— What are you… Cody, this is no time for… Hey!"

He spun me in a circle as the speakers blasted the band covering an old U2 ballad. Cody's cheek pressed against mine, sending dueling impulses firing through my body. Half of me wanted to stomp his foot, and the other half wanted to knee his groin.

"What are you doing? You're a mated wolf with a child, and you're dancing with the daughter of the red matron at your packling's wedding!"

"*Shh!!!*"

He pulled back only long enough to admonish me with his glare, before immediately resuming the white man shuffle. Even with the proximity, hearing his words was difficult. The realization that this was sort of the point set me at ease, and I fell into a left-right-left sway.

"Your heart doesn't speed up when you say his name."

"Who's name?"

The alpha huffed. "Your slayer."

"I'm not sure I'm following what—"

"When you touched me, your pulse spiked. Maybe you couldn't hear it, but I did, and I'm pretty sure Tobias did. I can read my pack's emotions in their mannerisms. You're *saying* one thing about your faith in this slayer, but Tobias is telling me you're not as sold on him as you seem to think."

"I'll remind you: I'm not in your pack. Hell, I'm not even in my mother's clan anymore. Besides, I have complete faith in Caleb's ability as a slayer, whether or not my heart speeds up."

"Good to hear, but I'm still having a hard time understanding his motivations. Your Caleb was on this path before he met you, and if he's as great a slayer as you say, why does he need you? More weight makes a heavy tow."

"You think he'd just, what, up and leave me behind?"

"He might. And if you break his heart on this epic quest halfway across the world, what happens to Tobias? What happens to you? Jesus, Geri, just love the guy, will you? Get over me, and let someone else into your heart. Your life might depend on it."

I didn't know when the music stopped. I didn't know when we'd become the center of attention. I did know, however, that every single wolf glaring at me throughout the hall reared to defense when I smacked their alpha.

I caught Lisa in the crowd over Cody's shoulder, shaking her head.

A dumbfounded Cody raised his hand to his face and rubbed the imprint of my palm on his cheek. "Once a hood, always a hood, huh?"

Proving I had no talent for knowing when to quit, I stood my ground. "How dare you or *anyone* tell me what to feel about you? In the last two years, have I once asked you to betray your wife? Have I ever used any of my abilities to cause a single member of this pack any harm? Even though it has cost me my family, my birthright, and may cost me my life, I've *never* asked for you to care a lick for me since the moment we were through. Since, one day after you asking me to marry you, I walked in on you in the arms of another woman. *Mated.* So don't you dare stand there now and try to order me to get over you, like it's just a decision I have to make and, poof, it will be done. No matter how much you think it, I'm not a member of your pack; alpha's prerogative doesn't work on me. You can't order me to stop loving you, and you sure as hell can't order me to love someone else. My heart is the one thing I won't sacrifice for you, or for anyone!"

It took to the end of my screed to realize at least six of the pack had formed a ring around their alpha, teeth bared, on the edge of taking on their wolves. Nothing lay between me and their anger but the order of their alpha. I looked into Cody's eyes, and for the first time, I knew the depth of heartbreak.

He sneered at me, at the ex-friend who represented regret and youthful indiscretions. At the outsider who he had welcomed into his pack, who now had betrayed that trust by showing him up in front of everyone. By calling him out and laying blame at his feet tailored by another, of forcing him to act.

My hands shook. Not with rage, but with nerves. The wall of words I'd just built stood between me and grace, and I'd dug the moats too deep to cross it.

"Oh, my god. Cody… I'm so… I don't know…"

"Rick!"

The beta of the Paradise Pack emerged from the crowd, gently pushing the awestruck bride aside.

"Yeah, Cody?"

"Accompany Miss Kline and her huey guest to their hotel. Advise them not to venture into the woods tonight. I can no longer guarantee their safety from the pack, especially on a full moon."

"You got it, Cody. Geri, you need to grab a purse or anything?"

Before I could answer, Amy was at my side, her fingers lacing mine and squeezing some strength into my resolve.

"I got her stuff, and I got her." Ignorant or ignoble? Either way, she stood with me against them. "We can find our way to the hotel just fine, thank you very much. I'll get us an Uber."

Rick cleared his throat. "There are no Ubers in Paradise, Miss."

Unperturbed, Amy hooked my elbow and forced me erect. "Fine then, we'll walk."

Tobias pushed his way forward. "I'll take them."

Cody shook his head. "I asked Rick to…"

"I said, *I will take them.*"

This time, Cody ceded, even as my heart sank deeper. What in the hell was he doing? It was one thing for me to tell off the alpha, but as a member of the pack, Tobias could get disowned for the same act. I couldn't let that happen to him again. I *wouldn't* let him become a rogue again because of me.

"Tobias, you don't have to. I'm not worth it."

The werewolf turned, leading the way through a crowd that parted before him, a blast of anger through narrowed eyes his only response.

When I'd left Paradise for Chicago two summers ago, fresh from my boyfriend being mated to another, I thought the seven-hour drive was the longest of my life. It didn't compare to the twelve minutes of eternity spent in the pickup truck, seated between Amy and a very rigid, silently seething Tobias.

NINE

"Are we getting more drunk, or less sober?"

"I'm more drunk, you're less sober. It's your first time drinking. Getting *more* drunk would require a basis of comparison."

I sighed as I swirled the little bit of liquid left in my glass. "My love life has finally driven me to drink. I held out twenty-two years almost. That's pretty good, right?"

"It's excellent! Only, now I guess I know why none of my prodding ever worked." Amy's hand rubbed my shoulder, as I, slumped over the bar, huffed. "Two years, and he could still hurt you that bad? You must have really been crazy over him."

A ping in the air kept me from having to comment right away. The message on the screen from Kim got straight to the point.

Don't worry about it. Made the wedding memorable.

Amy read the message over my shoulder and nodded. "I sold Kim short, I think."

"Yeah, but she's still pack. If Cody had said to rip me to shreds, Kim would have. They all would have."

"Not Tobias," Amy said. "Or that Rick guy. You might have been too distracted to realize it, but they were both sizing up the situation, looking for a way to intervene."

"Rick is a beta; one of his jobs is to keep Cody in check. A beta can counter an alpha without jeopardizing his place in the pack."

"What about Tobias then? What's his excuse?"

As I lifted my head off the bar, I realized that Amy was right; Tobias had stood up for me. Or had he? Werewolves weren't mindless drones; even though obeying the alpha was written into their DNA, at the end of the day, their opinions and their actions were their own. I played back the memory, analyzing the scene that had passed a few hours ago.

"Tobias didn't disobey," I finally admitted, both to myself and to Amy. "Cody's order was for Rick. If Cody had said point blank to fall back and let Rick bring us here, Tobias would have obeyed."

One could argue that Cody would have given that order, if Tobias hadn't cut him off.

"Still, given that everyone else in that room looked like they wanted to kill you, pretty brave of him."

"*Stupid,*" I amended. "The word you're looking for is *stupid.*"

"In what way?"

"Tobias is still pack. We still need Cody's permission for him to go to Istanbul with me."

"With *us.*"

Confusion turned my head. When I'd brought up the idea with Amy last night, she'd laughed at it. "You changed your mind?"

Amy took another sip of her second whiskey sour before smacking her palate. "I'm going to Istanbul with you. You said that these bad vampires…"

"SHHH!"

The bartender was busy talking to another customer at the opposite end of the bar, but still, I wasn't unaware that our voices had been growing louder in the two hours we'd been sitting at the bar, getting more and more drunk.

"Those bad *people*, then," Amy amended, whispering. "That they were the ones who attacked me, and that they'd try it again if they thought it would do any good. Well, I just helped you stand up to a pack of dogs, so I'm guessing any shot I had at claiming the title 'innocent bystander' is gone. So, yes. I'm coming with you, and you're going to teach me how to fight, okay? That's the deal. And in exchange, I'm going to teach you how to fall in love."

I attempted not to choke on my drink. "*You're* going to teach me how to fall in love?"

Amy blinked at me in rapid succession. "What, you think I don't know how? Geri, I almost fall in love five times a year. You don't think it's on accident, do you? It's a carefully controlled and deliberate process!"

"Granted, but what I need help with isn't falling in love. I did that just fine. What I need help with, apparently, is falling *out* of love."

"Silly Yooper, it's the same thing. There's no better way to get over the old guy than to get hung up on the next one."

"So you're telling me that you can teach me to fall in love with Caleb?"

Suddenly, the confident gambler decided to hedge her bets. "Caleb specifically? We can try. I mean, you just can't fall in love with *any* guy. He's got to have the right package. And no, I'm not just talking about genitals. Though, don't get me wrong, those are important too."

"I'm going to need another drink for this." I leaned over the bar, trying to ignore the way the room went along for the ride. Prior to tonight, I'd consumed alcohol on three occasions, each more ceremonial than celebratory. In the past ninety minutes, I'd set a lifetime personal best. Or worst. "Randy? Another?"

As the orientation of the room took time to catch up with me as I sat back up, I decided worst, definitely worst.

"Oh, my god. You really do know everybody here, don't you?" Amy asked. "I thought you were just joking, but you've been able to call everyone by their name since we got to the hotel."

"I don't know the tourists." With a wide swing of my arms, indicating the roomful of Johnny Detroits and Jenny Chicagos, I disavowed any suggestion of omnipotence. "But Randy here, he was my PE teacher in high school."

"And her driver's ed teacher," the balding, gray-haired man in his sixties said as he topped off my glass. "Speaking of which, I hope you're not planning on getting behind the wheel to head home after this tonight, Gerwalta."

"Nope! I'm staying here, pretending to be a tourist. Didn't you hear that my parents disowned me?"

Randy tried to hide his laugh. "Sounds like your mom hasn't changed. But your dad, too? He's always seemed to me like an okay guy, not the kind to turn out his daughter. Anything I can help with?"

"Not unless you can convince the old battle-ax to let me have my hood without being her minion, not really."

As Randy's face screwed up in confusion, Amy put both her hands on my shoulders. "Don't pay any attention to her. She's been babbling stuff like that for an hour. I should probably take her up to the room now."

She threw a stack of bills onto the counter, which Randy's fat hand pawed and swished away. Amy tried to tug me to my feet, but both my mind and my body refused to budge.

"But he just got my drink!" I protested, two hands, both seemingly connected to my right arm, swinging out to grab the glass. "I mean, *I* just got *my* drink. When I get upstairs, I'm going to pass out. If you're going to tell me how I'm supposed to fall in love, I need to know that now."

Amy leaned in, whispering in my ear. "If I tell you, will you promise to go after? You're getting kind of belligerent. People are starting to look at us."

"Tourists always gawk at the locals. We're like a zoo exhibit for them: 'Come see the amazing Yooper, who lives seven months a year in the snow, survives on a steady diet of pasties, and knows sixteen ways to use lake ice as a natural resource.'" I pounded the bar with my fist, making my refilled glass spill over the edge. "Now teach me, oh wise one. How do I fall in love?"

Amy huffed, but relented. "You need to assess four things. First, do they think the same thing about food as you? I don't care what so-called experts say: if you get to Thanksgiving, and one of you wants a turkey stuffed with pork sausage while the other wants a tofurkey, it's never going to work. Second, do you both want to live in the same kind of place? I can't tell you how many guys I've met whose bones I would have jumped posthaste, but it turned out they were country folks. I know it seems superficial, but so much about what we want out of life is wrapped up in where we want to live. Our pace, our shopping, our vacations, our expectations about family: all is geographically-oriented. If you've assessed those two factors, and the guy meets those conditions, you can move on to assessing quality three."

Her convoluted logic had me drawn in, and I was an acolyte sitting at the feet of the priest.

"What's number three? Job prospects?"

"No, silly, sex appeal." Amy said it like it was the most natural thing in the world. "If looking at him doesn't make you want to rip his clothes off three times an hour, then the relationship has no hope. Physical things only slow down with time. If you don't have that spark right at the beginning, you're never going to have it."

I ran the mesh of Amy's filters over the view of my current relationship. Food that we both liked? I guess we had that down. I mean, our dates often included going out to eat, and so far, we never ended up anywhere where there wasn't something each of us could eat. Sex appeal we definitely had down, excepting for some weird thing on my side that had so far prevented any actual sex. But as for wanting to live in the same place? The discussion had never come up.

"Wait," I said, realizing Amy's lesson wasn't done. "What about the fourth thing? You said there were four parts of the rubric."

"No one says rubric, Geri," she chided. "But yes, the fourth thing. This is crucial. You have to identify one thing about the guy you hate. And I'm talking really, really loathe here, like, makes you contemplate murder."

"And that's it? Three things you have in common, one thing you hate, and then boom: love?"

"Well, no, it's not that simple. But it's not much more than that. See, falling in love is the process of meeting someone, overlaying them into your life, and then, letting them sink into all your nooks and crannies. Don't give me that face, Gerwalta Kline, and get your mind out of the gutter! I'm talking about emotional nooks and crannies. The first few times you're meeting someone, you focus on just getting to know what those four factors are. Then, once you think you got them down, and he fits in on the first three factors, you sit down and talk to yourself. You say, 'Self, here is a man with the same appetites and the same goals as me, and who I want and seems to want me. And here is the one worst thing about him that I can say. Given that worst thing, am I willing to accept him for all those other reasons?' If the answer is yes, you let yourself fall in love. If the answer is no, dump him."

It was brilliant. And stupid. And genius. And ridiculous.

"And this is how you find yourself in love with a different guy every other month?"

Amy threw a hand over her heart. "Have I ever said I've been in love?"

"No. I just assumed that—"

Her upheld hand cut me off. "I *almost* fall in love frequently, but I've never bottomed out there. That last part, the worst reason ever? That's what gets me. So far, I haven't found anyone to make it over that hurdle."

"I did," I mumbled, remembering what had driven me to be where I was right now. "But you forgot rule five: if he's a werewolf mated to another, all bets are off."

"And with that, I think we're ready for bed, don't you? Thanks, Randy! Couple of bills for you here on the counter."

At three in the morning, the moon summoned me.

Green numbers on the clock next to the bed flashed four-forty-five. Four hours since I'd plopped down, with Amy's help, into my bed. It had been the only way to keep the room from spinning. I may have never been drunk before, but I'd heard enough stories to know recovery didn't come this quickly. As I sat up, what greeted me wasn't nausea; what greeted me was clarity. Crystal clear, clearer than I'd been in almost a year. Every sense reverberated: scent, taste, hearing, sight—even the ability to sense the wolves. I could feel them, out there, beyond the highway and the forest's edge. Under a cooperative nighttime sky, the pack darted around trees and bushes, chasing squirrels, rabbits, even a few deer. In their wolves, they were at one with nature. Stripped of their humanity, they reached the zenith of their inherent natures.

It was a dream. A glorious, enrapturing, surreal dream.

Silver daggers in the form of moonlight sprayed down from the sky, pierced the land, fell over my bare arms like raindrops, wetting my skin with power. Shoes were needless in this nocturnal walk. The pavement of the road between the hotel and the trees gave way to gravel beneath my feet, then the soft, downy grass of late spring. The forest and the human world dueled in a gentle fault line.

I didn't know how long I strolled in the woods, but at some measure, the sounds of the shore and Lake Superior's surf dissipated. The nearness to the pack pushed down on me, but so did the alpha's order to ignore me, not to approach me. Agreement, consensus, concurrence.

Dissension.

He hadn't listened to the alpha. He refused to turn his maw on me.

Tobias's wolf held a kind of grace even Cody had never had in my eyes. Was it because of the foreign climate in which he'd been raised that made his coat smoother, led his tuft to be slimmer? Other than perhaps Rick, he was certainly larger than the other members of the Paradise Pack, even in huey form. Tobias was just so… built. Broad shoulders, a firm chest, abs I could bounce a dime off. With his mix of red and brown fur, rings of white around his paws and his maw, he was the most beautiful wolf I'd ever seen.

And he was staring at me. Under the influence of a full moon. And me, here, in nothing more than a pair of boy shorts and a cami. Even in a dream, this seemed stupid. They were more beast than man under a full moon, and I'd never been more mortal.

But I'd been raised a hood, hadn't I? Even if I'd never succeeded in taking my fire, there was nothing wrong with my brain.

Other than the fact it was floating in booze.

Dogs could smell fear; a werewolf could taste it. Deep breaths, and focus. *I am a hood. Silver flows in my veins. No pest shall pester me. No beast or man shall conquer me. I am a red. I am the blood that flows through the veins of the earth. I am the warrior which keeps the wolf at bay. I am power. I am strength.*

I was no longer a hood. Mosquitoes, trying to tap my veins, found the deed insurmountable as the old teachings instilled in me all my life rang and became a mantra, though reality niggled at my confidence. Even if the bugs swarming around me thought otherwise, I was nothing more than a huey.

I held up my hands and flinched. "I'm not armed."

Tobias's head tilted to the side. If he'd been a man, he'd have been smirking at the idea a weapon would make any difference. That, or the animal within him was deciding how to best dispatch me.

Dream or not, I didn't want the memory of being ripped to shreds by a werewolf under a full moon. "What I mean to say is, I'm not going to try to hurt you. I'm just… dreaming. Even still, you shouldn't *try* to hurt me either. It might affect our friendship when I wake up."

Two more steps toward me, and I knew I should be running already. Both our eyes turned to the forest canopy as a crow made its presence known, cawing has he leapt from the branches of a fir to the leafy extension of a budding oak. A symbol, I was sure of it. I'd have to remember to google it later. When my eyes dragged back down to the earth, however, no interpretation was needed. A man stood before me: one with broad shoulders, a firm chest, and abs I could bounce a quarter off of. (My memory suggesting a mere dime before had proven faulty.)

"What are you doing here, Geri?"

Despite taking on his human, Tobias spoke with a growl. It had taken the man to reveal the anger of the animal within.

"Dreaming, of course. You?"

"You think you're dreaming?" He shook with silent laughter. "Maybe you're right. Maybe I am." A mud-caked hand dragged through sweat-drenched hair. "This can't be real."

"That's because it's not. I'm a huey now, and there's a full moon overhead. It should have no effect on me, and a more animalistic effect on you. Ipso facto: we're dreaming."

Three more steps, and he reached up to stroke my cheek. "If it's a dream, right now doesn't matter. It doesn't have to make sense."

"Nope. I suggest we try something crazy, then. I've always wanted to be a—"

But I was never able to admit to Tobias that I'd always wanted to feel what it was like to take on a wolf. Because the next moment, I couldn't say anything at all.

Tobias was kissing me.

Lips sweet with nectar, a brow wet with dew. His hands cupped my face, turning my head, letting me feel the intoxicating pull and suckle of his mouth. I moaned, reaching for his shoulders, wrapping my hands around his neck. His arms encircled me, pulling me hard against his body, firing the hood's soul within me. Old voices, long thought dead, spoke inside me.

Kiss him. Take him. Mate him.

As his mouth slid over my neck, all the feeling within me started to ebb. I closed my eyes, gasping, whimpering his name. My world turned upside down as Tobias swept my feet from under me. His chest felt so warm beneath my cheek. I leaned into his chest, letting his body heat reflect my own. The gentle left-right sway as he carried me through the forest lulled me. Soon, I couldn't keep my eyes open.

TEN

Amy called it a hangover. I called it proof of why cultures that shunned alcohol had things right.

Tobias arrived to pick us up the next morning, though I drove all the way back to Chicago while he and Amy napped in the back of the crew cab. Too many times, I caught myself snatching peeks in the rearview mirror, wondering if the lips which looked chapped in the light of day could be soft in the night.

And then I reminded myself that I already had a boyfriend, and that one dream didn't magically make Tobias any less of a widower wolf who would be forever bonded to his mate.

Back in Chicago, a message from Inga's office informed us that she and Caleb had left already, traveling to Istanbul via Tel Aviv.

"Israel?" Amy asked, reading the note over my shoulder. "Why?"

"Old vampires don't like email or phone calls or even fax machines. Inga's been corresponding with old friends, trying to find one the Ravens have approached to offer their life serum thing to. She's hoping one of them will lead us to their exact location. Right now, we don't know for sure."

"Okay, then why is Caleb with her?"

I shrugged, not wanting to admit aloud that that same thought passed through my head five times a day. "She's very protective of him."

"Yeah, well he's *your* boyfriend, so she better not try anything sketchy or I'm going to let her have it."

"You haven't even met him yet. What if you think he's scum or a player or something?"

"You, pick someone bad?" Amy's face screwed up. "I don't see that happening."

"Remind me later to tell you why Jess and I broke up."

A box on my bed with a note from Caleb passed along regrets for missing my graduation, but the present inside almost made up for it.

Just because you can no longer wield it, doesn't mean you can't make it shine. Very proud of you. Love you.

Amy snatched the card from my hand and held it at arm's length, whereupon she examined the page with the intensity of a homicide detective. "Geri, if you're serious about this guy, then get serious about this guy. You're going to lose him if you don't."

"What?" I grabbed the note back. "How in the hell do you know something like that from twenty words?"

"Because I'm looking at the only ones that matter. '*Love you.*'" Her finger pointed out the key text. "There's no 'I' there. He's— what's the phrase?—tipping his heart. He wants to show you what he feels, but he's scared of rejection. Scared, because he has a lot more invested in the relationship than you do."

Tobias cursed as he finally emerged out of the bedroom a few hours after sunset, the first words he'd said other than "I'll pump" since leaving Paradise.

"What the bloody hell is she talking about?" he said to me,

vaguely motioning to Amy.

"She's pretending to be the love guru again," I said, opening the box and holding up the contents for the werewolf's inspection. A silver crossbow charm the size of a dime pivoted from a thick chain of the same material. "Inga and Caleb left early. This is Caleb's graduation present to me."

Tobias grimaced. "Perfect. Now if I try to strangle you, I'll get third-degree burns in the process."

"So your alpha *has* ordered my execution."

"On the contrary, he's officially instructed me to accompany you to Istanbul because, and I quote, 'Geri's too irrational right now, and if something happens to her you could have prevented, her bitch of a mother will take it out on the whole pack.'" The werewolf coughed a laugh into the orange juice container as he stood in front of the open fridge. "Might be willing to test that theory after what happened."

I white-knuckled the handle of the fridge door as I pushed him back to close it. "Damned alpha."

"Can we get back to what's really important here?" Amy interjected. "If this Caleb guy is really as hot and sexy and sweet as you say, why are you not treating him better?" Her suspicious glare turned on Tobias. "Or do you have something to do with that?"

"Me?" Tobias stuck a thumb into his own chest. "Don't lay this at my paws. I've been telling her for months to sleep with the guy."

I threw up my hands at both of them. "As much as I appreciate you both trying to engineer the cashing in of my v-card, let me reassure you, I'm making that move only when I'm ready."

"Well, of course, sweetie!" Amy's mannerism shifted from grilling best friend to sympathetic sister. "No, I'm not saying put out before he gets out. No! I'm just saying, if you got a great guy, why are you being so resistant to building a *real* relationship with him?"

Tobias took a bite of bagel and shrugged. "I don't care, I'm just sick of having to wait around at WWL for you. If you started staying whole nights with him, I'd get half my life back."

Amy snapped her fingers. "Another great reason. Look, I have to go change over my laundry downstairs. When I come back, you and I are going to sit down, talk this out, and make a plan."

Finally, with Amy out of the room and Tobias talking again, I could bring up the were-elephant in the room.

"So Cody isn't that mad with me?"

The werewolf looked at me like I'd just suggested dumplings were disgusting. "Actually, I'd say he's right pissed. You called him out in front of the pack and, by the way, made a fool of yourself in the process. If you were pack, he probably would have renounced you to save maw."

A fool of myself? How dare he? "Like your alpha did with you?"

My verbal arrow hit its mark, and Tobias flinched. "It's not the same."

"Okay, I'll grant you it's not *exactly* the same. You were trying to prove to your alpha that vampires were involved in your brother's murder and your mate's disappearance, but you acted out of love."

"You telling your ex-boyfriend—your married-and-mated-with-a-child ex-boyfriend—that you were still in love with him wasn't heroic, Geri. You weren't trying to right a wrong or alert others to danger; you were just shopping for sympathy."

"Sympathy?" I spit the term back in his face. "May I remind you that *Cody* was the one who brought up my feelings to begin with?"

"Because every time you look at him, all dreamy-eyed and lovestruck, you weaken his position as alpha. He—" Tobias stumbled over his own realization as his flashing eyes went from me to the ceiling. "He set you up. He knew exactly how you would react, and he did it on purpose to create a scene so he could save face."

The notion turned over in my head only for a moment before my mind filled in the other part of that conclusion. "He did it because that was the only way he could let you go with me to Istanbul for the summer. He had to solidify his authority *and* make me look pitiful, so the others wouldn't question why he was letting you go chasing after a hood. Not even a real hood anymore, a former hood."

Tobias ran a hand through hair badly in need of a cut. "Cody might be better at pack politics than I thought him capable of." The werewolf extended a hand. "Peace?"

I wrapped my hand in Tobias's. "Until the next time we have a reason to fight."

ELEVEN

"What about your parents, Geri?" Mrs. Popowitz asked as Amy and I posed for pictures in caps and gowns. "Did they make it into town for graduation? Amy says you're from Minnesota. That's not too far away, is it?"

"Michigan, actually," I corrected. "Unfortunately, my parents are very occupied running the family business. They couldn't make it."

Truth be told, I'd been a little upset by the fact that neither my dad nor my mom had talked to me since last summer. But, as Amy's parents reminded me, I didn't have an exclusive on dysfunctional family drama. She had a feather of a mother and a stone of a father.

"Yes, I understand how hard it could be to get away," Mr. Popowitz grumbled. "Yet, somehow, I managed to do it, and I run a Manhattan law firm."

"Never you mind him, dear." Mrs. Popowitz practically cooed as she ran a gloved hand over my cheek. I didn't know if it was good genetics, or a great plastic surgeon, but she didn't look to be more than a few years older than her daughter. "But is there no one here at all for you? How tragic."

I bit my lip. It didn't feel tragic until she had said something. But then, wading through the crowd, wearing the darkest pair of sunglasses I had ever seen, strode my unwitting bodyguard.

"Actually, there's one person."

I squealed as his embrace picked me up off the floor and set my legs pinwheeling through the air.

"Damned proud of you, Little Red. Even though I don't understand what the hell it is you're going to do with that degree."

"It's just official documentation that I'm smarter than you."

"Could have told you that without you wasting all that money on tuition."

My feet tingled by the time Tobias set me down. He played nice, shaking hands with Amy's parents, then asking what they thought about their daughter's plan to join us in Istanbul for the summer.

Mr. Popowitz's face screwed up, as though he'd just smelled something foul. "Istanbul?" He turned to his daughter. "I thought you said you were going to Europe for the summer."

"Istanbul *is* in Europe," Amy sighed. "Or at least, half of it is."

You could have polished a blade on his sharpened eyes. "Amy Helene Popowitz, how can you even think to go to such a backward country for the whole summer?"

I snatched the werewolf's hand before he could try to slither away. If he had opened this can of worms, the least he could do was stick around to watch them crawl out.

Amy, however, must have anticipated her father's objection, and came out fighting with silver-studded facts. "Actually, *Daddy*, Turkey has a higher GDP than both Switzerland and Austria, is one of the world's leading producers of textiles, hazelnuts, and tobacco, and has the highest levels of education of any Muslim country in the region. *They've* even had a woman prime minister—something America still hasn't managed."

Mr. Popowitz looked off in the distance at nothing in particular. "If there was a woman worthy who'd run, we would have."

"But… Turkey," Mrs. Popowitz persisted. "It's rather dangerous, isn't it?"

"How is New York City different? Or the United States?"

Her father pushed his black-rimmed glasses up his nose. "And when do you leave for this escapade?"

"Tomorrow night. We have a direct flight out of O'Hare."

Mrs. Popowitz took me and her daughter by the hand and walked us toward the door. "Oh, that's soon! Let's make sure you both are well fed before then. I hear they don't have any pork in that country. Can you imagine? A whole summer without bacon."

Tobias winced as I elbowed his ribs.

"I can't believe a place like this really exists."

Ignorance was a fertile field in which surprises grow.

I'd been to large cities before: Detroit, Frankfurt, Munich. And of course, two years living in Chicago. Metropolises on their own, I'd thought, were interchangeable, after you got past a few distinguishing landmarks or sports stadiums.

Istanbul was a city defined by landmarks, one which a modern city had managed to grow into the cracks of and cocoon over the outside. Even Schloss Wolfsretter, the majestic, ancestral home of the House of Red and current de facto United Nations building for my entire species, would fade into the background among such colossal edifices. As I looked out over the European side's skyline from the cabin of the massive SUV Igor had waiting for us at the airport, snaking its way up the Asian coastline, a crick in my neck began to throb from all my head turning.

Igor grinned, although he too kept his eyes fixed on the living museum landscape. "Five hundred years since I first saw her, and she still has the power to make my heart beat."

"Wait, you mean your heart's not beating?"

Amy's question proved to be a bucket of cold water that awoke all of us to reality. Istanbul released its mystical hold on our attention, and our conversation turned inward.

Igor smiled. "Beating might be an exaggeration, but it functions, just in a much different way, from what I've been able to gather." Once he'd learned that Amy was definitely and enthusiastically in the know about the supernatural world, he'd decided that knowledge trumped ignorance, even if he wasn't sure of this particular huey's trustworthiness as yet. "It's been difficult to know much about how vampirism changes the internal organs and biochemistry of the subject. As we heal from minor injury so quickly, and given that when we do die, our corpses turn to ash as soon as they're struck by sunlight, it's been impossible to learn much through postmortem examination."

"But you're obviously still able to function humanly," Amy countered. "How, without a pulse? How do your muscles get oxygenated? Wouldn't you have continual strokes without it going to your brain? And what about digestion? You drink blood, which doesn't have that many nutrients or other essential things like fiber? How in the hell do you survive?"

"I still exercise regularly."

The attempt at humor fell flat. Igor cleared his throat and continued.

"All good questions, and ones I myself long to learn the answers to, Miss Popowitz. Despite centuries of study, both in books and on my own person, the best I've been able to deduce is that *that* is the primary reason we drink blood. Whatever infests or infects us when we become vampire—call it a virus or call it magic—keeps our bodies in a perpetual state of rejuvenation. It cannot, however, deliver oxygenation. In effect, we drink blood to breathe."

Amy's expression soured. "But you'd need to drink it, like, all the time."

Igor allowed an acknowledging nod, then added, "Then again, with practice, one can hold one's breath for a very long time."

Amy could accept that Igor was a vampire, but she couldn't accept that he had as quick of an intellect as she did. She settled back in her seat and turned her eyes back to the city. "You can't hold your breath forever."

According to Igor, I shouldn't be deluded into thinking that traffic would always be so accommodating, as the drive from one side of the Golden Horn to the other usually took several hours. Our advantage? At two AM, streets were merely crowded instead of congested.

Tobias looked down at the waves below the bridge when we passed over, each rise kissed by light from both sides of the strait. "There's more history in the square mile around us than England and America hold together. Really makes you ponder things, don't it? How insignificant our existence is in the bigger frame of things?" His bottom lip pulled in, and a glisten on his cheek gave away what he struggled to hide in his voice. "Kara would have loved this."

Like the city reflecting in the waters below, I turned my thoughts back to the mangled histories that had brought each of us to this moment. If I hadn't hesitated to say *yes* when Cody had asked me to mate him, I would be his wife now. Perhaps I'd even be sitting by his side this very moment, bouncing our baby on my knee. If Tobias had convinced me sooner to help him, Kara might still be alive. But then, who would be here to fight the Ravens?

I leaned into him, resting my head on his shoulder. "She would have."

As Igor paid the driver (and selectively poked at his memory to delete too much detail about us), the rest of us unloaded our bags from the back of the car.

"It smells like fish and piss," Tobias grumbled.

Amy paused, taking a moment to thoroughly scent the air herself. "I'm only getting the piss. Your nose must be better than mine." When Tobias gave her a *I'm a werewolf, remember?* glare, she followed up with, "Oh, right, yeah. Well, I'd rather be able to smell the fish, frankly."

"And I'd rather smell anything." I sucked down another lungful of air. Supernatural abilities denied, the profile proved limited. "Seriously, all I'm getting is…"

"Bread." Igor cut me off as the car pulled away. "There's a bakery across the street. You're smelling the yeast proofing the bread. In an hour or so, when the ovens fire up, you'll swear you were back in your mother's kitchen."

We all turned deadpanned expressions on him.

"Seriously, none of your mothers baked bread?" Igor shifted his weight. "We'll get a loaf in the evening when I rise, if they're still open. It's the next best thing. Empires universally result in two things: slavery and fine cuisine. The latter remains after the former has arisen."

The sidewalk leading toward the house before us seemed to be more worn down than welcoming. The structure, three stories high but only the width of two cars, still held an echo of beauty. At its zenith, it must have drawn the eye and inspired envy. Its wooden boards had long ago let go any hold of paint. The door, a dark-stained thing laced over with iron girders, looked like something salvaged from a pirate ship.

"Suddenly, I'm thinking coming to Istanbul wasn't my best idea." Amy examined the home with a displeased eye. She turned to Igor. "You're, like, an ancient vampire. Aren't you supposed to have luxurious mansions all over the world?"

Igor shrunk back, throwing his coat over his arm. "I suppose you also think I should only wear black capes with high red collars and seduce young virgins with my radiant sex appeal."

"One: ew, you're old. And two..." She pointed to exhibit A: a three-story structure held together by nostalgia and a few remaining nails. "If there was a building in Manhattan that looked like this, it would be surrounded by a security fence and plastered over with signs saying *condemned*."

Igor found a key underneath a pot of pink flowers resting on a stoop before the front door, a metal relic longer than his hand that may have been as old as he was.

"That is by design. We're here to find the Ravens, hopefully while not being found ourselves. We want to lie low. I do have a house here—a beautiful home out on one of the Prince Islands. I'm certain Vlad would have someone watching it. Too risky to stay there."

"If this isn't *your* home, whose is it then?"

Tobias's question echoed my thoughts. Immediately following which was, why here? For the past three minutes, I'd been scanning the run-down building's edifice for security concerns. Other than the bars overlapping the windows of the first floor and the front door, little inspired hope in me that this house would stand up to a rainstorm, let alone a Raven.

Igor turned the key. "I rented it online. Please remember, if any of the neighbors asks, we're a group from the university, here doing research about street cats. Also, let me tell you one thing about this country: it teaches you not to focus on outward appearance. There is often something surprising hidden behind the veil."

I stepped around Amy, pressed forward by hope. "Are Inga and Caleb here? I got a text from him yesterday saying they were on their way to Istanbul."

The vampire, his hand flattened against the door, paused. "None of you are supposed to be using any devices."

Amy looked up from a tiny lit screen. "I thought that meant just for the flight."

Before my friend could blink, our honorary *in loco parentis* had her device in his hand.

"George Orwell failed to foresee that you all would be the ones holding the cameras on yourselves." With one simple gesture, Igor closed his hand, reducing the phone to e-waste. "No smartphones, no computers, no telephone calls. Inga will be bringing devices we can use that are guaranteed to be secure."

While Amy mumbled her grievances, I was still stuck on the one thing with which I couldn't reckon. "Caleb?"

Igor motioned me into the house. "Soon, Geri. I promise."

He'd been right about one thing: the exterior concealed what the interior revealed. Not to say that I felt like we'd just stepped into something swanky like Caleb's WWL flat or posh like a suite at the Ritz, but the home held its own in terms of quality. Hardwood floors were covered in aged yet intricately-patterned rugs. Clean, white-washed walls hosted a gallery's worth of paintings and prints, many of which framed the very skyline we'd observed driving in.

Igor set down his bag inside the door. "That over there," he pointed to the right, "is the sitting room, though they call it a salon here. The kitchen is at the back of the house, along with a bathroom if any of you want to freshen up. There's only two bedrooms upstairs, but they're both pretty big. The third floor is one large room, empty of furniture at my request. I thought you all could use it for sparring and as a space to train Amy, like you were talking about."

"Only two bedrooms?" Amy asked. "So, who gets what?"

Igor seemed confused by the question. "I thought it would be obvious: the women get one. The men, the other."

Embarrassment warmed my cheeks. "I thought Caleb and I would get our own room?"

"So I'd get Tobias?" The blonde licked her lips. "Sounds good to me."

"No." Tobias put his paw down. "Don't take this the wrong way,

Amy, but no. There's no way I'm sharing a room with you."

"Amy and I will share a room," I said, stepping in to play diplomat. Caleb would just have to join me at the negotiating table when he arrived. But something still didn't add up. "What about you and Inga, Igor? Where will you stay?"

"Ah, yes! Where is—Ah! Here it is." In the middle of the house, between the entryway and what I assumed was the kitchen, the vampire opened an old wooden door that echoed the front door's style. Beyond, a staircase descended into a dark pit. Must and dew scented the air. "*This* is why this house," he said. "A cistern. Empty, of course. In the old part of the city, there's hundreds of them. Every grand home or even apartment block in Byzantine or Ottoman times had one, and a number of them still survive in one form or another today. A favorite of vampires for day rest, of course."

Amy's nose turned up. "Ew, you sleep in water?"

"Not so much these days, but once upon a time, it was quite usual for a vampire to prefer a water bed, if you'll forgive the pun. You see, nature likes balances. Ours is a slayer, of course. But even they, in turn, have a weakness, don't they?"

"I was thinking the weakness was that whole not-being-undead thing," I deadpanned.

The professor continued very professorially. "Water, Geri. A slayer can conjure a solarium and burn a vampire to ash, but they cannot do so while standing in water. Yes, back in the day, a cistern was the very height of vampiric sleeping arrangements."

I bent down over my suitcase and foisted out a smaller bag from within. "Whatever floats your boat. Or, your body."

Tobias side-eyed me. "Please tell me that isn't what I think it is."

"Of course, it is."

"But they won't even do you any good anymore."

"They make me *feel* safer." The silver tchotchkes clanked as I palmed two of them and pulled them out. "They're small, and I'll make sure they're nowhere that you're going to just casually rub up against one of them."

Amy crossed her arms. "So, you're going to stuff them into your bra then?"

TWELVE

"I've never understood the term *food coma*, but I think I'm going into some kind of torpor."

Amy folded her arms over her stomach and fell back, groaning. By the time we'd awoken late in the afternoon the following day, most of the bakery's stock had been depleted and was already turning hard. Still, food was food. Crumbs were all that remained of the second loaf of bread we'd polished off.

Her eyes swung around the room as another smile crept onto her face. "Can you believe places like this exist? Igor wasn't kidding when he said 'behind the veil,' was he?"

I dipped my chin. "It certainly wasn't what I expected when we first pulled up outside, that's for sure."

Yes, the interior of the house was just as aged as the exterior, but it wore its years clinging to remnants of a former glory. Instead of individual pieces of repositionable furniture, a permanent row of low, wide couches ringed the edge of the room, festooned with lace coverlets. At the center of this U-shaped configuration, a table which looked more like a giant copper plate sat atop a collapsible base of wooden peg legs, its circumference edged with poufy floor cushions. This, I came to understand, was also the dining table.

"We'll have to make sure to get some lira soon," I said as I lay down on one of the couches. "We were lucky that guy at the counter was willing to take pity on a few American tourists who only had dollars."

Amy lay on the floor parallel to me, her blonde hair a contrast to the red-tinted rugs covering the floor throughout the house. "I told you, I could have used my card. They accepted them; it said so on the door."

"No, we're here on the down-low, remember? We want to avoid electronic breadcrumbs as much as possible. No credit cards."

"There's no way they'd know to follow my records, though. I mean, I only decided to come with you a week ago, and I shouldn't be any interest to them. I'm just a looney."

"*Huey*, Amy. The term is *huey*. Like, a human-y creature: *huey*. Not sure who came up with it, but—"

The front door had opened, and both our resident vampire and werewolf were still asleep. I'd rolled off the couch and drawn the blade from my hair before Amy could even blink.

"Geri, w—"

"*Shh!*"

Putting a finger to my mouth, I ordered her silence. Amy was a quick learner; she sat up but didn't make another peep. A drawn-out, deliberate creek of a floorboard near the entrance suggested an intruder moving with deliberate haste, but in our direction. Jumping on the couches let me move toward the door without the same giveaway, but the element of surprise would only last until we could look each other in the eye.

Years of training took over, as I began to categorize assets and liabilities. *Huey behind me, so I can't run away. Silver blade would be ineffective if it's a vampire, but given that it's still daylight, it probably isn't. They might have a weapon. A gun or a knife. A knife I can handle. If it's a gun, only try to take him down if the physical match is pretty close, and get control of the gun ASAP. Scream for Tobias as soon as silence is no longer a benefit. Get Amy to run away if you can't control the situation. Hostages, not homicides. Anyone here isn't here by accident. Hold and interrogate. Find out who sent them, and what they were sent here to do.*

"Igor?"

The voice struck at the chords of my memory, but the tune seemed out of place. My hand planted on the floor; it would be my ballast point so I could round out a kick low and sweep out the intruder's feet.

"Hello? Anyone here? Geri? *Oofff…*"

With the coordination of a tiger's pounce, I dropped my blade and had him on the ground, my legs thrown over his hips and my hands on either side of his head. Only my goal wasn't to incapacitate any longer; it was to hold and to kiss.

Caleb laced his fingers behind his head as he slipped into his mask of smugness, a golden grin greeting me. "Looks like somebody missed me."

"Maybe a little."

I giggled as he rolled up, exchanging our positions. A solid weight against my thigh told me he'd finally taken my advice on always having a weapon. As Caleb leaned down and renewed our kiss, a halo of blonde hair emerged from the background.

"Please tell me this is the boyfriend."

I almost burst out laughing when Caleb pulled away and found a stranger brandishing a vase of dry flowers as an improvised weapon. Realizing we were no longer preparing for a real-life action movie fight scene, Amy let the vase lower as her eyes glassed over.

"On second thought, please tell me he's *not* the boyfriend. Wow."

Caleb turned back to me. "Is she a werewolf? And mind, I only ask because she's drooling."

"No, she's a huey, and she's only drooling because my boyfriend is hot and there's nothing Amy likes more than hot men. Now, stand up and let me introduce you to her properly. After that, you're going to tell me what the hell you and Inga have been up to."

"If you insist. But after that, you're going to tell me why in the hell there's a huey in our house, wielding flower vases."

Our house. That phrase shouldn't have sent my mind abuzz, but… *buzz buzz.*

"Fair enough."

THIRTEEN

"Technically, I haven't aged in centuries, but for some reason, I feel suddenly very old. Did I just walk onto the set of some new CW series where an ex-hood, a slayer, a werewolf, and a token huey have to fight evil monsters on the streets of the city?"

Igor sized up the four twentysomethings lounging in the living room. Tobias had just joined us a few minutes ago. The vampire's head swung to take in the scope of the room.

"Where is Inga?"

"A 'hello' to you, too, professor." Caleb stood and cleared his throat, shaking Igor's hand, before they both took seats on the couches. "Inga's still in Üsküdar, over on the Asian side. At least, she was when I left the hotel this morning. We got in last night, but that's as far as we could make it from the new airport before dawn. I'm going to guess when she woke up a few minutes ago and found me gone, she smoked out of there pretty quickly."

"You crossed the city alone?" Igor Karmarov had never fit the "disapproving father figure" role better. "Caleb, you of all people know how dangerous this city is for someone like you. For anyone, frankly."

"It was daytime. I wasn't going to be tagged by any fangs," my boyfriend returned. "I've barely seen Geri for the last three months. Knowing she was just a ferry ride and steady walk away, I couldn't wait anymore. It was fine. Besides, you forget two key facts: one,

I was born here. I know the city. And, two…" A ball the size of a tangerine burst into existence on his open palm. "I could have handled a vampire if one wanted to tango."

Amy's mouth dropped to the floor. "He's Harry freaking Potter."

Tobias yawned and stretched both his physical muscles and his sarcastic ones. "And how, exactly, did you get into our ultra-secure facility?"

The slayer pointed his free hand over his shoulder, back toward the door. "Found a key under a pot of flowers out there. Maybe not the best place to leave that?"

Igor failed to be impressed, despite blinking as the solarium stung his irises. "This isn't Chicago. These aren't little offshoot clutches spun out from the Old World. We're in the Belt of Blood, and the Ravens circle it daily."

"Belt of Blood?" Looking to Tobias, I saw he was just as perplexed. "What is that?"

The vampire grimaced. "The traditional territory of the Dracule clutches. It spreads from Vienna, down through Asia Minor, then up into the caucuses. There's a reason this region is known for its vampire lore. It came of age with the Byzantines, fled west and east with Christians into the Hapsburg and the Czars' courts, then folded back in once the Ottomans seated themselves."

"That last part thanks to Vlad Tepeş," Caleb added.

Thank goodness that I had Amy, whose innocence couldn't be condemned, to ask the questions that would have revealed my ignorance. "Wasn't Vlad the Prince of Transylvania? Why is he so obsessed with Istanbul?"

"It's a bit Freirean, I'm afraid."

Our blank faces drove Igor to frustration.

"Seriously? Two of you just graduated from university in the last forty-eight hours, and nothing?"

"If it was a biochem thing, I'd know it," I offered. "Obviously, it's not some kind of molecule."

More annoyed scowling. It was almost like being back at home with my mom.

"It's the concept that an affronted or oppressed population will assume the characteristics of their oppressors when they gain power," Igor explained. "As a human, Vlad and his people—That would be Wallachia, Amy. Transylvania refers to the region at large.—were at the mercy of the Ottomans. His entire royal line ruled at the leisure of the sultan. As children, Vlad and his brother Radu were even political prisoners at the sultan's court."

Caleb nodded, presumably heading off our confused expressions. "It was a very common practice in the ancient world, and not just for the Ottomans. A good way to ensure that a conquered people didn't rise up against you was to give incentive for toeing the line. Even Augustus took Cleopatra and Marc Antony's children into his own home after they died."

"Even though the children were technically prisoners, they were treated as royal guests, given an education and furnished with a lifestyle nearly on par to the sultan's own children," Igor resumed. "But Vlad never forgot who reigned over his people, though his brother sided with the Turks, even helping them conquer Constantinople in 1453. It left an imprint. When he escaped the confinement we'd placed him in, he came here, vowing to live out the luxurious life his people's blood and tears paid for, by literally living off the blood of his enemy's descendant."

Amy's eyes couldn't get any wider. "If Shakespeare had known about this, he might have written a vampire play."

Igor waved off the comment. "Politics is a constant, perpetual motion. The only difference is the players."

The growl rumbling through Tobias's chest preceded his shift, and within moments, all hell had broken loose. The werewolf tensed his haunches, balancing on all fours amid a pile of ravaged clothing, as I in turn drew my blade and covered Amy. It seemed to happen all at once: the front door flying open, the bank of smoke that rushed into the room, the smoke taking form, slamming Caleb against the wall, and Igor rolling his eyes at it all.

"You bastard!" Inga Rosethorn practiced control like a Zen master. A foot off the floor and pinned in a vampire's grip, Caleb looked nonplussed. "How dare you pull a stunt like that? I thought you were dead! I thought they'd gotten you. I thought after everything, I'd failed."

"But I left you a note on the dresser."

"I KNOW YOU LEFT ME A NOTE ON THE DRESSER!" Her nails nicked his neck, and I had to fight the urge to leap in and pull Inga's hands off my man. "Which was even more stupid. What if the Ravens had come for you? They'd know exactly where to find you. Do you ever think about *any* of the consequences of your actions? How pussy-whipped are you?"

"I object to that." My words turned a spotlight onto my presence, and a vampire seething anger lashed out in my direction. "Most hood women would consider such dominance over their beau a compliment."

Caleb took his protector/attacker's wrists in his hands. "I'm fine, and look around: no ravens. Not even sparrows."

"Inga, enough," Igor said. "I've already lectured him. Let it go, and by that, I mean him. He's a man in love. They do irrational things."

"If he doesn't learn to master his emotions, the irrationality is going to get him killed," Inga grumbled as Caleb resumed his feet. Now free to observe the room at large, her eyes fell upon a somewhat flushed huey. "Who are you?"

The blonde stood and threw out a hand to the seething vampire. "Amy Popowitz, and I'm apparently the token honey."

"Huey!"

"Huey," Amy corrected. "I'm assuming you're the beautiful Inga Rosethorn I heard so much about."

Inga took a moment to look at Amy's hand as though inspecting it for defects. Finally, her tensions eased, and she gently slid her own out to meet the greeting in kind, if without kindness.

"Miss Popowitz, a pleasure." The words were flat, emotionless, scripted. "But you should not have come. This is no mission for a huey. I doubt even Gerwalta's readiness."

"Oh, I know. From what she's told me, she's pretty much useless now."

"Hey!" My hackles raised in the wake of my best friend's betrayal.

Amy continued as though I'd said nothing. "But since I was attacked by a vampire in front of a theater full of people, I thought if I came along, I'd stand a better chance of surviving with you, Igor, and Caleb around."

Inga raised a suspicious eyebrow. "And Tobias?"

Amy swatted the air. "What's a werewolf going to do to a vampire? Bark at it?"

Tobias took on his human, complete with outrage. "Bark at it? Don't forget who—"

I lashed my arm out over Tobias's chest, keeping him from pouncing. Maybe he didn't yet see what was going on, but I'd certainly caught on. Genius. Amy was a diplomatic genius. In a few brief moments, she'd managed to turn a centuries-old vampire to her favor.

The corners of Inga's mouth ticked up. "Indeed. Well, I still think it foolish that you are here, but at least you will prove to be most entertaining."

"Inga?"

The female vampire's head snapped to her vampiric father.

"You said something about what you found out in Tel Aviv?" he continued. "I think we should all hear that. Let me make some tea, and then I want you to tell *all of us* what you've learned."

We sat dispersed on the couches, drinking from the tulip-shaped cups that had perplexed me when I saw them in the kitchen earlier. Igor handed each of us a spoon about half the size of a normal one.

"Tea is the lubricant of the tongue in Turkey, as well as the wallet. Even if you don't like it now, you need to acquire a taste for it. It will be given to you everywhere you go, and I mean everywhere. Learn to drink vast quantities of it in a way that doesn't stress your pulse or your bladder."

The brew, a mildly bitter tonic with hints of bergamot, didn't quite satisfy the palate like coffee, but it did warm the insides. Despite the fact that it was now early June, something about the house made the drafty interior a bit chilly.

"As we suspected, the Ravens still make their clutch in Istanbul. As in the ancient world, it is still one of the most convenient bases from which to operate."

"Operate?" I asked. "That's an interesting word choice."

"It is an intentional one," Inga confirmed. "We knew that Vlad's discovery of the power of werewolf blueblood to sustain vampire life after the natural death was due had been used for political advantage. Seems he's also using it for financial gain as well."

"He's still selective about who he allows into his inner circle," Caleb added, even as his fingers traced lines over my palm. "Not just anyone is chosen for the treatments. A run-of-the-mill clutch holds no interest for him. He grows friends in gardens of influence, and seeds it very carefully. Our contact assured us that one does not seek out the Ravens; the Ravens seek out you."

Tobias set his untouched tea down on the copper table. "But how would the Ravens even know who to approach? How are they getting their information about potential clients?"

Inga and Caleb exchanged a weighted look, one that then turned on me.

"No." It was impossible. How would that even happen? "Not the hood's tracking software? But that's only used to keep a tab on werewolf populations, to help create matches between different packs and flag potential lone wolves."

Tobias mumbled into his shoulder. "Big brother, watch thyself."

"It is the same software the hoods use, but the hoods are not the ones who created it. *That* dubious achievement came from the Line of Dracule. Your mother—or some other matron—received it from us."

Tobias leaned back on the sofa, looking oddly Roman as he held up his half-empty cup and swirled it, setting the tea leaves collected at the bottom spinning. "So vampire tech was implemented by hood overlords to control werewolf populations. If they weren't all dead, I'd say the slayers are the only clean ones in this."

"I'm not dead." Caleb's fingers laced through mine. "But I'll admit that I'm not that clean. I can, in fact, be very dirty."

"Yeah, well good luck with that," Amy muttered. "You're sharing a room with Tobias."

Inga pushed on as though no one had interrupted. No doubt she was accustomed to Caleb's twisted tongue. "A tool isn't inherently good or evil. It's the intent the user brings to it that determines its utility. In any event, it seems that Vlad and the Ravens are very good at what they do. Several I contacted in Amman and Tel Aviv have been approached. None have any idea how to find the Ravens on purpose or where they're located."

"That's a shitty attempt at building a client relationship," Amy said. "There's something missing there. They'd have to know that some would stew over a decision like that, and want to change their minds. How were these vampires told to get in touch if that happens?"

Inga grinned. My little huey roomie proved impressive when pitching in the big leagues. "They were told if they changed their minds, they were to come to Istanbul. No further instructions than that, not even if they should come to the Asian or the European side."

I chewed over the revelations. "There's something fishy about that. Something missing. Can vampires sense each other's proximity the ways hoods and wolves can?"

"Wait, you know when each other are near?" Caleb passed narrowed eyes over Tobias and me.

"Not me anymore. But yeah, before my mother did her little disowning ceremony."

"The only good thing to come of that whole event," Tobias added. "I'm no longer a living Geri-emotion-meter. Thank god that happened before this trip."

I turned over my shoulder to examine the werewolf lounging on the couch behind me, managing to stay serious despite the comic vision of him, naked, with a pink throw pillow covering up his unmentionables. "What's that supposed to mean?"

"Nothing. Just… I'm in a crowded city, stuck indoors, and I'm jet-lagged. In short, Red, I'm in a foul mood."

"So our first objective should be finding out where the clutch rests during the day."

Inga's statement made my eyes twitch. "Why?"

Beside me, Caleb released my hand and rolled to the front of the cushion. "Because that's the best time to kill them, when they're asleep."

"Kill them?" I nearly choked on the words. "Without even talking to them?"

My boyfriend looked like a deer caught in headlights, not really sure if there was more danger in staying where he was or dashing off in another direction. "Baby, that's the whole reason we're here."

"It's not entirely why we're here." Tobias sat up finally, putting an emptied cup of tea on the table. "They're going to die, trust that. But sounds like Vlad Inc. isn't just an old boy's cricket club. If they're distributing, they have a network—whether that's a handful of others or hundreds. We off them without understanding what kind of network they've built up, we'll just be clearing the corner for someone else to set up shop."

Igor, who had remained silent, finally stirred. "I agree with Tobias, though I do think we need to be cautious. The moment he feels you're a threat, he'll destroy you."

"What, and you're safe?" Amy asked.

"We are of his blood," Inga said to the unaware. "A vampire cannot kill another of his bloodline. It destroys him in the process."

Amy snapped her fingers. "Well, isn't that a meatball?"

Caleb poured himself another cup of tea. "With all due respect, Igor, I think we're better off destroying the Ravens and letting the chips fall where they may. Once it gets around that there's one slayer still out there and he killed off the most infamous vampire of all time, anyone else will think twice about following in old Vlad's footsteps."

"I am in agreement with Caleb," Inga said. "We tried to be rational before, Igor. We thought we could handle this problem ourselves by sealing the Ravens away until their time to expire had passed. Somehow they survived, and now, we must deal with the consequences in a way that leaves no opportunity for survival. Every moment they're left to live, we risk the lives of all supes. We're not trying to defeat our enemy, we're trying to destroy him."

"So where do we look?" I posed. "I mean, this is a HUGE city. Something like ten million?"

"Plus five million more," Tobias said. "You really did *no* research before coming here, did you?"

"Not the kind that would go into a third-grade geography report, no. But I now have a very thorough and appreciative knowledge of the weapons used by the Ottoman military over its very long history."

Tobias rolled his eyes as if to say "Hoods!" Igor, however, stayed focused.

"The city keeps adding new neighborhoods on its edges, but I'm pretty sure Vlad will have selected a location in the old parts of town, more than likely on the European side. Remember: he's dangerous, and in part because he's learned to be tactical. Wherever it is, he'll have chosen a place that is easily defensible and has access to sufficient humans for feeding."

"In one of the biggest tourist destinations in the world?" I asked. "That doesn't narrow it down at all."

FOURTEEN

Each of us came from a different lineage: slayer, hood, werewolf, and huey, but we had one thing in common. Jet lag had turned our world on end. Even Caleb, who had come from Tel Aviv, a single hour of difference, reeled from the shift.

"Don't expect this to be common, Amy," Tobias warned. "As soon as we adjust to the time difference, we'll be sleeping through the day. I'm so knackered right now."

"I'm not exactly bouncing off walls here," Amy returned. "But if I'm not allowed to go outside at all by myself at night, and only in the daytime with a 'special' chaperone, then you'll be up and dragging my ass around the city whenever *I* like."

"If you let me train you, I'm sure we can get that changed."

She rolled her eyes at my platitudes. "Like me knowing how to throw a knife is going to do me any good."

"It's not just knowing how to fight, you know." Caleb turned the corner, leading us into a crowded corridor lined on both sides with what looked like a flea market. "Most people like you know how to tell when a situation is suspicious, and most people like us only want easy targets. You figure out how to recognize when you should just leave some place because something doesn't add up, you'll be ten steps ahead of where you are now. The best defense is a good offense, as they say."

"Actually, I think it's the other way around. And lest you forget, when I was attacked, it was on a crowded stage in front of… well, a crowd." Amy coughed as we passed through a flume of smoke rising up from a brazier on the side of the road. "Where in the hell are you taking us? This looks like something out of *Aladdin*."

Caleb stopped and swung around. "You know *Aladdin*?"

"Of course, I do. It's only one of the best animated movies ever made. Answer my question."

Caleb grinned, took Amy by the hand, and walked her backward under an archway bearing the seal of the Ottoman Sultan.

"Manhattan Barbie, welcome to Shangri-La."

If not for the fact that I knew this wasn't a Christian culture, I would have sworn we'd discovered Santa's workshop. We were mice in a maze, and cheese lay in every direction, making it impossible to know which way to run first. Ahead: leather, spices, exotic and massive glassworks designed in intricate patterns. To the left, polished metal, most of it jewel-encrusted, sparkled. Even without my supernatural abilities, the sight of so much silver made my insides hum. To our right, bags, books, buttons… Anything a heart could desire outside of illegal activities had its place.

Amy roused herself from her reverie with a clap of her hands. "I'm going to buy one of everything."

Tobias raised one eyebrow. "You don't even know all of what's in there."

"Doesn't matter." She could barely move forward with anything but her eyes. "I'll figure out what it all is later."

Two hours later, I'd learned two new things about Amy. One, she had a penchant for painted tea sets, and two, she could haggle with a tenacity that left Caleb wondrous.

"I used to think no one could negotiate a price like the Turks," he said, shifting a bag filled with silk scarves from one arm to the other. "But Amy? She could talk a potato out of its own skin."

I nodded. "And she's limited by the fact that I'm only letting her use cash. Think of the damage she could do if I told her she could use her credit cards."

The slayer sucked in air through pursed lips. "That might actually cause an earthquake when we went back to the rental. So much weight might shift tectonic plates."

"Fifty-five!" An olive-skinned man standing three inches shorter than the New Yorker pushed five sausage fingers and a bunch of attitude into Amy's face.

"Fifty!" Amy held her ground. Her own fingers she left at her side. "And that's still more than it's worth."

A series of Turkish curses followed, after which Amy shoved her purse back into a bag at her side and walked away.

"That's it?" I asked. "Fifteen minutes of back-and-forth, and you're going to walk over five lira?"

"Oh, Geri…" She grinned a smile that failed to conceal mischief, deliberately moving slowly to where we waited. "Watch and learn."

Just as we all turned to walk away, the man from the booth called out, "Miss! Miss! Come back. Fifty, but only because you are beautiful."

Caleb leaned into me as the victorious blonde turned to close her deal. "With that sort of cachet, you could probably get some things for free while we're here."

"Caleb Helsing, did you just call me beautiful?"

"Implied it, actually. Why don't you try for one of those skimpy belly dancer costumes over there?" He lifted his free hand and pointed to a diaphanous concoction of muslin, bedazzled by belts of silver coins. "I know it looks pretty flimsy, but remember: you won't be wearing it for long."

"Is our relationship at the 'will you wear this lingerie for me' stage?"

"We'll never know unless we give it an honest try."

"Oh, please." Tobias, two stalls away and looking at some woolen socks, of course could hear us just fine. "At least warn me if you guys are going to talk about your sex life so I can—"

When a dog caught on to a suspicious noise, what followed was a typical series of mannerisms. He'd stop all action, go still as the dead, and tilt his head in the direction from which the noise had emanated. Werewolves were no different.

"Caleb, get Amy." I wasted no time in explanations, and Caleb thankfully didn't ask for any. He went about the errand as I made my way to the wolf. "What is it?"

Tobias sniffed, tasted the air, then sniffed again. Even I was picking up on the subtle hints of lupine essence swirling in the air.

My sense of smell might be average now, but it had been finely attuned to that particular profile.

"How many?"

He didn't look at me but, instead, began to turn a slow circle. "One, but mixed with recent scents from at least a dozen others. She's alone, but she's not a loner."

"She?" I didn't know why I expected the werewolf to be male, but a little nudge in my gut told me the eyes of a man were upon me. Then again, in this crowded venue, that could be coming from any corner, from any kind of creature.

Tobias lifted a hand, pointing at a booth a few stalls up, to a little shop selling leather goods and postcards for tourists. "There."

Amy and Caleb rejoined us, the former with no reserve of cool about being pulled away from her hard-won victory. "This had better be good."

"Geri, look." Above the entry to the door, a silver plate embossed with looping, decorative script hung. "Caleb, can you read it?"

My boyfriend clicked his tongue. "I can read Turkish but only in Latin script. If it is in Turkish, it's from the era when they still used the Arab alphabet. That means at least a hundred years ago."

"Sounds right. We haven't used these in about that long." I took another step toward the shop, sending a chill of anticipation up my spine. "It's a Writ of Authority."

Tobias huffed. "Jesus Christ, even the crazy greens in England did away with those in Victorian times. That can't seriously be current, can it? I mean, this whole building is hundreds of years old. It has to just be a relic, right?"

"It might be, except there's definitely a wolf in that store, standing under an ancient hood marker declaring them in compliance with its enforcement. Something tells me no proud wolf would leave that up for just decoration."

"Wolf?" Amy's complexion went ashen. "As in, werewolf? Here, in the middle of the Grand Bazaar?"

Caleb's fingers crackled with power until I pulled at his fingers, forcing the solar rays to dampen. "She's scared. You're going to send her into a panic."

He proved incredulous. "And you know this… how?"

"Basic common sense." Though that wasn't the whole of it. I was basically a huey now; insights into wolf emotions were meant to have been a thing of the past. Nevertheless, something in my gut told me I was right. Chalk it up to experience. "Let me talk to her, tell her we don't mean any harm. Tobias will come with me."

The wolf stepped in front of me. "Let me lead. Let's not make her think I'm your bodyguard or anything."

I gave him my best fawning southern belle eye flutter. "But you *are* my bodyguard."

"Reason number five we need to get this wrapped up quickly. You're ruining my rep."

The shewolf froze from head to toe, except for her eyes. Those darted around, cataloging what weapons I might be carrying—two deep green marbles rolling in a game of chance. At her wrists, flesh twitched, as though she fought the instinct that told her to shift into a form better suited for fighting, before the *Homo sapiens* part of her brain kicked in and reminded her that she was in a crowded marketplace filled with thousands of huey tourists.

Standing behind Tobias, I raised my hands and showed naked palms. "I mean you no harm."

She flinched, but otherwise remained still.

"Shit, I should have asked Caleb to come with me. I assumed you'd speak English. All the other shopkeepers do."

When Tobias stepped forward, his shadow falling back over mine, backlit by a skylight at the top of the booth, she eased, even if just to allow him to approach without argument. Tobias ate up the space between them in cautious, tiny bites, until he stood just inches from her. For a moment, neither moved, locked into each other's gazes, until at last, her eyes shied to the floor. My werewolf leaned into this new one, scenting her neck as they both began to turn a slow circle. After a moment, he stood still and let her round him alone, all the time drawing scents off her person. It was… one of the most bizarre things I had ever seen, and yet seemed entirely appropriate.

After what seemed minutes but must have been only seconds, she lifted one hand to Tobias's brow. Instinct drove my hand to the base of my braid, where it gripped the handle of my grandmother's silver blade.

"Geri, wait!"

Tobias threw a hand out in my direction. The shewolf paused, waiting to see if I'd obey. When I did, her hand continued its northward trek, until delicate fingers touched Tobias between the eyes.

The werewolf sucked in a heavy breath. "Thank you."

What was he thanking her for? Regardless, a moment later, she turned to me with questioning eyes, and I realized she was asking him for guidance where I was concerned. Tobias's head turned toward the juncture of roof and ceiling, and the shewolf turned away from him and toward me, taking three light steps and no more.

"*Başliksiniz.*"

I looked to Tobias for guidance. He offered none.

Instead, it was the shewolf who clarified. "You are…" Her hand swept back over her thick black hair, then raked down her chin. "*Başlik.*"

"Oh, you mean a hood."

I knew the term for my kind in a few languages; Turkish was not one. One might think I should have learned, knowing I'd be spending at least my summer in Istanbul, but how could I have anticipated that here, in the midst of one of the largest metropolises in the world, I'd cross paths with a creature who loathed both cities and crowds?

"I am. I mean, I *was*. I…" I stuck my hand out, hoping this western tradition held. "My name is Gerwalta. *Geri.* Everyone calls me Geri."

"*Ben* Tobias. *Ben de kurt.*" Tobias's try at a foreign tongue was admirable, but muddled. Even having no idea what he was saying, I could tell. So could the shewolf, it seemed. "What's your name? Do you speak any English?"

"Little." The shewolf nodded and finally shook my hand. "I am Ayşe."

"Good, because beyond *I am a wolf*, my Turkish only includes the names of foods and a few of the colors."

Speak slowly, I wanted to say as I watched the wheels of Ayşe's mind spin, trying to suss out what the brawny foreigner had said.

"Are you alone? Are there others here?"

After a moment's contemplation, the shewolf sucked in her bottom lip. "This store? My pack store. This month, I run. Another month, somebody else run. Why hood?"

Her question was for him, though she gawked at me the whole time.

"She's my friend." A simplistic answer, but not an untrue one. "Your pack is near?"

She nodded. "We live near."

That took me by surprise. "Your pack lives here, *in* Istanbul? A whole pack, in a huge city like this?"

"Istanbul is not one city. It is many cities." Then, eyes back to Tobias. "You come eat us?"

He guffawed. "Cannibalism isn't my thing."

"I think she's asking you to dinner." Someone had to save the male from his own lack of social insight. For whose benefit I lowered my voice, I couldn't say. It wouldn't impact her ability to hear, that was for sure. "Say *yes*. There're supes in the city. They might know something about the Ravens."

"I know, but there's no way an unfamiliar pack is going to feel comfortable having a hood in their midst."

"But I'm not a hood, remember? Is there anything we could do to convince her I'm not a threat?"

He chuckled beneath his breath. "Yeah, but you won't like it."

"Something painful?"

He hedged his answer, looking off to the side. "Depends on how you define pain."

Even though I was a huey, I knew my tolerance was high, and passing up an opportunity like this would be foolish. Not to mention, our rushed words in low tones had Ayşe growing suspicious. We must have looked like a bickering couple, like I was some domineering wife refusing to let my husband go out for his bowling night.

"Do it."

His eyebrow arched. "You sure? Your boyfriend's not going to like it."

My back became a board, my shoulders squared. "If it helps lead us to the Ravens, he'll understand."

"Okay, I hope you're convincing."

The second Tobias's mouth lowered to my ear, instinct I'd thought dead sprang to life. *Kill him. Subdue him. Kiss him.* His hot breath on my neck heated not just the skin beneath my ear, but all along my chest. I longed to turn around, and put those lips on another part of my body. When his teeth grazed my skin, I had to suck on my upper lip to keep my breath from rushing out.

The words were forced, but his tone was clear. At least to a stranger who didn't understand the type of relationship we had.

"I *am* going to accept this invitation, Geri," he growled out. "You have no say in this decision."

"I wh—"

His hands threaded through my hair and pulled my head to the side, his elbow resting on my shoulder, and before I spoiled the ruse, I finally got with it. Eyes to the floor, I let my head fall to the side and my tongue go silent.

Tobias yanked back, examining me. Had I the will, I would have loved to see his face. I didn't doubt he was eating this up with a silver spoon.

Well, a tin spoon, anyhow.

The shewolf took two steps toward us, her hand up cautiously before her. On one of the shop's business cards, she jotted down an address. "Tonight, at eleven."

FIFTEEN

"Igor, will you talk some sense into Geri's head?"

The invoked vampire lowered a pink-tinted newspaper and looked at the slayer across the room. "I'm not sure I could stuff more in there. It's already pretty full."

Caleb threw up both his hands. "Oh, come on!" Pivoting, he began to join decades of former residents in wearing down the carpet beneath his feet. "We can't let a relinquished hood go traipsing about alone with a foreign pack of werewolves. Have you ever read a single fairy tale? These things don't end well."

Seeing that silence was not to be found through simplicity, Igor folded his paper and set it on the kitchen table. "Actually, if I recall *Little Red Riding Hood*, she survives just fine."

"And she's not going in alone." Tobias emerged from the stout refrigerator, an empty glass bottle in one hand and a milk mustache over his lip. "I can guarantee you, no way in hell I'm letting her be eaten."

Oddly enough, my boyfriend's nerves failed to be soothed. "Well, great. Now that I know that, go on ahead."

"They think I'm Tobias's looney." Dots of tangy pepper paste clung to my fingertips, a mess caused by haste. I sucked each off in turn. "And, can I remind you, I'm still a highly trained warrior. If things turn ugly, I know how to do ugly."

Igor blinked thrice. "They think you're insane?"

"No, not a looney. A *looney*, a werewolf groupie." I stood to take my plate to the sink. "Some packs and hood clans are loose on the no-humans-knowing thing. I'm not sure if it's a reference to the moon or to being crazy, but that's the term. Anyway, Tobias is smart. He put on a little dominance display that convinced the shewolf in the Grand Bazaar I was one."

Accusation burned in the crimson hue of Caleb's cheek as he turned to Tobias. "You *dominated* Geri?"

The werewolf shrugged. "Figured at least one of us should."

The solarium, the mere size of a pebble, whizzed by Tobias's head and singed a spot on the wall. Tobias might have pounced back, and Caleb dove forward, if I hadn't created a barrier between them the moment the words were out.

"Okay, boys, enough. Can we focus on our luck? There's a werewolf pack in Istanbul! Think about that: supes in the city who aren't vamps. It would be stupid of us not to try to see if they know anything more than what Ayşe already told us."

"Did she really tell you anything, though? You said her English wasn't that good. Baby..." Caleb cuffed my arms as he drew me in. "I know you can kick lupine ass, but a whole pack versus you and one other wolf? You have to see what a bad idea this is."

Rolling up on my tiptoes, I pressed a kiss to his lips. "We'll be home by dawn."

Amy had often boasted New York was the city that never slept. Istanbul was the city that never blinked.

"It's crowded and lacking wide open spaces, but I can see how this works for the nocturnal." Tobias surveyed the crowds milling through the long street, a stack of cafes, shops, and bars, past street performers forced to occasionally pull their acts aside and allow passage of a restored streetcar. "This is like Chicago in the middle of the day. Everything's open. Have you ever seen so many hueys running around on a Tuesday night?"

"It certainly is beaming with life. I don't like it. Too many people. It's making me nauseous."

The wolf side-eyed me. "Sure it's the crowd?"

"What else would it be?"

"Seems you and Caleb can't stop having rows."

"Relationships don't come prepackaged. They take work, and working out."

"They also take compatibility. And at some point, *intimacy*."

The pig squeal of a laugh leapt out of my throat. "One, that's none of your business. And two, we *are* intimate, even if that hasn't reached its…" I searched the air for the right word.

"Climax?" Tobias suggested, wearing a smirk. "I agree, it's not any of my business. And, god knows, I'll kill you if you give me details, but I can't help but recall a very unfortunate, very public spat you had with my alpha not too long ago. Can't help but thinking he might have had a point. Maybe you are hung up on past loves."

"What would you say if I said that to you? That you need to just get over Kara, that you're too young to spend the rest of your life pining over her?"

"I'd probably rip off your arms."

"How much do you like your arms, Tobias?" A rickety *chug-chug-chug* pushed the crowds to the side of the street, all of us compressing as the tram passed. "Speaking of which, how is this going to go over? I'm supposed to be a looney, but I'm guessing they know you're a widower."

"You heard Ayşe offer her condolences in the Bazaar, didn't you?" He didn't wait for my answer. "I've been asking myself since earlier today what my motivation for keeping a looney around would be. I'm guessing it comes down to sex."

"I'm not sleeping with you just to strike up a conversation with a few werewolves. I don't care if it lets us find out where Vlad buys toothpaste. Besides, I thought it was impossible for a mated wolf to be adulterous."

He grimaced. "Emotionally, it is. Physically, I hear it can be done. I've been told by a few wolves who've lost their mates that it's possible, just to scratch the physical itch. Takes years, though. I could suggest that because Kara and I only had a few months, and we were never officially mated under a full moon, our bond wasn't as strong."

"Sounds good, if you're comfortable with that." I sidestepped a man handing out flyers. "I don't get that. What would be the appeal of sex without the emotions?"

"Only a virgin would ask that."

"I hate you sometimes."

"Only sometimes? I must be doing something wrong."

Ayşe hooked us with gray eyes staring out from behind a black veil. In the market, she'd been dressed in slacks and a loose cotton shirt. Now she looked like someone freshly arrived from Tehran. Fear rimmed her irises, wide and glossy. It was enough to make us pick up our pace once we'd spotted her at the back of a crowd gathered around a man performing a puppet act.

"Is something wrong?" Tobias put a hand on her arm with a tenderness that made me question how *itchy* he was becoming.

"No wrong. Just…" Her eyes went to where buildings met sky, a luminous patch of stars dimly nodding in the background. "Tonight there is…"

"A hood." Tobias's eyes flashed to the sky. "She's nearby. I can sense her now, too."

I couldn't help my own impulses. I turned, surveying the visible, looking for the impossible. A black hood? I'd never actually met one, but I'd heard tell of their particular preferences in silverwielding. Scimitars, it was said, and daggers the size of a man's fist. But that wasn't what really thrilled me. The black hoods were famous among our kind for another reason.

They hunted with falcons.

"Is there something the pack has done to get their attention?"

Ayşe shook her head. "Only, I should not be on the street."

With my eyes still fixed against a barren blue-black sky, confusion closed in on me when Tobias wheeled me around, saying "You're fine. I'll protect you."

Protect me? Protect me from what? Only then did the moment return to me. I was supposed to be a looney. Ayşe recognized me as a hood in the Bazaar, though how, I still didn't understand. But as a hood-turned-looney, I was the worst form of apostate.

Never had my Betrayer namesake clung so tightly to my skin.

I feigned confusion and relief, nodding vigorously as Tobias's hands cuffed both my arms. "Thank you."

"Hurry." Ayşe pivoted and waved us along. "We must go before she is angry."

"Angry?" Tobias said. "About you being out on the street? That doesn't make any sense."

"My pack is not like other packs. Soon, you will understand."

SIXTEEN

Alleyways branched out from the main street, narrower by the turn, until at last, in a place without light and where my eyes struggled to distinguish motes from minarets, Ayşe stopped. The metallic clacking of keys was followed by the tenor groan of rebellious hinges yielding.

"You see, Geri?"

The same moment she asked the question, Tobias's hand pawed mine, lacing our fingers together. "I will be her eyes."

My pulse raced, *from surprise*, I told myself, and I wondered if he'd done it on purpose to help sell our ruse.

Three steps into the passageway, Tobias pulled me to a stop. "There's stairs, and the corridor is too narrow to go down side by side. You want to be behind me or in front of me?"

"Front, please."

With his hands on my hips, holding me out at arm's length, we descended.

"You can put hands on my shoulders," Ayşe offered in front of me. "The stairs are old. Not safe."

Pride warred with practicality. I looked over my shoulder to Tobias behind me, despite the fact that I couldn't actually see anything.

"Have I mentioned lately how much I hate being a huey?"

"Not in the last hour."

Twenty-six steps, then a downward-sloped passage with an irregular floor, and another flight of stairs, making a total of sixty steps.

"Ayşe, do the basements go down this far?"

She shook her head. "Basement? I do not know this word."

"Where are we going?" Tobias clarified.

"Home."

"Home?" I found the idea ridiculous. "You mean you live underground?"

Suddenly, light exploded around us, swallowing darkness. Pain pierced my retinas. A thousand lanterns burned on the periphery of my vision, birthed by one celestial orb in the middle. Even Tobias threw an arm over his eyes from the shock of it, though as a damned supe, he adjusted quickly.

There could be no doubt the man before us was a wolf. Tall and wide and replete with muscle, his frame radiated power and poise. Golden eyes took stock of us from a face fortressed by facial hair—black, with outshoots of gray whiskers. He held an electric lantern aloft and, wrapped in a tattered, floor-length black trench coat, presented a dominating appearance. Tobias slumped his shoulders, bowed his head, and lingered. All signs that could point to a single truth: this man was an alpha.

He must have been advised that we spoke no Turkish, as accented English tumbled from his mouth. "I am Serhan of Pack Pera. Who are you, and do you represent your pack?"

"No, alpha." I'd never heard Tobias so soft-spoken before, not even when addressing Cody. "My name is Tobias Somfield, of the Paradise Pack. Alpha's prerogative brought me here."

Serhan's eyebrow arched. "How is that?"

Without raising his eyes, Tobias jerked his head in my direction. "I protect this woman on his orders."

"She is not your consort then?" Suspicion filled his gaze. Ayşe had apparently told a different story.

Consort: I much preferred that word to *looney*.

"No, but she was an unmated consort to my alpha. She is a friend of wolves. Ayşe invited me at the Bazaar to dine with you tonight. It would be rude for me to refuse a share of your hunt, and because of the duty I hold to my alpha, I could not leave her behind. The shewolf likely told you of my display earlier today. I was not attempting to deceive, only to expedite. I ask welcome for me and my ward at your haunches, and bring no rival."

Who was this formal wolf and where had my Tobias, who earlier in the day had yelled at me to "get out of the pisser," gone?

Serhan's mouth cycled, as though chewing on Tobias's explanation. "She is a hood."

"Relinquished."

The alpha sneered. "What difference does that make? Istanbul is home to a hundred spiders weaving ten thousand webs. My pack wishes to be caught in none of them."

I grew tired of being spoken of in the third person. I knelt, holding out my arms for display and rolling my head to the side. "My name is Gerwalta Kline, daughter of Brünhild Kline, Red Matron of the

Americas. I seek only peace and conversation at your fire."

The alpha blinked his surprise. "You have a talent for lupine etiquette."

"I was the consort of an alpha," I said, weaving the loose ends of my truth with the slack weave of Tobias's lie. "I know many things."

Tension built palaces in the space of a few moments. In the midst of our conversation, the shadows had grown shapes, sulking out of the darkness, a dozen eyes burning me in effigy.

At last, the alpha abated. He raised his left hand, turning it once as though screwing in a light bulb. In that motion, his pack eased. Where animosity had festered, hospitality emerged. Tobias took my hand again, pulling me along as wolves, young and old, female and male, fell in behind us, urging us along. When the ceiling above us rose and the walls tapered out, both Tobias and I were struck dumb.

Neither cave nor chamber, the space in which we found ourselves merited confusion. As high as a cathedral, and yet, with earthen walls like one of the old day shelters of the Black Forest, the wolves dwelled in an archaeological wonder. In the midst of it, a fire burned. Not too large; so deep beneath the ground, I suspected that the temperature remained largely unchanged through the years. No, the fire was merely for light and, perhaps, comfort. The smoke rose, filtering through a ceiling from which pipes dropped and plants grew down.

"A place for dead." Ayşe had managed to sidle up to me without my realizing. She'd rid herself of the traditional cover in the interim, adding to my suspicions of why she felt the need to wear it on the huey streets above. "How do you say… a tom?"

"A tomb," I corrected, then looked instinctively for crevices where coffins rested. None could I find, but perhaps the pack had removed them? "Ayşe, is this where you live?"

She nodded. "Some of the time."

"But why? Why are you here in the middle of the city, and not out in the mountains or the woods?"

"Because here are jobs," she said. "Our place in the Bazaar? It feeds us all."

"The leather shop," Tobias said. "The labors of your hunt?"

Serhan laughed, inviting us to sit by the fire. Several younger wolves, no more than nine or ten years old, vacated the space. "Have you seen a single cow or sheep in this city since you arrived?"

A woman appeared, wearing a brown skirt from under which her bare, besmirched feet shuffled, her hair tied back in a white scarf like an extra from *Fiddler on the Roof*. She deposited bowls of a thick stew into our hands, then dropped a quarter loaf of the same type of crusty bread Amy and I had gorged ourselves on a few days ago atop it. Given that there was no utensil, I suspected the bread was meant to serve as both side dish and spoon.

"Only this, and on the plates of the cafes in the street above." Tobias played the conversation like a string section called on to answer a bellow of horns. As one trained all my life for diplomatic pursuit—though, my mother had sneered, diplomacy was art beyond the grasp of most wolves—I had to admire the ease with which he took to the calling. "Another pack provides the product then?"

Serhan acknowledged it. "All with permission of the onyx hoods. Permission purchased by a steep percentage of the proceeds."

The anger that shot through me wasn't because I took any offense on behalf of the hoods, but because I couldn't believe the unfairness of it.

Serhan seated himself across from me, examining me. "Something troubles you, Miss Kline?"

"I recognized a silver decree posted above your shop today, even if it was in another language." *Pause to swallow the lamb stew.* "A Writ of Authority, official permission to operate your shop? The reds outlawed that sort of practice a century ago. And you, living here, stories below the city in a crypt, forced to stay out of sight? What kind of old-world practices are these?"

Serhan leaned forward. "Where is it you suppose you are at? This is not the Americas, or England. Nor are we in the gleaming shadow of Schloss Wolfsretter. This is Istanbul. This is Constantinople. This is Byzantium. We are not some privileged, pampered pack. Your modern world is all boxes. A cradle when you are a baby. A house when you are an adult. A coffin when you die. We are the *gökkurt*, descended from Asena himself. No one will confine us in a box, not even the onyx."

I leaned forward, searching for recognition in Tobias's expression, but he seemed just as clueless as I was, confirmed a moment later when, his mouth full of potatoes and lamb, he leaned forward.

"Asena?"

"Yes, Asena. The father of us all. Come, now, Tobias, you must know?"

A dribble of broth raced down his chin. "I'm sorry, no."

A grin crossed Serhan's face. He rose to his feet, encouraged at intervals by the claps, the cheers, the shouts of his pack. From out of nowhere, a violin rang out, scratching against the surface in an echo of the daily calls to prayer the city above rang out with five times a day.

"*Aramızda kim Asena'yı tanımıyor?*" His arms akimbo, Serhan spun. His wolves shouted a response as he pointed to several in turn. Then, back to us, he brought his long, dirt-encrusted finger. "What wolf does not know of Asena? A wolf who does not know Asena does not know how he is a wolf."

"I am a wolf because my father and mother were wolves."

The alpha shooed away Tobias's retort with a wave of his hand. "But why was your father? And his father before him? And his before him? Because of Asena. We are *all* his children. It was he whom the shewolf chose to father our people, and she by him who gave birth to the ten packs. So werewolves came into the world, but we... we are sons of the eldest pup born of Asena, Ashina. We are the truest wolves."

I elbowed Tobias in the side. "So maybe you're not English after all. You're descended from Turks."

My guardian ignored me. Rightfully.

"And have you been in Istanbul all this time?" Tobias asked. "Living here, beneath the city?"

"We have always been Turks, and so our packlands have moved with the fate of our ancestors, as have the Turkish hueys. From the Steppe, to the Caucasus, to Anatolia, and into the Balkans. Our pack was among those who took the city from the Romans."

But that brought up a question in my head that the others didn't seem concerned with. "And what about hoods? Um... *başlık?*" I asked. The mere utterance of the word sent a hush of the gaiety of the pack. "Where did they come from?"

Serhan's smile flatlined. "Do not you know? Your kind who flies? Your kind who speaks to birds?"

"Birds?" I almost tugged Tobias's shirt sleeve clear off. "Tobias…"

His hand lay over mine, stilling it and my words. "Protecting this relinquished hood is not the only reason I… *we* are in Istanbul, Serhan Bey. We're here trying to find someone. Several someones, actually."

Serhan fanned the air. "In a city like this, finding one is difficult. Finding many, easy. Who is it you seek?"

"He has had many names," I said. "A vampire. A *very* old vampire. Most know him as Vlad."

The name. So simple: four letters, one syllable. For all that, *v-l-a-d* might have spelled *stop* or *silence*. Even the wolves who stayed some distance from the fires on the edges of the crypt stilled. In the chamber, a chill descended upon me, upon *us*. I felt at once old worries rise. A moment ago, I'd been surrounded by a clan of people who had welcomed me into their home, such as it was. Now, I felt the weight of lupine curses.

And only one wolf who would defend me.

I focused in on Serhan as I shot to my feet, my hand clutching the silver dagger's hilt. The alpha needed but give an order, and the pack would take their wolves and rip me limb from limb. Instead, Serhan turned to Ayşe, barking out gruff foreign words before, without any further explanation, he whirled, trouncing off into the darkness, diving into shadow.

Ayşe's disappointment was palpable as she began to lead us

back the way we'd come in. Neither Tobias nor I needed ask what had transpired, though I was certain that he, like me, desperately wished to learn the *why*. As we reached the street, Ayşe covered herself and led us back toward the main street.

"We can find our way from here, Ayşe," Tobias offered. "That hood is still nearby. I can sense her. Both Geri and I apologize for any offense we committed. We never meant to upset you."

"It is not… the word you use, *offense*?" The shewolf rounded a corner, practically clinging to the walls. "It is *haram*. You say, I think, forbidden? Yes, *forbidden*, for us to talk about the Ravens."

I fisted Tobias's shirt. "You do know about them!" Despite the daggers Tobias shot me, I couldn't let this go. "Please, Ayşe, tell us what you know. We promise, we won't tell anyone."

Tobias sighed. "Geri, she's under alpha orders. She can't say a thing. Come, the hood that's patrolling is very close. Let's not get anyone into trouble, or get noticed ourselves. Good night, Ayşe. Thank you for letting us sit at your fire."

The girl nodded once, turned to go back into their subterranean landscape, then halted. Inner conflict pulled tight the expression on her face. "Advice?"

Was she asking for it, or offering to give it? Tobias nodded some sort of acceptance.

"Birds that hunt need to soar high," Ayşe said. "But please, do not look for them. You will die. That is all I can say."

SEVENTEEN

"Baby, you have to let this go."

I was trying. Damn it, I was trying. "But they were opening up to us! And then I had to make a mountain out of a molehill. One tiny mention of birds, and I blurted out Vlad's name, and then we were personae non gratae. I swear I have that 'awkward non-sequitur' award of the year cinched this year."

I could only hope that Tobias had some luck in getting them to accept our apology. When he told me earlier in the morning he was going to find Ayşe at the Bazaar and offer our regrets, I had begged to come along. He'd insisted that it would go over better without me there. When even Caleb agreed it was probably better to let the wolves work it out among themselves, I deferred.

Amy, however, had not. The second she found out Tobias was on his way back to that magnificent place, she was out of bed and on the prowl in record time.

Caleb continued massaging my shoulders, relieving the tension that had me wound up his primary objective. "One, let's try to limit Latin phrases to one per statement. And two, I don't think there's any casual way to bring up the Prince of Darkness in polite conversation. You saw an open window, you jumped for it. I would have done the same thing."

"No, you would have gotten one of the female wolves alone, then turned on your awesome sex-god powers and charmed the information out of her. In Turkish too."

His mouth came down the juncture of my neck and my collarbone. "Sex-god powers? How would you know about those?"

With the shifting mood, I softened my voice. "I've never left your place unsatisfied."

"*Mmm*, true, but you've never left my place entirely… fulfilled."

"If the brochure is that great, I can only imagine the actual view is mind-blowing."

"Oh, it's *blowing*." His hot breath funneled through pursed lips as he blew on my ear, sending a wave of anticipation up my spine. "We're home alone. We should take advantage of that."

My head tilted to the side, giving Caleb de facto permission to ply willing flesh with his demanding mouth. "Technically, Inga and Igor are home, even if they're in torpor in the cistern."

"They won't hear us if we go upstairs, which leaves only one question: your room or mine?"

I could see it in my mind, how simple this would be. I'd stand, turn to Caleb, offer him my hand. He'd take it, stand as well, and kiss me. We'd fumble our way upstairs, taking only brief glances beyond each other to navigate the climb and then, the door, and then the bed. We'd take turns robbing each other of clothing, piece by piece surrendered to the floor, until ultimately, we'd stand before each other wearing only the balance of our confidences.

I'd call out his name when he entered me, and think of another…

That broke the vision, and suddenly, what my body had wanted, my heart denied.

I needed more time. I needed more distance. I needed to just convince myself that I had to move on.

I needed an excuse.

"Caleb?"

His voice vibrated against my skin. "Mmm?"

"I've been thinking." I swallowed hard, trying to block out the sensations he sent spiraling around my body as his hands encircled me from behind, one of them sneaking its way under my shirt. "This is going to sound…" *Crazy? Puritan? Prudish?* "…old-fashioned, but I think I want to wait."

Clearly, his blood had already vacated his brain for other parts of his body, as he asked in a dreamy tone, "Wait for what?"

"Wait for this," I said, pulling away, turning to face him. "I never thought I'd be so traditional, but where I come from, this—" I motioned between us. "This doesn't happen until marriage. I thought I could do this, but you've seen what happens when I try. I think it's because, deep in my heart, I know that I want to wait."

Undeterred, the slayer leaned forward, balancing on his hands as he ghosted a kiss over my lips. "I bet parts of you deeper down think otherwise. And I'm willing to go searching for those parts. Way—" *Kiss.* "Deep—" *Kiss.* "Down."

He fell facedown onto the couch as I took to my feet. He'd only sat himself up when I turned to face him from the hall.

"I'm sorry, but I'm not negotiable on this."

EIGHTEEN

They dragged themselves in before the morning light, each wearier than the last. Igor and Tobias had scouted most of the districts on the Asian side, each night ringing out further into districts springing to life on the edges of the eternally-growing city. Three weeks of effort, and nothing more to show for it than the discovery of a few good all-night kebab houses. Inga and Caleb, in the meantime, had cut lines through the European neighborhoods, testing even the endurance of an immortal.

"Cities should not be allowed to grow so vast," the vampire lamented as she fell back on the couch, brown hair falling like a halo around her. "Damn Istanbul. It's like a cancer, a giant, pulsing tumor spreading across continents. Give it another hundred years, and this city will cover the world and strangle the whole planet."

Amy managed to wander in just as the vampires made it home. "I think it's going to bump into Beijing and, well, frankly, all of China before that can happen. Morning, Geri. We still on for the boat ride today?"

Tobias looked up from his breakfast of fried sausage and egg. "Boat ride?"

"We're taking a Bosporus cruise."

Caleb ran a hand over his face. "Great. We'll spend our nights looking for villainous vampires, but you guys pretend to be tourists and take in all the sights. What's the point in having that training space upstairs if you're only going to use it for yoga?"

"First, Geri has actually been teaching me a few attack forms, so there." Amy peeked over the fridge, a carafe of orange juice in hand. "And two, we thought it might be a good idea to see the city from a different perspective—especially since you won't let the poor hueys go out at night all defenseless and alone. Seriously, you guys have been at this for three weeks, and have nothing to show for it but a cryptic message from a werewolf who now refuses to talk to you. The worst thing that happens is that we get nothing out of it."

Caleb sat up. "And the best thing that happens is that you get *someone* out of it." He turned to me with begging eyes. "Geri, come on, you know she only agreed to this to scope out guys, right?"

"Caleb Helsing, are you calling Amy a flirt?"

"I'm calling Amy the female version of me." He blushed under my scornful gaze. "The old me. Before I was with you, I mean."

I slipped my cell phone and bottle of water into a backpack and threw it over my shoulder. "I'll make sure she behaves. And uses protection, if it comes to it. In the meantime, you guys get rest. Only two nights until full moon. We'll have to spend tonight finding someplace to stash our own werewolf during it."

"I still volunteer my room."

The slayer's hand lashed out in response to Amy's quip. "See? That's what I'm talking about."

The only revelation that emerged from our two-hour cruise was that there were dolphins in the Bosporus Strait, something which made total sense in hindsight but which I hadn't anticipated.

Amy folded her hands and leaned against the railing. "It really is a beautiful city. Isn't it?"

"Indeed."

"And you still want to go back to Paradise?"

I shrugged. "Not Paradise, maybe. But someplace like it, not too far away. Sault Ste. Marie, maybe."

Sunlight bounded off the water, forcing Amy to shield her eyes. "And then?"

"And then… what?"

With a sway of her arm, she indicated the city, as though it were evidence in some court proceedings. "The world is so big. You got your degree, you can go so many places with it. What are you going to do in the backwoods of Michigan? What is Caleb going to do? I picked up on his type the moment I met him: likes fashion, fancy restaurants, clubbing. One-hundred-percent city boy. You think he's going to go along with the Suey Ain't Mary plan?"

"Sault Ste. Marie," I corrected. "Why is it that he'd have to go along with it?"

"Hello? Because he's your boyfriend, and he's going to either want to be in the same place as you, or stop being *with* you. Seriously, Geri, what was your goal when you came to Chicago to begin with? Let me interrupt you, because you probably don't know, and I do: You were trying to escape Paradise. Even if you're not willing to admit that to yourself, that's what you were after. You either have to accept that Caleb is part of that escape, or let him go."

The words struck me harder than if I'd fallen in the waters below. "You're blowing things way out of proportion here. I'm only twenty-two. *Barely* twenty-two. I don't have to make those kind of long-term decisions yet."

"Sorry, but you do," she countered. "Didn't you tell me just a few days ago that, before the two of you hit it off, he was a bit of a lady's man?"

"By his own admission. And Inga's reports. So?"

She rolled her eyes. Something I was saying really watered the stupid tree. "If a guy like that goes cold turkey it means he's found—and believe me, even I can't believe I'm using this term—'the one.' Caleb is planning a life with you, and if you're not doing the same, you got to let him know. Trust me on this."

In the eddies swirling off the boat in the waters below, murky visions of a life with Caleb emerged. Running from city to city, always in hiding, unless under the protection of a vampire who already admitted she was living on borrowed time. Tall buildings, landscapes of concrete, crowds of people everywhere. Everywhere. So many people. And kids. He'd want kids. Lots of them. He was the last of his kind, after all. At the very least, it was his duty to procreate. And what would I be then, but a breeding sow, raising slayers who I couldn't even get to understand the kind of person I'd been before my mother had relinquished me?

Amy's hand settled on my back. "You see it, right?"

"I do." The words cracked when forced over a dry palate. "But he loves me."

A softness overcame her. "All the more reason to end it."

Only a blind man could stare at the sun and deny its light. "Damn it, you're right."

"I know I am. Now, let's talk about Tobias…"

My hands went up. "Whoa, remember that big talk about werewolves and hoods you and I had a few weeks ago? Tobias was mated, and wolves mate for life. No exceptions."

"I know," she said. "But there's something between the two of you, something… dare I say, primal? You two just click. Like, platonically, even if the physical stuff is never a part of it. Which I can't believe I, of all people, am saying, but that's not so bad, is it?"

"Oh, yeah, we'd be great together. Long walks through the woods, baking cookies, sighing mournfully in unison each morning. Twice on Sundays. No, Amy. A life with Tobias means living with the Paradise Pack. It's me watching Cody and Lisa and their perfect little cubs running around for the rest of my life under the shadow of my mother's domain. It's about the worst thing I could think of."

"Yeah, I suppose so." Her eyes settled on one of the boat's crew handing out glasses of tea on the aft deck. Igor had been right; tea really was everywhere. "Too bad Tobias didn't get hit with that serum stuff that vamps have. It could solve all of this."

"That serum was designed to work on alphas and betas," I said. "Tobias is neither."

"How do you know?"

"Because he's not. It's that simple. Cody's his alpha, Rick's his beta."

"And back in England…?"

"His dad, then his brother, then… I'm not sure. Someone else who kicked him out."

"And Kara was a beta in her pack. Isn't that what he said?"

I nodded. "What are you getting at?"

"Nothing, just based on everything I've learned about werewolves and hoods and slayers so far, there's a lot of heriditary stuff involved in the way you guys determine leadership. Now, I might think it outdated and undemocratic, but if that's the way y'all roll, fine. *But* in that case, wouldn't political marriages be a thing? Wouldn't it be weird for Tobias, son and brother of an alpha, to be mated to another pack's beta?"

"Amy, I don't know where you hide all these smarts, but they're amazing."

"Mostly I keep them in my bra. If guys are going to stare at the girls anyway, they might as well get an education in the process."

"I think several of your recent boyfriends should be given honorary doctorates, then." Master's degrees at least. "But even if it's true, that he has the genetic inclination for being a pack leader, that doesn't make him an alpha."

Amy now turned all her attention on me, forgetting about the tea guy. "What would?"

"You mean, how does a wolf become an alpha?"

"Yeah, I guess."

"Well, that's simple," I said. "The previous alpha dies, and he rises to take his place—whether that's through the agreement of the pack, or through a formal challenge for leadership. Or he starts his own pack, but that's something that hardly ever happens. It takes a wolf of extreme strength, both physical and mental, to do something like that—not to mention the fact that he risks lunacity in the process."

Amy's head tilted to the side. "Lunacity?"

Even if the last few weeks had seen Amy take a crash course in all things supernatural, there were still some gaps in her knowledge.

"Lunacity," I repeated. "Or what we usually call moon madness. Wolves are so orientated towards pack that their psychology hinges on it during full moons. They can only go a few lunar cycles away or they become their wolf forever. It drives them crazy, makes them very dangerous. It's an obligation of the hoods to eliminate a wolf who gets to that point. I've seen three in my life." My chest tightened at the recollection, of being at my mother's side as she dispatched a creature trapped in fur but with remnants of a human soul I could still sense. "I hope I never have to see it again."

"But what does that have to do with becoming a new alpha?"

"A wolf who decides to try and be his own alpha has to have three things: an ability to make it through three lunar cycles away from his pack without going insane, the release of his previous alpha, and a beta wolf who's willing to risk the break as well. That's the part that stops most defections. One can rebel, but getting a beta to buy in at the risk of going insane and permanently wolf is almost impossible. It's generally only done in times of war and famine, to give the pack the best hope of surviving by immigrating into new regions."

"I see." Amy laced her fingers together. "Maybe you can live in Suey Ain't Marie and he can commute to the pack? Is that a thing?"

"Afraid not."

"Damn it. Well, then, I might have to resume my get-Geri-hooked-up campaign."

"I could jump into this water right now, Amy."

"Go ahead. I double dog dare you. More than that, I double *wolf* dare you."

NINETEEN

Tobias stood at the door, staring at his upturned palm.

Stalling.

I put down the book I'd been reading, a droll history of the Ottoman system of government. "You seem to be treading water there, chief. You sure you're comfortable with this?"

A wispy grimace preceded his words. "What choice do I have? Unless you want to tie a saddle to me and ride me through the streets."

I snapped my fingers. "Damn, I didn't pack my saddle, and I never learned to ride bareback…"

"Based on your tepid love life, seems you haven't learned to ride *barefront* either."

Switching the subject ASAP was the only way to keep from blanching. "Scared you can't trust the Pera Pack?"

He barely bobbed his head. "Ayşe's sticking to orders; she still hasn't uttered a single word to me when I've approached her in the Bazaar. Luckily, she still *listens*. I told her I needed shelter for the full moon, and that I'd wait down the street for an answer. A half-hour later, another wolf came to tell me I could pass the night with them, as a lupine courtesy."

"The last thing the alpha of a pack trying to avoid attention wants is some foreign wolf to run about on full moon, causing trouble with hueys," I concurred. "If I had my hood, I'd build a silver cage for you in your bedroom upstairs."

"So your suggestion for an alternative to passing the moon with a local pack would be to imprison me. You still want to claim you're not into BDSM?"

"Try chaining me up sometime and see."

His eyes jolted away as a spark of crimson warmed his neck. Were Tobias's jabs about rough play a cover for his own proclivities? How interesting.

"I still can't believe Caleb convinced Inga to go with Igor to Spain for the weekend." The werewolf shoved his overseer-approved phone into his back pocket. "I guess you were right about his charm, huh? Even convinced the daughter of Dracula herself to give in to him. How did he manage to do that?"

"By promising we wouldn't step a foot out of the house after dark until they got back. I think he even pinky-promised."

"So you, Amy, and Caleb are planning a quiet night at home?"

"Oh, hell no. Amy would open a pop-up Kama Sutra studio. Caleb and I are going out to dinner, then he said something about going to see Hagia Sophia."

"He lied to Inga?"

"He prefers to think of it as a technicality. We aren't stepping *a* foot out. We're using both feet."

Tobias laughed. "Remind me never to get into a negotiation with a slayer. Slippery eel, that boyfriend of yours. Hagia Sophia… That's that big church-turned-mosque thing, right? Is it even open at night?"

"I think we're just going to walk by it. He said there's a beauty to it you can only see at night."

He grinned and tapped me on the shoulder. "So he thinks taking you to a huge church is going to finally get you into bed? Told you telling him you were 'waiting for marriage' would make him think you're a religious nut."

"My sex life is not a venue for your comedic efforts."

"No, it's the venue for your own."

The sepia orb crawled its way out from behind the city skyline, pulling me in a way I hadn't felt in months: anticipation, dread, longing, desire. A familiar swirl of extremes that, in my huey existence, left me anxious. Or, maybe it was because I'd planned to talk to my boyfriend about how I didn't see our relationship as having legs—despite the fact that it brought us all the way to Istanbul to track down an infamous vampire and, eventually, kill him.

"The moon sure is pretty tonight."

Caleb turned a smile to me that made the cosmos in the sky above dim in comparison. "It's not the only thing."

"Caleb…"

Any effort to peel away was met with an equal effort on his part to pull me closer, which ultimately resulted in his tugging my arms behind my back and holding them there.

"You need to just accept the fact that you're beautiful, Geri. Every time I bring it up, it's 'oh, Caleb, stop.' It's like you don't want me to compliment you."

"Oh, god no. Compliment away. It's just…"

Not yet. Not out of nowhere.

"Predictable."

He brushed a kiss over my lips, and I tried not to notice how good it felt, how my bottom lip tingled, how my body instinctively leaned into his, chasing the kiss.

"It's possible," he admitted as he pulled away and we resumed our leisurely stroll along the avenue. "You're the first woman I've been with long enough for my wit to become seasoned. I'll try harder in the future."

Worms crawled through my belly. *Change the subject.* Beside us, an ancient wall stood, each of its stones meticulously shaped and placed, like a puzzle. "I thought you were taking me to see Hagia Sophia. Isn't this the old hippodrome?"

Just then, a doorway emerged in the wall, an old (though probably hundreds of years newer than the stonework surrounding it), heavy metal thing that looked like it had been recommissioned from a submarine.

Caleb flicked the padlock that held it closed. "That's new."

"That's new?" I repeated. "You've been wherever this leads before?"

"Not in about a decade or so, but yeah."

"What is it?"

The slayer shifted his body, blocking the view of his hands from a group of nearby Asian tourists. If they saw the glow that radiated from his palm, turning the obstacle into a molten sludge, they probably just thought it was a cell phone screen lighting up. Liquid metal dripped to the ground as hinges groaned, pulled on for the first time in who knew how long.

"It's like Hagia Sophia's slayers-and-guests-only entrance."

Doubts refused to be dismissed. "You sure you know where this goes?"

"Unless a two-thousand-year-old passageway has been rerouted in the last decade. Don't be nervous. It's full moon, the weakest time of the month for vampires, and I was running through these tunnels before I could read."

I feigned surprise. "I didn't know you could read."

"There's a lot of things I can do that you still haven't found out about."

Caleb's solarium became a lantern, giving definition to a passage sloping downward. I was getting jealous of how many diverse applications there were for the slayer talents.

"First, werewolves living in an old Byzantine crypt, and now, slayer passages underneath one of the most historical parts of the city?" I stepped over an old drainage pipe laid over our path. "It's like this city is built over a foundation of supernatural haunts."

"This city is built over a foundation of everything," Caleb said. "This part was a passage of the Roman hippodrome. The Byzantines ignored it, but then the Ottomans built stuff on top of that. Istanbul is like cultural moussaka. Slayers have been in this city since it first took shape, but Hagia Sophia and these passages are some of the only remnants of that history."

I pulled my hand back out of his. "Slayers had something to do with building Hagia Sophia?"

"Not building it, just *how* it was built. Whoa, just a second."

I tried to blink definition into being as Caleb's solarium faltered, plunging us into darkness. The slayer slowed our pace, and a moment later, I realized why. Since we'd entered the tunnel, there'd been the sound of dripping, of water pooling at the bottom of walls. As I stepped forward into a cool stream deep enough to cover my ankle, I hoped to high heaven the source was underground and not runoff from the streets or, worse, bubbling up from the sewer.

"It would be really great if you could turn the lights back on. I'd like to see what I'm stepping in so I know if I'm going to need a tetanus shot."

His sloshing feet at least gave me a direction to follow.

"Should be just a few more steps. And yeah, we're through."

My feet cleared the stream just as the cavern around us illuminated anew.

Caleb bounced the relit solarium on his hand. "One defect with these little things: they can't be conjured when I'm standing in water."

A memory resurfaced, of Igor saying much the same thing when we'd first arrived at the rental house. "That was only, like, three inches of water. That tiny bit is enough to flatline you? Maybe those solaria aren't all they're cracked up to be."

"Oh, they're cracked. Just wait until you see why." He took my hand back and hurried me along the path as it twisted and pivoted underneath the streets above. "It will be easier to show you when we're inside. Come on, it's not too much farther."

I could search through a thousand libraries, each with ten thousand books, for a hundred thousand years, and never find words sufficient enough to describe it.

Caleb let go of my hand, allowing me to drift on the breezes of beauty and history, interwoven with stone and light. Hagia Sophia struck me dumb and left me incredulous. It rose above, around, tunneled underneath. It captured the limits of my imagination then mocked it. It was like man had tried to cage heaven. Mineral veins and dozens of stone panels lay over walls and beneath my feet, drawing my attention to a ceiling circumscribed in Arabic letters around a mighty dome above us, punctuated with uncovered mosaics in the apses.

"I have never felt more huey… More *mortal*, than I do at this moment."

Caleb nodded. "My mom used to say that peasants and sultans were equals when they entered here, that it was the only building on the face of the earth so vast in scope it rendered the arrogance of small differences mute. It's… I mean, look at it! It's maybe mankind's greatest achievement, am I right? But it's more than just a church, or even a mosque. Remember what I said about slayers influencing how it was built?"

"Yeah, but how?"

Shyness grabbed a man who'd rarely known its company. "Geri, for all we know, I'm the last slayer."

I cocked my head. "What does that have to do with Hagia Sophia?"

"Because this building, Geri… This big, boisterous, beautiful building is part of my legacy. Inga and Igor have, um… you know, *donations* from me. If I die, they may be able to rescue my kind back from extinction. But being a slayer isn't just genetics, it's training and culture. Igor says he talked to you about hoods training slayers if it ever came to that, but someone needs to carry on our *legacy* too."

"Caleb, I still have no idea what you're talking about."

"Here, let me show you."

He extended his right hand and conjured a solarium. The lemon-sized balls of light were powerful little things, powerful enough to kill a vampire, to turn him to ash. But as it rose at a measured pace upward, controlled, I assumed, by Caleb's will, the most magnificent thing began to happen. Not only did its light cast a warm glow over the interior of the structure, but the beams began to fracture, to turn in on themselves and bounce off mosaic-covered walls. Reds, greens, golds, yellows: a spectrum of brilliance turned into the center, collecting below.

I had to hold up a hand to protect my eyes, stung from the magnificent display. "What is this?"

"This is why this building was made the way it was," Caleb said. "Before the Ottomans converted it to a mosque, every inch of that dome and most of the walls were covered in glass mosaics, all designed specifically for this. This building is both a place of worship, and one of defense. In the Byzantine times, slayers protected this city from vampires. Vlad changed that. Vlad made this his sanctuary. Someday, Geri, a slayer might be able to stand here as I do now, and if the Ravens are here, it will be enough to destroy them all. I hope."

Already boggled by the structure for its own sake, I could hardly grasp the revelation. "This is why we're here, isn't it?"

He didn't deny it. "If we spook one Raven, all we'll do is send him flying. We have to get them all here—or somewhere like it. And when Vlad and the others stand here, they'll die. Inga knows this, Igor knows it, and now you know it."

"But what do you expect me to do with this? Why did you tell me?"

He dropped his hand, and despite the act, the solarium continued to shine above. "Because one day, it may be one of our children who has to undertake this."

"One of our… Caleb, I—"

The heat of his kiss made the ball of solar rays above seem cold by comparison. I'd tasted desire, and longing, and lust, and love. Caleb's mouth on mine spoke of it all and more. It spoke of negotiations, offerings, outcomes. It promised family, a place, meaning. It proffered all this to me with a bonus of pleasure.

This man would do his damnedest to make me happy. He'd make me his.

"Caleb, stop."

In the most technical sense, he did. His lips lingered just beyond mine as our breath mingled. When had I begun breathing so hard? When had I come to be completely wrapped in his embrace? With open eyes, I could see just how brilliantly his light shown, as though the fire of desire uncurling within him, within us, fueled the solarium in the dome above.

"If this is because I told you I wanted to wait until marriage—"

"It's not." He licked lips which then curled into a smile. "I mean, that's a bonus, but that's not why I'm asking. I don't want to go through any more of this life without you. I can wield the sun, but you are my light." He reached up, laced his fingers through my hair.

A touch, a kiss, a brush of his lips on my neck. His sunlight shone above, and the moonlight fell on the building from outside. Both born of the same fire, separated by the lattice of history and purpose. It stirred my veins, lit my desire. I wanted him. God help me, no matter how selfish it was, I wanted him. Let his light outshine mine; I'd be warm in his.

His lips went to my ear. "I love you, Geri. Please say *yes*."

"Caleb, I…" My heart fell back into shadow, and my body shook. "…can't."

The brilliance turned blistering. His solarium doubled, tripled in size.

"What?"

I pulled back from him as flares licked up his arms, singing the sleeves of his shirt.

"I want to. God, Caleb, you have no idea how much I want to believe that you and I could work, that we could make a future together. But we have completely different expectations about what we want, about where we see ourselves."

"How can you know that?" With both hands on either side of my face, he pressed a hard kiss to my lips. "All I want is you. We'll find a way to make it work."

I shook my head, even as he held it. "But I know what I want, and as much as I *like* you, Caleb, and no matter how much I tell myself to just let a good thing happen for once, I don't love you. I won't do that to you. I won't make promises that someday it could change, when I know it won't."

In a snap, hope turned bitter.

"How can you know?" Caleb dropped his hands and backed away. The brilliant sphere above began to descend, moving in parallel with him. "You don't even know who or what you are. You're too wrapped up in who you *used* to be to think about who you could become."

"I know you're angry, but you don't need to—"

"Or maybe Cody was right. Maybe you are too in love with him to ever give anyone else a chance."

Now the heat radiating in the place was my own. "How do you know about that?"

"Just because you won't talk to me doesn't mean the others won't."

My fist clenched so tightly my nails cut flesh. "Amy."

"Tobias, actually. And here's the kicker on that one." His arms flailed through one revolution. "He did it because he actually thought Cody was right. He told me—*begged* me to step up if I had any intentions of being with you, and get you to forget about him. But you can't, can you?"

"*Tobias* told you?" But that didn't make any sense. Yes, he was *my* friend, but Tobias hated Caleb. Why would he encourage the very man he told me wasn't good enough for me to woo me? "It's not about Cody. That was all over two years ago."

"Ha! That's who you think *him* is?" He threw his head back and barked a laugh, and as I faced the slayer, I saw my shadow stretch before me. "You think you can never love me? If that were true, Geri, you'd see the relationship you're choosing over ours. That you've already chosen. Fine, good luck with that. Just remember, when you wake up from that fantasy, that you and I can actually work. Better hurry, though, because I can't wait forever."

I began to run even before he'd finished turning, making to exit from one of the main doors instead of back through the underground passage we'd used to sneak onto the grounds, even as the aurora of Caleb's solarium chased along.

"Please, Caleb! Don't—"

My words died in a blaze of red and orange. Fire blinded me, bound me. It seeped into my veins, trying to consume me.

I wouldn't let it. I breathed it in, and made myself its master.

Little made sense when I walked in the door: how I got back, where I had been, how much time had passed. All I knew was that I was tired. So crushingly, utterly tired. Every bone and every muscle ached. If this house had a bathtub, I'd draw one up and probably drown falling asleep in the soothing waters. My skin felt two sizes too small for my body, and scorched.

The full moon dipped low in the sky, taking my determination with it. My body surrendered to gravity as I fell back into the low couches in the parlor. Tea. I wanted tea. I didn't have the strength to make it. Habit took my hand down to my pants pocket. Maybe someone had texted. The device proved useless, however, its plastic frame bubbled from the heat of the solarium. The cracked screen wouldn't even light.

The night outside waned, and I wanted to chase it as it blinked out. I closed my eyes, and ran into its oblivion.

TWENTY

The tide pulled in, the tide pulled out. Each wave rolled me, a gentle cycle of taking and giving. The water became flesh and wrapped itself around me.

My head rolled into his shoulder as he scooped me off the couch. "Why are you sleeping down here? I thought Caleb said you guys were staying down at some fancy hotel in Beşiktaş."

How did he know about that? No matter, I shook my head as he navigated the narrow staircase. "Never made it."

"Please tell me you guys didn't do it like dogs in some back alley." A chuckle rumbled in his chest. "As a dog, even I look down on that."

"We didn't do anything. We broke up."

He stopped, and my legs gave out beneath me as he set me on my feet. "What do you mean, you broke up?"

I could barely get my eyes open. God, why was I so tired? Depression? Stress? "He asked me to… I don't know, he wanted me to teach our children something? I think he might have asked me to marry him."

The werewolf sniffed the air. "I'm guessing, by the fact that Caleb's not here, you said *no*."

He could know the truth, but he didn't need to know the whole truth. "In so many words."

"And how did he take that?"

"He hit me with a solarium."

"He what?" With a jerk on my shoulder, Tobias spun me around, examining me for damage. "I'm going to kill him. What happened? Where are you hurt?"

"I'm fine?" A hint of surprise took my voice up a few notes. "No damage, other than a ruined cell phone. I must have just caught the edge of it."

"Thank god." The werewolf ran a hand through his hair. Fretting. My reliable, tough werewolf was fretting. "You smell different, though. Did he at least apologize?"

I tried to think back to the aftermath, but all I could draw was a huge blank. "I'm not sure. It's no big deal. I'm obviously okay. I'm not even sad about the break-up, except we still need him to be a part of what we're doing here. Has he called you at all? Texted?"

"Only once saying I shouldn't worry about walking in on you two because of the fancy hotel thing. He's probably there, licking his wounds. Come on, let's get you into bed."

"Can I… Can I come sleep in your room?"

Tobias gasped out a laugh. "Geri, that's hardly…"

"What?" I asked. "Appropriate? A good idea? We slept in the same room in Chicago for almost a year while I was dating Caleb. How is it a worse idea now that I've broken up with him?"

"Because you're…" He held up his hands, fingers splayed, as though he could gather the explanation from the air and press it into a ball. "…grieving."

"I am *not* grieving." I could cock a hip with the best of them. "Fine. I'll go to sleep in my…"

I had barely turned to storm away when, seizing me by the arm, Tobias tugged me back the opposite way.

"You're so frustrating, you know that? You think this is about you. Seriously, how can you be the singularly most informed hood I've ever known when it comes to werewolf behavior and still be so utterly clueless?"

He pulled me into the bedroom he and Caleb shared. The footprint was identical to the one Amy and I had on the other side of the house, the exception being a blanket hung over an east-facing window to block out morning light. It made sense for two nocturnal beings, but I was surprised at the relief I felt in the dark. The door shut with a little too much force. I didn't need my old hood skills to see I'd ticked off the wolf somehow.

"I can go back to the couch if I'm that much of a nuisance."

"Makes no difference. My Geri-meter has never turned off."

I blinked as his form took shape in the darkness, features inking themselves on my irises. Maybe the room wasn't as dark as I thought.

"What does that mean?"

"The others can't sense you anymore," he said as he peeled off his shirt and pelted it against the floor. "And you can't sense them. But you… The intensity changes, but I can still sense *you*. It hit me like a brick wall about a block away: your sadness, your confusion, your guilt. I'm awash in it. *Grief*, Geri. Don't think for a moment I'm not familiar with its markers. I've been stewing in it since the day my brother died, since my mate was kidnapped."

"I might be a little down, but it would be insulting to you to say breaking up with Caleb affected me even one-tenth the way losing Kara did you."

"Yes, it would be." His hands went to his belt, undoing the buckle. Suddenly, my emotions could be described as anything but grief. "But a small cut still bleeds, even if it doesn't take off an arm. If another of my pack suffered, I'd comfort them. My instincts say to… *comfort* you? I suppose that's as good a word as any."

A tiny drop of conflict rose in my stomach, even as Tobias's pants dropped to the floor. Yes, he was a wolf—which included, on full moon nights as last night had been, going commando.

"Meaning?"

He pointed to the bed. *His* bed, not Caleb's. "Lie down."

I swallowed. "And you?"

"I can't sleep in his bed, if that's what you're asking," he said. "That slayer wears too much damned cologne."

The laughter came despite its improbability.

"I'll take the floor, just like back in Chicago."

"In your wolf?"

He turned the other cheek. Literally. "Yeah, so?"

"Right after a full moon? Aren't you tired as hell?"

"On so many levels. What's the difference?"

"Then share the bed with me." I couldn't believe what I was saying. "Besides, I… I need you to be…"

"Comforted." He turned, and I managed to keep my eyes locked on his. "But we both understand that comfort has definitive limits. Right?"

I nodded. "Right."

TWENTY-ONE

Instinct told me we'd slept through the day, even if the blanket over the window kept the changing angles of sunlight from confirming it. Oxygen flooded my muscles as I stretched long, then let my body go limp. I couldn't remember the last time I'd felt so rested.

Tobias's arm fell over me, pulling my body back into his. Air flooded my lungs as I drew in a breath. He held me. Tobias held me. I was a relinquished hood in bed… with a wolf. And I *wanted* him to hold me.

"I'm so hungry, I could eat a whole lamb."

"Me, too. I'm famished."

"Famished?" Tobias lifted his head enough to glance at me through one open eye as I looked back over my shoulder. "I think my English is rubbing off on you."

"We say *famished* where I come from."

"Do not."

"Do too."

"I have never heard an American use the word *famished*, ever."

"Can we get back to the discussion about the lamb?"

"Indeed." His head collapsed into the pillow. "Lamb dumplings, with that tomato sauce they put on it. We should get dressed and have breakfast at that place down the street again."

"Dumplings. God, I want a whole plate of them."

He squeezed me, which I convinced myself was the same thing as a hug, even if his side of the hug came without any clothing.

"Ask Amy if she wants to go. I need to get some clothes on."

"It's still daylight. She might not even be here."

"She's right outside the door."

I shot bolt upright. "How do you know?"

Tobias grinned as he rolled off the bed. Naked.

Still naked.

"I'm a wolf, remember? I can hear her."

No sooner had he made the declaration than the pounding started at the door. "Gerwalta Kline, I know you're in there. Tell Caleb he's had you long enough. I need details!"

Tobias turned to me, his brow furrowed.

"She thinks I've been in here with Caleb since last night."

"Reasonable conclusion. I don't think she knew about the fancy hotel either. What are you going to tell her?"

I headed for the door. "What do you mean? I'm going to tell her the truth."

"Geri, wait. Let me at least—"

But it was too late. The second I opened the door, Amy's eyes filled with the scene: me, in the clothes I had worn last night; Tobias, wearing nothing but the blanket he'd just ripped off the bed to cover his wolfie bits.

No Caleb.

"Oh. My. God."

My hands flailed about in a mad attempt at distraction. "This isn't what it looks like."

The blonde stuck out one accusatory finger. "So you didn't spend the whole day curled up in bed with Tobias?"

"We only slept together."

I shot daggers at the wolf, even as he scrambled to pull up boxers under the protection of our bedspread. "That kind of statement is not helping."

Turning back to Amy, I continued. "Yes, we slept together. *Literally*, and only *literally*."

Confusion pulled her quirked expression out into broader definition. "So you *metaphorically* slept with Caleb, then came home and crawled in bed with Tobias for some *literal* sleep? Is this some sort of ritualistic, supernatural mate-swap thing?"

"Oh, my god." Tobias growled as he pulled a shirt over his head. "I don't know if it's a girl thing, or an American thing, but do you really just up and ask about each other's sex lives without a thought?"

Big words from a wolf who was constantly on me about mine.

Amy enumerated her virtues on her fingers. "One, it's more of an Amy thing than anything else. And two, you said there was no sex. Did you want to revise that statement?"

The wolf brushed past us. "It remains none of your business."

And with a *thwack!*, the bathroom door was closed and the shower came on.

Alone, she assaulted me and dragged me down the stairs. "Start at the beginning, tell me everything. I thought you said you were going to break up with Caleb last night?"

"I did break up with him. But unfortunately, not until after he'd asked me to marry him. Mate him. Be his baby mama? I'm not sure which one he was going for, but he didn't take it well."

I then explained the fact that he'd whacked me with a solarium, which turned the blonde into a banshee bent on revenge.

"That bastard!"

"I don't think he meant to hit me. I think he was just pulling the energy back into himself, and I got in between. It didn't hurt me. I mean, I don't think it did. I don't remember being in any pain. In fact, now that I think of it, I can't really remember anything that happened after that."

Amy's brow furrowed. "How did you get home?"

I scraped at reluctant memories. "I'm not sure. I just remember walking in the door an hour or so before sunrise and collapsing on the couch."

"And Caleb?"

A big blank spot there too. "Probably just needs some time. Actually, can you text him and make sure he's okay? My phone kinda melted."

She grimaced, even as she pulled out her device. "You still haven't explained how it was that you came to be sleeping next to a naked werewolf all day long."

Heat prickled across my chest. "I just didn't want to be alone, is all. I swear, we didn't do anything. Remember, he can't."

Amy held one hand up. "Look, Geri, I'm not your mother. God knows I'm not, given how much time I spent the last two years trying to get you hooked up with someone. Which… was my fault. You're not the hook-up type. You're the automatic long-term commitment type; I see that now. Anyways, the point is, I'm not going to stand here and pretend like I have any business telling you what to do with your love life, but I will say this: allow for more than twenty-four hours between breaking up with your slayer boyfriend before curling up next to your I-swear-he's-just-a-friend werewolf buddy. Even if it's platonic, and even if it's platonic because of some weird mates-for-life condition. You guys are still here on a mission, and if you have to continue to work together, you need to… well, continue to work together."

A knock at the door below drew my attention away, and I spoke to Amy over my shoulder as we went down the stairs. "It was a moment of weakness. And when Caleb comes home, I'll make sure he knows how much of a friend I still consider him. Has he texted back yet?"

"In the last sixty seconds? No."

"He could be asleep. The sun just set, after all."

The man standing outside the door was no doubt a local: A button-down shirt, black hair, olive skin, and a mustache that looked like he'd chopped off a squirrel's tail and glued it to his upper lip. He said a few words in his native tongue, none of which either Amy or I understood.

"He says he has a package for the woman of the house."

Amy and I both looked at Tobias like he'd grown a second head as he joined us in the entryway.

"How in the hell do you know that?" I asked.

"Unlike the two of you, I've actually been studying Turkish while we've been here." The werewolf said a few words back, highly shaped by an English inflection, and dug a few coins out of his pocket. The man nodded his thanks, placing a linen envelope in Tobias's hand in exchange for the tip. "*Teşekkür ederim.*"

I closed the door and engaged both its locks. "Must be a message from Igor. He *loves* being a pen pal and it reeks of vampire."

"Faintly. Like it's been near one but not touched by one." Tobias put the missive to his nose, inhaling. "*You* can smell that?"

"Of course, I can smell it." Then, what Tobias had actually said hit me. "Not touched by one? Is Igor using scribes now?"

Two questions which needed to be answered immediately. When Amy put her hand on my shoulder, I wondered why. Only when her fingers massaged my tension did I realize how clenched up I'd become.

Fine linen paper turned to scraps as Tobias ripped open the envelope.

"Well," I said after a few tense seconds of his eyes playing a tennis match across the page. "What does it say?"

He shook his head. "I don't know. It's not English. It's not even in English letters."

"You mean roman script," Amy corrected as she grabbed the paper from the werewolf's hands. "This is Cyrillic."

"And you read Cyrillic?" I asked hopefully.

The blonde grimaced. "Cyrillic isn't a language. It's an alphabet."

"So what languages use it then?"

"Lots. Russian, Ukrainian… It's used for most of the Balkan languages."

Even as I asked it, even as Amy's eyes went unfocused as she looked into her memory, the pieces had started to fall into place. "Romanian?"

She pondered that a moment, her mouth pursed, lips pulled left. "No, though maybe once upon a time. I mean, Turkish used to be written with Arabic script, didn't it? Why?"

Tobias and I exchanged a look.

"Because," the werewolf said, "Vlad was Romanian." Tobias pulled out his phone, plucking out digits. "We need to get Igor or Inga on the phone now."

"And Caleb!" Amy added, pulling out her own phone.

I pushed her device back down. "There's no point trying again. The Ravens have him."

TWENTY-TWO

"If I had only told him what he wanted to hear…"

"Then you would have been lying."

Amy's rebuke nipped my latest downward spiral of guilt in the bud, even if only temporarily. An hour had passed since the delivery of the letter, and though we still had no idea what it said, couldn't even state with certainty that Caleb was in fact a hostage, we all felt it. Only, where the others were merely perplexed and worried, I was manufacturing self-blame like I was planning to sell it wholesale.

"The last slayer is dead, or will be," I muttered, staring off into space. "And it's all because of me."

"Seriously, you have to stop. We don't know anything. You're jumping to conclusions. Plus, can I remind you that the only one to blame for any crime is the criminal?"

A scratch at the front door made both of us jump. An hour ago, when I'd opened the door to the messenger, I'd done it without a second thought. The last tendrils of sunlight had still streaked across the sky, and that fact had filled me with a false sense of security. Now, with night having descended over Istanbul, every person in the street had become a monster in my mind. A city of fifteen million heinous creatures, all wanting to destroy us. I'd even convinced myself that my ability to sense wolves had returned. The Pera Pack would mount an attack posthaste, as contact with us would eventually lead to retribution on their account.

Amy, however, had found a way to keep a level head, even as my nerves wrapped me in a ball. She looked at the peephole then, bearing some frustration, opened the door just enough to look out.

Tobias's snout pushed into the opening, the precursor to his giant wolf's frame making its way inside. He shook off the mist that clung to the night, spraying the air. The moment the door was closed behind him, he shifted back to his upright form.

I stood, handing him the pile of clothes he'd discarded before heading out. "Anything?"

The werewolf shook his head. "As soon as I got out to the main street, there were too many scents for me to pick out that messenger's. I would have tried going a few blocks in other directions, but I was already getting a lot of worried looks from the locals." He pulled up his jeans and buckled them. For once, Amy seemed not to take any delight in having a naked man in her presence. "There may be plenty of street dogs in Istanbul, but a wolf the size of a pony still sets everyone's teeth on edge. Anything from Igor or Inga?"

Amy pulled out her phone and looked at the screen. "No, but Spain is two hours behind here; it still won't be sunset there for another hour."

"And you sent them a picture of the letter?"

"Of course, but I don't think we have to wait."

She held up her phone and turned the screen our way. On it, a photo of the letter we'd received and, overlaying the lines of text, boxes outlined in red, on top of which English words were superimposed.

She turned the screen back in her direction. "These online

translation engines aren't exact, but it's more than we know now. It'd be better if it was printed instead of handwritten."

"Enough, woman!" Tobias exclaimed. "What does it say?"

"Remember, this may not be completely accurate, but..." Amy focused on her phone. "*Think you victor my field? I keep your crusader, want monarch. Throw yourself. I am finding where raptors sit in a high place.*"

She shrugged as the two of us gawked at her.

"I told you, it's not perfect. Look, just try to think *around* the literal translation. The first sentence, 'think you victor my field,' sounds like some arrogant ass boasting about something. Heard enough lines like that through many a break-up."

Tobias balanced his chin on a cupped fist. "One thing we know about Vlad, about all the Ravens, is that they're very full of themselves, so that fits. The crusader is probably Caleb, but sounds like they wanted someone else instead."

Already I was pulling on my boots. "I don't care who they wanted. Who they're getting is me."

"Like hell, they are." Tobias seized me by the forearm, pulling me to my feet. "What do you think you're going to do, Geri? Even with your hood abilities, what *could* you do? Silver doesn't harm them."

"Not on its own, but I still haven't met something that can survive without a head."

"So, what? You're going to magically find a highly-dangerous clutch of vampires we've been searching fruitlessly for for over a month and chop off all their heads, just like that? And without a weapon? I thought you were the one who said we needed to interrogate them first."

"That was before they kidnapped my boyfriend."

"Ex-boyfriend." Amy slid her phone back into her pants pocket. "You two broke up, or don't you remember that part?"

Of course, I remembered! But what had happened afterward? The recollection stunned me for a moment, and I saw myself last night in my mind's eye, running after Caleb as he slayer-walked out of the museum. He'd been moving so fast, what possibly could have caught him? I couldn't. Not that I was as fast as a slayer, not even when I'd been a nascent hood. The only thing as fast as a slayer was a…

"They were there." Realization slapped me in the face. "The dome of Hagia Sophia has windows. Anyone could have seen the light of that solarium."

Amy passed Tobias a look of confusion. The werewolf only grimaced and shook his head. The historical pictures that covered the walls of the rental house had been telling us the answer the whole time. Hell, even Ayşe had told us. We'd wasted so much time when the answer had been in front of us since we'd arrived.

"Remember what Ayşe told us last time she was talking to us? I thought it was a metaphor, telling us not to mess with the Ravens, because they were too dangerous. It wasn't a metaphor at all."

I crossed to the living room, where, over one of the low-slung couches, a painting of Istanbul at its height under the Ottomans hung. The modern city lay anchored on so many of its great monuments. Many of these buildings had been raised under the early sultans, but some of them stretched back to Byzantine times.

"Think. What did Inga and Igor tell us about the Ravens? About

Vlad?"

Tobias pulled alongside me. Was he starting to see it too?

"They'd be somewhere that was easily defended," he said.

"Somewhere that wasn't built by the Ottomans. Somewhere that had large crowds nearby," Amy added, making us a trio before the painting. "A place where there were lots of tourists without places to be, people to be accountable to. Easily fed from. Easily used without anyone noticing."

"Vampires can't smell worth a shit, but they can see the faintest light," I said. "Caleb thought we were inside, on a full moon night nonetheless. He didn't think there would be any danger in showing me. But they saw it. They can see almost the whole city from there. It was like a… Like a…"

"A giant bug zapper."

The werewolf and I both gawked at the huey.

"What?" Amy asked. "You've never seen one of those? It's like a cone and the light attracts bugs and then it zaps them—"

"We know what a bug zapper is!" Tobias growled back. He refocused on the scene before us. "The whole time, and we've been running around in its shadow." The werewolf cupped his hand over his chin, pulling on a beard that became more permanent by the day. "It's the perfect place. They're protected by a thousand eyes, and by the fact that they're in a fucking tower. It will be hard, but I think I can do it."

I rounded on him with speed a cheetah would envy. "You're not going anywhere near the Ravens. It's my fault they got Caleb, and I'll be the one to get him back."

"Unless we're going to wait for Inga and Igor to come back, which I'm guessing would be tomorrow night at the soonest, assuming that the professor can't leave Spain until he gets a belly full of his special diet blood, then it has to be me. I'm not going to let two hueys get themselves killed by Count Dracula."

A squeak erupted out of our token huey. "Oh, I have no intention of going anywhere near them. Got my fill of intimate time with a bad vampire when one turned into the smoke monster and tried to kill me in front of a live studio audience. But Geri's right, Tobias. It can't be you."

"Amy, no matter how much you've learned about our kind since you came into the fold, you don't know what you're talking about."

"Actually, she does." Shame took my eyes to the ground. "Your brother and your father were both alphas. Even if you weren't an alpha, you still have the blood markers to be one. Remember what Igor said? Alpha-beta blood is one of the most powerful elixirs for a vampire to extend his life."

Tobias's teeth ground. "I can't let you go in there defenseless, even if that's true."

"I'm not defenseless. I have a lifetime of hood training in both combat and negotiating. Just because I can't move as fast as I used to or that I'm not as strong doesn't change that. Besides, being a huey in this circumstance might be an advantage. I'm still the daughter of a red matron, and I doubt a vampire as arrogant and self-involved as Vlad or the other Ravens would know that I've been relinquished. Knowing I'm a matron's daughter will make him think twice about killing me. Worst-case scenario: he decides to feed from me."

The werewolf let me speak my piece, then shook his head. "You really think that's the worst-case scenario?"

"It's the worst one I'll let myself think about."

TWENTY-THREE

All my life, I'd known the weight of eyes. My mother's admonishing glare, my father's sympathetic gaze, the pensive stares from werewolves as I accompanied different members of my clan on rounds to regional packs. The scowls of other hoods during summer training trips in Germany when I would best them in competition after competition. Eyes had mass, gravity. I felt it now, the anchor of a dozen eyes upon me as I stood at the base of Galata Tower, weighing me down with expectation, confusion, surprise.

Intrigue.

Despite the crowds of tourists milling about, some chatting, some seated at nearby cafes, taking in an early dinner, others snapping pictures of the tower above the square, I felt utterly singular. Was this really so different from the forests and rivers and stones I knew as home? Only there, my goal was to sneak up on the prey without it knowing. This time, I had to attract the hunter, being just another beast.

The hunter needed bait, however. I lifted a hand to my head and wrapped my fingers around the hilt of my dagger. The familial weapon sighed from the sheath buried in my braid. Balancing the blade on the tip of my finger garnered little in the way of attention from the crowd. When I started to toss it into the air in a series of complex routines, however, a small crowd gathered. When I added fighting forms to the presentation, they fanned the edges.

I felt like my old self in this moment: driven to the middle of an expanse, waiting for the challenge that would soon make itself known. Even though I'd made Tobias promise not to come anywhere near here, I felt his stare too. The liar. Familiar, comforting, almost like a warm blanket on a cold night. I swept the crowd, wondering if I could catch sight of him, but when I came about three-quarters of the way through my turn, a man stood before me who had not been there a moment ago.

Black hair, feathered, haphazardly tossed and styled. A shirt as blue as the tiles that decorated so many of the Ottoman architectural wonders, opened down to the third button to show the sculptured, fuzzy chest beneath. Gray slacks and a suit jacket. A thick mustache that seemed the fashion among the natives. Native: he looked like one, but an air of otherness about him suggested anything but to trained eyes. He snatched my hand, his black eyes fixed on the drop of blood that pearled where my blade had nicked a finger.

"Merhaba, canım. Dün gece nereye köştünüz?"

I shook my head. "Don't speak Turkish."

He grinned. Such white teeth. No fangs. They must be retracted. "English, then?"

"Or some really basic South American Spanish."

"Alas, my Spanish hasn't advanced beyond the sixteenth century. Your owning of a pulse suggests yours was born after that." He looked at me with a more intense inspection, as though determining what dress would best suit me. "Most hueys would consider escaping from us a blessing. How intriguing that you returned to be captured willingly."

Escape? I escaped the Ravens?

Despite the mixture of pride and confusion warring inside me, I had to maintain outward indifference, annoyance. Disdain. *If you make their concerns seem petty, you make their players feel powerless,* my mother would say. *Set them ill at ease by letting them think their goals have no value for you. Then they must appease you in some other way to get what they want. Then, you can make demands.*

"What makes you think my being here has anything to do with you?"

He lifted my finger up to the level of his eyes, examining the trickle of blood that had begun to crust over. "Either you're not as skilled with a blade as you assumed, or you yourself set a beautiful trap to get our attention. I understand you Americans have a concept called 'finger food.' I must admit, I did not think it so literal."

I managed to snap my hand back seconds before his lips closed over the injury, leaving him holding air.

"Where I come from, people like you have to ask permission to feed. I haven't given it."

He dropped his hand and stepped to me, bringing our chests into contact. He'd seemed taller a moment ago, but I realized, as our gazes locked, that he was, indeed, the same height as I. His slender fingers petted down my hair, tracing an eventual line over my chin.

"A Raven is not given permission to do as he wishes. He takes what he desires."

An adversary must be equal at the very least. I mirrored the vampire's action, raising my own hand to cup the dominant jawline. Anyone else seeing us in the crowd would think us lovers.

"So I've learned. Give him back to me, or I'll be forced to take him back. I promise, if it comes to that, the consequences will be drastic."

The glint in his eye sharpened. Possibly from amusement. Possibly from the longing sparked by my racing pulse. Or both.

"Vlad will find you most interesting."

"I imagine the feeling will be likewise." I dropped my hand. Now that he'd confirmed he was one of Dracula's clutch, and not the man himself, I wouldn't touch him. It would suggest equity. "Summon him."

The vampire took the hint that the locus of this cat-and-mouse game had shifted. I'd played myself beyond the first maze.

"He's not here."

"How convenient."

"Do you suppose we reside *here*?" The vampire motioned to the tower overhead. "It's merely our... official place of business. He suspected you'd come tonight. He made sure we had someone waiting for you when you arrived."

"Sorry, who?"

The vampire shook with silent laughter. "In time, you will call him *master*."

TWENTY-FOUR

Boot heels pounded on cobblestones. Tourists and locals swirled in a miasma. Ten steps from the tower, a sharp right, fifteen steps along the adjacent street, two steps off the curb into the black SUV that had arrived right on cue. A slamming door, and the weight of his stare lifted. Tobias had lost sight of me behind tinted glass. There was no doubt the werewolf was in the crowd, or that he was now panicking about what to do. On two legs, he'd never keep up with a vehicle, even in Istanbul traffic. On four legs, the feat was possible, but impractical. A two-hundred-plus-pound wolf in a highly-packed tourist area running as though he were hunting prey, though? The huey authorities would shoot to kill without a second thought.

The Ravens had chosen their perch well.

Two men sat in the front seat, textbook goons: slicked-back hair, three-piece suits, holstered guns peeking out. Vampires or enthralled hueys, I didn't know. The man who'd harvested me slid into the backseat from the other side and leaned over, a slip of cloth in his hands.

"May I?"

I very much doubted that. "Why not just enthrall me? Erase my memory when I leave?"

He didn't wait for permission to secure the blindfold over my eyes. "*If* you leave. And if you leave, it must be for certain you will not return."

"Am I being taken prisoner?"

The goons in the front seat chuckled. They understood English. Was that important?

The vampire beside me wore his smile in his voice. "You are an honored guest, until such time you give us a reason to dishonor you. No matter what my sister claimed, we are not bloodthirsty monsters."

"So, I'm not a prisoner, but my boyfriend is?"

No answer to that. This vamp either was unaware of Caleb's capture, held an opinion on his detainment contrary to his master's, or had been instructed not to discuss the matter with me. No point in further attempts at information; he wouldn't provide it.

"Do I at least get to know your name?"

"I thought my sister would have told you that already."

"I know the names of all the Ravens, but I don't know which you are."

After a few moments, his answer came out clipped. "Timur."

"Timur," I repeated, inking the feel of it on my lips.

"And you?"

"I am eager to meet Vlad."

Power wasn't about who knew the most; it was about who was able to share the least and still get what they wanted.

Perhaps an hour had passed when the SUV parked. Timur and I kept our silence, though the driver and other passenger kept up a conversation I could make neither heads nor tails of. When the car came to its final stop, Timur circled to my side to open the door, guided me out by the hand, and gave the car time to drive away before the blindfold was removed.

The structure before me looked more like something from Prague or Vienna than Istanbul. Six stories high and covered in vines, the mansion was definitely fit for a prince. Though its size blocked my view of the exterior and periphery, the taste of the air and the profile of the soundscape convinced me it was either right on the water, or within a block or two of it.

"Does my master's abode meet your expectations, *yenge*?"

That word I knew. Literally, it meant *aunt*, but it was also used casually the way Americans used *ma'am*.

"I don't frequent with fifteenth-century Wallachian princes-turned-vampiric-sultans, so my expectation had no basis. It's a very nice home, if that's what you're asking. Does my opinion matter?"

"A question I myself am asking."

Timur opened the front door and led me into a hall donned with appointments that reflected the exterior's luxury. The floor: marble. The walls: fine linen wallpaper. I would bet a ten-spot that the frame of the mirror we passed was gold-leaf.

"We rarely entertain outside our own community, so the level of luminosity was somewhat debated. Do let us know if it needs correcting."

Meaning, normally the house was kept dark. Vampires only needed the dimmest light for efficient vision, far less than a hood or even a werewolf. Though, as I realized in reflection, it could also be that any huey victim gathered for feasting might not be able to detect their attackers.

"It's sufficient. Thank you for the consideration."

"Of course."

When we entered the main salon, I would have bet that I'd been magically transported to Buckingham Palace or Versailles. Not that I'd visited either, but I'd seen pictures. Every furnishing evidenced extravagance, every material and means of decorating, precise and expertly arranged. A marble fireplace captured my attention. In the midsummer, no flames danced within. Instead, its craftsmanship blazed, as did the red-haired, fair-skinned woman sitting before it in an ivory wingback chair, a mound of yarn on her lap.

She flashed big blue eyes at me, knitting needles frozen in place. Having expected the legendary Nosferatu himself, I wasn't sure what to make of her. She, likewise, gawked at me, unmoving. Was she shocked? Scared? Disturbed at my presence? Her plaintive expression suggested all and nothing.

"Alexandra." Timur assumed a place at my side in utter silence. "Would you please allow the room? *He* would like to have a private audience with…"

"Alexandra may stay."

Mist became man, and myth became material. How I could have

wondered if Timur might be Vlad back at the tower dumbfounded me now. Vlad's artists had painted him well, and the only thing time had touched were his fashions. The coffee-colored hair no longer dropped in gentle waves about his shoulders. It was trimmed, feathered but short, and his face no longer naked, but bearded. His billowy, black pants reminded me of something from a Middle Eastern fairy tale. He didn't wear a shirt. I traced back to memories of my year of study in preparation for this moment, and couldn't bring to mind one authentic rendering of him bare-chested, but I doubted any artist could have accurately captured it.

Maybe the stonecutter who'd perfected the fireplace, since it seemed to be of the same material.

"Timur, see that our guest has tea?"

As the lesser Raven pushed a tulip-shaped glass to a heated samovar on a nearby table, Alexandra stood, holding her work tight into her stomach. A tiny slipper peeked out from the bundle of yarn. "I'd prefer to leave, my lord. Her kind scares me."

Vlad grinned. "My dear, what harm do you suppose a relinquished hood could deliver from which I could not save you?"

Timur handed me my tea, even as tension dug into my gut. Somehow, the truth of my condition had found its way to Istanbul.

A faltering smile flickered on the woman's face. "None, my love. You would save me from any danger. But I'm weary at the moment. I would, with your leave, rest."

Vlad took the woman's hand and planted a kiss. "Of course. Go, I will come to you later tonight."

My veins iced over from her frosty glare as she passed me on her way out. Only, between her ire and her stately manner, the purpose and source of her disdain sat in a mire I couldn't digest. When she was gone, Vlad turned his attention to me, replacing tenderness with annoyance.

"My message was meant for Inga."

"Inga is in receipt of your message." I assumed by now she'd be awake in Spain. I wondered what Amy had told her?

"If that were true, you wouldn't be here, Gerwalta Kline."

It didn't faze me that he knew my name. Or, at least, that was what I told myself.

"You took Caleb. I want him back."

"No, and not merely because Mr. Helsing's residence with us has been most efficacious," he said, motioning to another seating area away from the fireplace, in a corner of the room before two massive, arched windows through which the lights of the opposite shore and of the few boats bobbing on the waves shimmered on the water. "Is that why you've come, in some vain attempt to recover Inga's pet slayer?"

My mother's lessons echoed in my brain. Sitting tall I hoped made me look more formidable, though what effect, if any, that would have on a legendary vampire, who knew? As I caught sight again of the silver-plated samovar, I longed for the abilities of a righteous hood. If I could draw it to me and shape it into a disk, I'd just slice this bastard's head off.

"I'd also like you to tell me who else knows about the power of unmated alpha blood, what the serum is that Cynthia derived to undo the mating bond, and where you store that serum so that I can destroy every last drop of it. But for the moment, let's start with you returning my mate."

"Your *mate*?" Vlad's eyebrow rose. "I thought only werewolves took mates. There are no werewolves here, not unless your token beast managed to track you across twenty kilometers of traffic. What did Caleb say his name was again? Oh, that's right." A grin emerged, one tailored to show off prominently extended fangs. "Tobias."

I hoped he saw the embers burning in my cheeks. "I'm talking about Caleb. We're a couple, or didn't he tell you that part?"

He may have tried to hide it, or perhaps Vlad assumed that a relinquished hood, a de facto huey, had eyesight too poor to see how he winced. In this moment, I knew that part of our lives, Caleb had managed to keep hidden. Why, though? Was it because remembering my response to his proposal hurt too much, or because his feelings, despite the rejection, were strong enough he'd done it in an effort to protect me? If the latter, then Vlad wanted something from him. Something that he was refusing to offer up, and he feared that having me would create leverage the Ravens could use to force his hand. Either way, I'd have to play this out very close to the chest.

The vampire changed directions. "You don't seem to be frightened, Miss Kline. You do know that it would take me only a few bats of the eye to sink my teeth into your neck and rip out your throat, don't you?"

"If you're simply playing with your food before eating it, then I'm dead already and there's no point in fretting. Even if I am relinquished, I was raised a hood. Women of my kind do not fear men."

Vlad splayed his hands out. "Perhaps this is why the slayer is so resistant to our encouragements. Perhaps you have trained him to fear you more than he fears any vampire."

Yes, they were negotiating with him, but for what? "You'd be wise to learn from his lesson."

The vampire threw back his head and laughed. Unlike the suggestions in any number of horror films I'd scoffed at through the years, Vlad's laughter was full-bellied, whimsical. Lightening.

Attractive.

"So, Caleb is yours." Taking to his feet, he grabbed me by the hand. My untouched tea crashed to the floor, sending a shatter of glass and spray of drink over the tile.

Vlad watched with some amusement as the liquid became a rivulet heading toward the fireplace. His eyes tracked its path, as did mine in turn. The stream ran over the hearth and into the fireplace proper. Only, instead of pooling, it fell into oblivion. That fact alone was curious, but I found myself focusing on the cleanest grate I'd ever seen. Silver? With gold leaf on all of the nearby knickknacks, should it surprise me that Dracula burned his winter fires on a grate made of precious metal?

"A simple accident. Don't worry, it will be dealt with." After a moment, Vlad pulled me up. "Would you like to see your mate, Miss Kline?"

"I wouldn't *like* to see him." Despite the fact that it gave away my excitement, there was no way to slow my racing pulse. "I *demand* to see him."

Vlad turned another amused smile on me as he guided me towards a staircase at the edge of the room. "Oh, I find that, despite myself, I do *like* you, Miss Kline. Very much, indeed."

Whereas the bottom floor had high ceilings and an open concept, the vampire's head barely gained clearance upstairs. We emerged in a hallway dimly lit, wide and long but with few doors. Not a single window in sight, not even at the end of the hall where it reached a dead end. The walls on this floor had been painted a dark blue, crisscrossed by a repeating geometric pattern not unlike those I'd seen decorating lamps and plates in the Bazaar.

"For a Romanian prince, so many of your tastes seem local."

Vlad gave my comment a nod of acknowledgment. "For many years after my father turned me, I was a raving nationalist, I must admit. Do you know my story, Miss Kline? I do not wish to bore you by repeating things you already know."

"I know a story about you. Whether or not it aligns with the one you know of yourself, I can't say."

"Bravery and wisdom," Vlad said. "I see why so many are so drawn to you. I, too, have tried to use my many years to gain wisdom. I like to think that, in this house, I have cultivated an artifact to that growth."

"Oh?"

"Indeed. Over the centuries, I've even learned to embrace certain aspects of the Ottoman's legacy. For example,…" His hand fanned out, indicating the wall. "…the motifs. And another system I had not the scope to recognize until I had learned to let go of my human attachments to concepts like nationality and tribe."

In this course, we reached a door. Surveying left and right, I realized it was the only door on this side of the hall. Vlad's hand curled around the knob, just as a devilish smile curled the corners of his mouth.

"And though it took me many years to understand how to properly implement it, they also had the best way to assure the survival of their bloodlines."

When the door opened, I wasn't quite sure what it was I was seeing. An open space, a room two stories high with a loft above, open to below. In the loft, a dozen or so beds sat at intervals, and below lay a lounging space populated with cushions, couches, and low tables. And women. Lots of women, as many as there were beds above. Finely dressed, all sitting about on luxurious couches. Some did needlework, some drank tea, some even played instruments in a corner. Alexandra sat among them, her eyes still in her knitting.

The edges of my face pulled tight as I turned to the vampire. "You keep a harem?"

"With one important difference."

"Geri?"

I took two steps into the room, pivoted. It couldn't be. "Caleb?"

There, in a puffed-up imitation of an armchair, wearing three beautiful women as clothing, sat Caleb. Swollen lips and purple blooms over his neck suggested just how warm they had kept him too.

From behind, Vlad leaned down to whisper in my ear. "As you see, he's simply pined over you since he's been here."

The slayer stood, his lampreys falling off with a pop. In the space of a few blinks, he'd crossed the room and stood before me. "Why are you here?"

"To rescue you, of course. Here I was thinking you were being tortured and drained for some kind of Ravens' blood-bender, and instead, you've spent the last twenty-four hours making out with half the harem?"

A low rumble bounced off the walls as the vampire laughed, echoed in moments by any number of the blood slaves sitting at intervals throughout the room.

"Oh, my dear," Vlad said. "Is that what Inga led you to believe? That the moment I got my hands on your dear *mate*, I would hang him by his heels and let his precious blood flow into a trough?"

Caleb stepped to the side to look around me at Vlad. "Mate?"

"Did you not know that you were mated to her, Helsing?" Vlad asked. "She seemed quite insistent that you were."

The mate in question righted himself, his hands balled into oppressive fists. "My recollection about what she wanted from me in a relationship is quite different."

"Seriously?" I pointed around the lavish suite, at its in-floor fountain, at its pitchers of fruit water. Seriously, fucking fruit water? "This is okay with you?"

"It is, Geri. It's more than okay. In fact, you can say I've had a sort of awakening."

Just then, a third hand grew out of Caleb's side. Or so I thought, until it was soon joined by an arm attached to a body. A body that most girls would kill for. A body that "old Caleb" would have loved to spend some time with.

"Come back to us, Caleb. We're getting lonely without you."

Caleb smiled back over his shoulder. "In a moment, Konstantina. I have to deal with something first."

The black-haired beauty rolled up on her feet and pressed her lips to the slayer's ear, sucking on his earlobe as she slowly extracted her hand from him. When she pulled away and retreated, I didn't miss the "awakening" going on in his pants.

Taking three steps toward me, Caleb stared me down, his face only inches from mine. "You shouldn't have come here, Geri. Inga lied. The Ravens haven't killed the slayers at all. They've preserved them. They've freed them from oppression."

"They've freed…" The words died at the back of my throat. Who was this man, and what had he done with my Caleb? "How can you say that? They killed your parents. They killed all the slayers."

Caleb shook his head and stepped back, even as each of the dozen women in the room rose to their feet. The familiar orb glowed atop Caleb's hand as he held out his arm and opened his palm to the sky. My eyes went wide as each of the women mirrored the act, conjuring tiny balls of sunlight like his. Only Alexandra remained sitting, her knitting now in her lap.

Slayers. They were all slayers.

"*These* are my people," Caleb said. "These are the slayers. And it's with them, not you, that I'll find happiness. Good-bye, Geri. Good-bye forever."

I couldn't find it in me to resist when Vlad's arm draped over my shoulders. "Come now, Miss Kline. Your *mate* has had his say. Unless, you'd care to join him here?"

Caleb paused in his retreat, turning his head back over his shoulder. Even as shivers chased up my body, I saw it: the momentary flinch in his expression.

"Like I said, *Sultanim*, she's nothing more than a huey now. The women here would eat her alive. If you didn't, that is."

Vlad balanced my fate in his grin. "Either might be entertaining."

"If you want my continued cooperation, you'll strongly consider how much her presence disturbs me."

Wait, he didn't want my help? He knew that I was still highly capable of kicking ass. We had been sparring together for a year. We knew each other's rhythms, and joining the harem would be a ticket to set me up under the nose of the enemy. There was only one thing I could think of to explain his words: he *was* playing a part. He didn't want *me* to be here, either. There was a plan afoot, one he needed Inga to trigger. I was only getting in the way. I was only going to get myself killed.

That, or it wasn't a plan at all. He really meant it.

Impossible, but without the ability to get him alone, what could I do but play along? I had to be the hood. I had to be in control.

"You've enchanted my mate somehow, Vlad." I swallowed my nerves. "Which leaves me to wonder, are you making me an offer, or an ultimatum?"

"I do not kill in such haste, no matter what Inga suggested." Again, the prince paid attention to my neck, this time with his mouth, not his tongue. "I have tasted hoods before, but never relinquished hood. The bouquet of your skin is earthen, metallic. Does silver still run in your blood?"

"Not likely." I was, as he so duly noted, relinquished. "Are you planning on drinking me?"

He pulled back, holding me at arms' length. "I would love to do so much more than that. Miss Kline, you've managed to pique my interest in a way few can. What kind of relinquished hood seeks out vampires and claims, even if in a poor attempt at some ill-conceived rescue, that a slayer is her mate? Most hoods I've met would curl in disgust at the prospect of having to partner outside their own bloodline, let alone across the divide. Yes, I would have you, if you would consent, but alas, to what end? Vampires cannot chase scents as do wolves, but did you know we can *smell* emotions?"

A prickle chased up my spine, sending all my hairs standing on end.

Vlad fingered the ends of my braid, pulling it to his nose, inhaling my secrets. "Heartache, longing. There is a scent about you, a remnant of another who holds your heart, but threw it away."

Cody. How strong must his hold be that even, two years later, the vampire could sense it?

"It is in this way I know you cannot be had in the way I take women."

The collection of female slayers dispersed around the room, all still balancing balls of sunlight on their hands, giggled like some sadistic Greek chorus.

Vlad finally peeled himself away from me and circled the room. "They laugh with joy. I love each of my beauties. But in turn, they love only me. Isn't that right?"

"Yes, *Sultanimiz*," they cooed in unison.

He ran a hand tenderly over the ebony cheek of a particularly statuesque slayer. "I demand complete obeisance. I would be the only man you'd owe fealty. So, unless you're willing to surrender your love for whomever this man is who wound up your emotions so tightly..."

"Good luck with that," Caleb mumbled under his breath. At last, he closed his hand, and with it, the female slayers did too.

The vampire feigned disappointment. "Then, to the dungeon with you."

"What the hell?" My inner Geri erupted out of my mouth before I could stop her. "You said it wasn't an ultimatum!"

"Not where your life is concerned. But you didn't just expect that I'd let you walk out of here of your own free will, did you?" Vlad clicked his tongue. "Come now, Miss Kline. And here I had attributed to you such intelligence. Did you or did you not come in response to summons I sent my sister? Did you not surrender yourself to me in her stead?"

"I…" Did I? "I don't recall mentioning the word 'surrender' at all."

He flicked away the inconvenience of small differences. "All the same."

I didn't remember making the decision to turn and run; I just did, exploding into the extensive corridor through which I'd first come. Almost at once, the soft lights dimmed, leaving all sides inked black. Though, perhaps, not as dark as I thought. After a blink or two, with my pulse pounding in my ears, my eyes adjusted somewhat. Details remained concealed, but structure took on definition. How I managed to get to the stairs without any of them catching up with me, I'd never know. The last several stairs were managed in a single leap, as I pivoted and turned back towards the front of the house. The grounds were enclosed, I knew that much. How I intended to break out of a secured clutch, I couldn't fathom. One step at a time: first, to get outside.

"Not so fast."

Icy fingers lashed around my neck, and the lower half of my body, subject to physics, swung forward, making a pendulum of my legs. Timur held me with such little effort, it surprised me that he didn't just break my neck in two.

"We offer you hospitality, and you respond with—"

Silver streaked the air. Blade rent flesh. This song I knew like a lullaby.

The world rose to smack me as the vampire released his grip. Hungry lungs, flattened by the impact, gasped for air. Somehow, I managed my feet, ignoring the gurgling of the creature behind me, and propelled myself forward.

Just beyond a gate, presiding over the corpse of one of the men who earlier had driven me across the city, was a dominating, broad-shouldered man cloaked in red. His face was obscured, but I knew him on sight. It didn't mean I understood how he'd come to be here.

Suddenly, Markus called out in warning. "Geri, behind you!"

I turned just in time to see fangs and death. Only, seconds before the other man who'd been in the car sunk his fangs into me, he burned into dust in a terrific orange glow. Through a curtain of his ashes, a familiar face: Alexandra.

She'd thrown the solarium? But, why?

"Hurry, or they'll be upon us. Flee!"

I shook my head. "Caleb—"

"Is safe as long as he continues his ruse," Alexandra said, cutting me off. "Run, fool. Return only when your victory is assured."

With that, Markus took my hand, and we fled into the night.

TWENTY-FIVE

Amber fingers, luminescent strains of gold and red, beamed from behind patchy storm clouds, smacking my retinas as Markus drove us over the bridge between Eminönü and Karaköy, absent of cars at this early hour.

"You know you won't be safe in that house you've been staying in anymore, right?" He kept his wincing eyes pointed ahead. "Come nightfall, they're going to descend on that place like harpies."

The first words he'd spoken since helping me flee the Ravens' compound formed a lecture. My mother would be proud. He'd allowed me silence after he'd told me to get into the car parked just outside the gates of the mansion, though that might have also been self-preservation. We were two hoods wrapped up in a vampire family drama; neither of us should be here. Both had reasons to call the other out.

"How long have you been following me?"

"I arrived in Istanbul before you did, by an hour or so, anyways," Markus reported matter-of-factly. "As soon as I got word that you'd boarded the plane in Chicago, I hopped on the next departing flight out of Frankfurt."

"Frankfurt?" It didn't take me but a moment to put together the pieces. "My mother's at Schloss Wolfsretter?"

"No, your mom is still in Paradise, but she's had me there on standby since the beginning of June."

"Why would she send you to spy on *me*? She's already disowned me. Relinquished me. She's never cared about vampires killing other vampires."

"I'm not here to spy on you." His stoic face crumbled under the weight of his own lie. "Okay, yes, that's one of the reasons she sent me. But believe it or not, my primary mission here is to protect you. You have to stop thinking your mother is some kind of monolith who only casts one long shadow. She might have banished you from the clan, but that doesn't mean she loves you any less. Come on, you're still her daughter."

"If you think, for a single moment, I'm going to buy that on any level, you're crazy." Then, grabbing at any scrap of humility I could muster, I added, "But I probably would have been locked in yet another vampire dungeon if you hadn't helped me, so thanks. Speaking of which, what the hell is it with vampires and dungeons?"

He pulled up outside the house I'd been sharing with the others. No sooner had I gained my feet getting out of the car than the front door opened and a massive lupine form bounded out, leapt clear over my head, and landed atop the sedan Markus had stolen off the streets.

My cousin, still decked out in his hood, silver still brocaded over his chest in wait for his command, held out his hands. "Easy, wolf. I'm not here to hurt you, but if needs be…"

"Tobias!"

The brindle wolf swung his head in my direction.

"He's from my clan," I explained, pointing. "And one of my best—"

"Freeze!"

That the werewolf would pounce towards an unfamiliar hood after what had happened last night didn't surprise me. What did surprise me was Amy in the doorway, pointing a small handgun (pink, no less) into the street.

The silver plate over Markus's chest shimmered. He'd weaponize it quicker than any huey pulling a trigger if he really thought there was a threat.

I threw my hands into the air. "Oh, my god. We're separated for a couple hours, and suddenly both of you are crazy." I turned and pointed at the blonde. "Amy, put that away, and Tobias…" My accusing gesture swung to the wolf. "…come inside and change back. We have to talk and we don't have a lot of time."

Amy kept the weapon squared. "Who's the hood?"

"His name is Markus. He's my cousin."

"Your cousin?" As the barrel of the gun sank toward the ground, Amy's eyes rose toward Markus. "Is he single?"

Markus scoffed. "Hardly."

That was news. "You have someone now?"

He nodded, his glee practically misting the air. "Yan. He's quite a looker. Oh, and I look. *Often.*"

Amy's face fell. "Why do the hottest ones already have boyfriends?"

Tobias skittered through the door and past Amy. The moment he was safely out of view of the street, the familiar groan of a body reforming itself spilled beyond the doorway.

The wolf merged into the conversation without even slowing down. "What is one of your mother's minions doing in Istanbul?"

"Me?" Markus pointed mockingly at his own chest. "Oh, nothing. Taking in the sights. Saving my cousin from Dracula's compound. You know, the usual tourist things."

That knocked the wolf on his ass. "What?"

The shock of Markus's statement created an opening for us to get in off the street. As soon as the door was shut, I set about explaining what had happened after I disappeared from under the tower. By the time I'd finished, Amy had put away her gun, and Tobias, his apprehension.

"When he drove away with you, I did everything I could to keep up," the wolf said. Luckily, he'd managed to shimmy into a pair of sweatpants while I spoke. "I lost you after a few blocks. Speaking of which…" He pivoted to Markus. "…how were you able to follow them?"

"By understanding my enemy, and by accepting my own limitations." My cousin laughed and pulled out his phone, waving it about as Exhibit A. "Only a slayer can run down a vampire, and I don't know this city well enough to outdrive them. Thank goodness for technology."

"A tracker?" Tobias asked. "How?"

"Embedded in silver and moving with the target." Markus tapped his chest, sending a ripple over the liquid metal clinging to it like armor. "Hoods can make silver do whatever we want. Not really that hard."

The wolf took my hands and pulled them to his lap. "I'm so fecking sorry, Geri. I shouldn't have given up so easily. I ringed the district until I started to get worried about Amy here alone. I was hoping you'd shake them and make your way back."

I put my hand on his shoulder. "It's not important. What we have to focus on now is that the Ravens know where we are, and at nightfall, you can bet they're coming for us. We have to find somewhere else to go, somewhere they don't know about or wouldn't dare come."

Tobias crossed his arms. "Agreed, but where?"

The pivotal question. None of us really knew the city very well, definitely not as well as the Ravens. If only Inga and Igor were back.

"Have we heard from our vampires yet?"

Amy jerked her head. "They said they'll fly back first thing after sunset tomorrow, but that still won't get them here until about midnight local time. They also agreed with me that you were stupid to go after Caleb on your own. Inga says she can handle things."

"I know just how Inga would *handle* things," I said. "She'd have gone in there and killed Caleb instead of let Vlad have him alive. Text her back, Amy. Tell them I'm okay."

The blonde pulled out her phone and began keying in the message. "Should I ask them where we should go hide?"

"Not unless you want them to give you directions to your own grave," Markus piped up. "This isn't some fifteenth-century blood gang. I saw the security system they had in place at that compound. Motion sensors, laser lines, infrared. I have no doubt they have your phones tapped at this point. Anything you send back and forth with them is going to give you away."

Amy dropped her device, her face ashen.

"Don't worry, Amy. I doubt you've told the Ravens anything they don't already know."

I picked up the device. A glare was all it took to get Tobias to present his phone as well. He pulled it out from some of the cushions on the couch and handed it over. I took both devices to the door of the cistern, and walked away satisfied when I heard the plop below.

"We're in the same situation if we leave anything written here," I continued. "We have to worry about ourselves right now. Reconnecting with Inga and Igor comes later. Markus?"

My cousin stood to attention. "Yes, matron?"

I didn't know if he meant it as a dig, or if he was just so well trained to respond to a commanding hood female. "One, don't call me that. I'm not even a hood anymore, let alone a matron. And two, you've been stalking around this city for over a month. Any suggestions?"

"I've been following *you* around. I only know the places you went. So unless you're going to spend the rest of your time in Hagia Sophia…"

I perked up. "Hagia Sophia? Why do you say that?"

"Just that the vampires who attacked you there seemed unwilling to go in for some reason."

My hands went to my temples, squeezing as if this would somehow press the memories up and out. "We were attacked by vamps?"

Markus's eyebrows lowered; he examined me for signs of sanity. "Don't you remember?"

My hands dropped as I shook my head. "I can't remember anything between being hit by Caleb's solarium and coming home the next morning. You were following me?" This time, the tone was optimistic. "What happened? What did you see?"

But all my hopes fell to the floor with his expression. "You disappeared."

"Disappeared?" I asked. "What the hell does that mean?"

"I don't mean into thin air," Markus clarified. "As soon as that Caleb guy came out, he saw the vamps and he did this, like, swishy thing with his arm?" The hood demonstrated a move that looked like someone bowling without a ball. "Then the solarium—side note: how awesome is that? Just like I read about!—followed him out of the museum. I saw you for a second when it hit you instead. Looked like it knocked you out, though why it didn't burn you to a crisp, I'm not sure. Your boyfriend couldn't conjure up another one before the vamps took him. As soon as the goons cleared out, I scrambled down from my hiding spot and came to help you, but I couldn't find you anywhere. I'd assumed you'd run back from wherever it was you got in to start with."

I replayed the events leading up to Hagia Sophia in my head. "But Caleb and I came in through old slayer tunnels underground. You didn't follow us down there. Even if I am relinquished, one of us would have heard you. How did you know we ended up at Hagia Sophia?"

"That tracking device I mentioned? It *is* embedded in silver." The hood at the end of my glare flinched. "In the handle of your dagger, specifically."

"What?" My hands went to the weapon's usual hiding place, buried in the wrapping of my braid. I pulled out the silver dagger that had been my constant companion since I was thirteen, a gift bequeathed by my paternal grandmother upon her death. "How in the hell?"

Then the pieces all fell into place. How easily my mother had known when I was in the packlands, how she descended on my attempt to be awakened by my distant cousin, the yellow hood Consuela, how she never seemed to worry about me while I was in Chicago.

I dropped the dagger to the floor. "All this time… And it's been…"

Markus groaned. "We're wasting time. We can catch up on what I know as soon as we get somewhere safe. Come on, we need to think! Where can we lie low?"

Amy spoke with peculiar softness. "Lie low?"

"Yeah, somewhere that's not friendly to vamps," Tobias repeated.

The blonde rolled through a slow nod. "Vampires don't like werewolves, do they?"

The only member of the species in attendance quirked an eyebrow. "Not traditionally. Why, you want to all line up behind me and hide?"

Amy grinned, a daring light in her eyes. "As much as I'd like to have any excuse to stand behind you and do anything, that's not what I'm getting at. I was just thinking, though, you said that the pack of the girl from the Bazaar, that they keep hidden from all the other supes in town. Do you think they'd give us a place to hide?"

Tobias and I exchanged a weighted look, before the werewolf said, "Serhan specifically told us he didn't want to get mixed up with anything."

"I know, and I want to respect that," I said. "But Amy's right. And it's the only thing we have on such short notice."

TWENTY-SIX

"It's weird. I didn't expect the daylight to reach down this far underground. Sure is a lot easier to see my way around this time."

Tobias paused the briefest moment to look back at me over his shoulder before resuming our downward trek into the abyss that was the Pera Pack's crypt.

"It's not any lighter," he said. "Not that I can tell. Markus, what do you think?"

That made me halt. Like in some cliché TV sitcom, Amy slammed into me. Luckily, unlike some cliché TV sitcom, it didn't knock me over or send me facedown into some awkward-yet-sexy position with Tobias.

I helped my friend gain her footing on the step next to me and turned to my cousin at the tail end of our procession. "When were you down here?"

But it was Tobias who responded. "Don't you remember when we were here the first time?" he said. "The wolves all sensed a hood. They assumed it was one of the black hoods, but there are no black hoods in Istanbul. Are there, Markus?"

My cousin only held out an attempt at innocence for a moment. Markus had many qualities as a person and as a hood, good and bad. An ability to lie was not one of them.

"The Pera Pack isn't in the Wolfsretter registry," he confirmed, referring to the database the matrons had for tracking packs. "If there ever was a hood patrolling this area, she did so without any guidance from the black matron based near Bayburt."

"So this is an illegal pack?" I asked. The term tasted like ash on my tongue; even hating the overlord tendency of my mother and other matrons like her, I still jumped right back into their lexicon on the spur of the moment, didn't I? I rounded on Tobias, eager to offer up an apology, but the disappointment in his expression convinced me not to try. Instead, I turned back to Markus. "So you followed us down here before? And I suppose you immediately reported it back to my mother?"

"I'm a righteous hood, Geri, but I'm not an asshole. I don't report anything back to your mother that she didn't *very specifically* tell me to report. At no point did Brünhild say to me, 'Markus, if you find any evidence of an unrecorded pack living in a decrepit tomb under the city, let me know.' Besides, *you* would know what would happen if I did, and I repeat, I'm not an asshole."

Amy, who uncharacteristically had kept pretty mum since we'd entered the tunnels under Istiklal Street, finally piped up. "What would happen?"

The shame I'd felt moments ago tripled in mass. "The matron of the region has the right to order the execution of its alpha and relocate the remaining pack members in any way she sees fit. It's been decades since something like that was done, though. I can't imagine any matron today doing something so heinous."

"The Wolfsretter database wasn't even around until the 1980s," Tobias said. "That means this pack has been in hiding at least since then, but I'm not convinced it was the hoods they were trying to avoid."

Weariness leaked into the cracks of my suspicions. "Who, then?"

Tobias shook his head. "Later. Geri, help Amy. We need to get a move on; if Serhan refuses to shelter us, we only have a few more hours of sunlight to find somewhere else."

When Tobias and I visited the Pera Pack before, I remembered that it seemed to take forever to descend, the whole time thinking I was about to trip over the edge of an abyss in the dark and fall to my death. This trip felt longer. Maybe the fact I could see this time tricked my brain into perceiving time through a strainer.

"Shouldn't we be there by—"

"*Shhh!*" Tobias whipped around, a finger pressed over his lips. Why he thought keeping quiet would help, I wasn't sure. A werewolf's sense of hearing put a huey's to shame, and even I had been able to hear the footfalls ahead of us. If I could hear them, they had no doubt heard us for much longer. The pack knew that someone was approaching; the only question was why they hadn't confronted us already.

And then I realized why: because a hood walked among us.

No sooner had the truth dawned on me than fur and fury flew before my eyes.

Serhan's wolf cleared Tobias easily, the alpha's ability impressive even more so due to the fact that he made the leap both over a really tall man and up stairs. Within moments, the rest of the pack were upon us. Snarls, yips, growls. *Posturing,* I hoped. Years of training overrode logic, and before I could ridicule my own response, I had the handle of my blade pressed into my palm.

To my surprise, the alpha let Markus be. I, however, was on my back before I could mount a counterattack. A maw dripping with saliva opened, sending hot breath smelling of carrion wafting over my face. Somehow, I'd managed to take the blow unharmed, though a wolf of Serhan's size could break every bone in a huey. His back paws anchored on the ground, while his front paws pinned my shoulders. My blade could still give a werewolf a wound that would take weeks to heal. The task wasn't beyond me, not even in this diminished, relinquished body. But as Serhan's pack looked on from the edges of the fracas, I knew that offing their alpha would be pushing down one domino in a line I'd need to topple to survive.

"Please." Gritted teeth deformed the word. "I don't want to hurt you, but I'll protect my own."

The alpha barked, a mocking sound approaching laughter. His maw jerked to the right, alerting me to the state of the faceoff: Markus lay under a pure white wolf, while Amy, looking as scared as I'd ever seen her, had her back against the wall and a small brown wolf inches from her upheld hands. My cousin retained his dagger, but the member of the pack holding him had his wrist clamped in his jaw, blood trickling down. The pain must have been immense, but Markus's discipline kept him contained. A pack would swarm wounded prey.

Tobias remained in his mortal form, the lone member of our party unmolested. Part of me wished he'd take on his wolf and kick Serhan's ass; the other half of me swelled with pride when, instead of lash out, he attempted to negotiate.

"Alpha, hear us out." Tobias sunk to his knees as his chin tucked into his chest. "I beg you."

The wolf lording over me turned; the dagger in my hand lowered slightly. A series of yips and low growls built a wall of language I barely understood but in which Tobias was fluent.

"I give my word, they mean you no harm," Tobias responded, chancing to bring his head up just enough for his eyes to catch mine. "Geri, please?"

Metal on stone sent a dull ping echoing through the air. Moments later, Markus's blade joined mine on the floor, though I couldn't say if he'd dropped it on purpose or lost the ability to hold it against the pain.

Either because wolfspeak wasn't as universal as I thought, or because he wanted me to taste the bile in his words, Serhan took on his mortal form, paws becoming hands, long fingers hooking over my collarbones.

"I told you never to bring this hood here!" the alpha belted out. A moment of confusion passed before I realized that, in fact, I hadn't been in this exact part of the underground before. The reason it seemed to be taking longer than last time wasn't my imagination; at some point, Tobias had redirected us. "And now, you bring not only one, but two, and a huey too? I could have your scruff for this."

Even knowing I lived at his pleasure, I couldn't tamp the ire that rose in my gut. "Hurt a single hair of his hide, and I will divest yours of every strand, one at a time, with excruciating and deliberate slowness."

The alpha spared me one disgusted glance before lashing out at Tobias. "You said she wasn't your consort. You said her feelings were for your alpha. And now, *this*? Explain."

Did he care so little for his pack that he wouldn't rip apart anyone who tried to harm one of them? Would he expect me to do any less? Of course, I'd defend and avenge Tobias, just like he'd do for me. Just like he was doing for Kara. Because that's what you did for someone you loved; you protected them no matter what.

For someone you loved…

Truth fell upon me like light through a door opening to a dark room, illuminating a path to escape my own haze of confusion. No sooner had I admitted it to myself than Tobias spoke it aloud.

"She's in love with me."

Markus squealed out a laugh, but Amy grinned, like the rest of the world had finally woken up to what had been obvious to her all along.

Serhan pushed himself off of me. Clearly, a woman in love wasn't a threat. He rounded on Tobias. "And you? Do you love this wolf killer? Have you betrayed your own kind?"

"No. My moon eclipsed with the passing of my Kara. I will forever be her true mate."

Even though I knew Tobias's words weren't meant to cause pain, his response cut through my soul. No time to adjust, however. Revealed and reviled from one moment to the next, he sped to clarify.

"But she is a warrior, and a friend, and my alpha considers her pack. Geri isn't like other hoods; she cares for wolves. She's lost her clan, her birthright, and almost her life, all to help me avenge my kin and my mate."

A roar leapt from Serhan's throat, bouncing off the walls of the subterranean cavern. "A hood, a member of the pack? Ridiculous!"

"It's true," Tobias insisted, and even from my position on the ground, I could see his fists roll and tighten. He didn't jibe with being called a liar. "I swear on the mercy of your maw and my throat in kind."

Both Markus and I gasped, though in my peripheral vision Amy's head quirked to the side. Inside a pack, a wolf's life was always at the mercy of his alpha, though rare were the occasions where something so heinous caused one to lose it. It was a far worse fate to be disowned, to be sent into the world a loner, destined to go mad. Outside a pack, however, a wolf had few options to represent his loyalty. In offering his throat to the Pera Pack's alpha's maw, Tobias had presented his life in place of his honor should Serhan call for it, and Cody wouldn't have a leg to stand on for recompense. Tobias had potentially laid his life down… for me.

Not for you, stupid hood, a voice inside me mocked. *He just finished saying he doesn't love you, that he could* never *love you. He needs you to get to the Ravens. He needs you and Markus to lead him. Without you, he will never have his revenge.*

At last, the alpha's demeanor shifted. Serhan cocked a hip, amusement pulling up the corner of his mouth. "Never did I expect to see the day a wolf would offer up his throat to protect a hood."

Tobias nodded. "You and me both."

The alpha let out a single laugh as he moseyed over to where Markus remained pinned. The heel of Serhan's foot balanced on Markus's injured forearm, making my cousin wince. "And what of you, boy? Do you have any wolf who would risk his neck for you?"

Markus's red hood shimmered before dissolving into mist. Perhaps he thought he'd be less of a threat without his cloak on display. "My orders are only to protect Geri. If you're not a threat to her, then I'm not a threat to you."

With a jerk of the alpha's head, the wolf atop Markus took his leave and let my cousin sit up and tend to his wound.

"I'm not going to hurt anyone either." My former roomie blew a stray hair from her eyes. "And I don't think I'm ever going to get used to wolves transforming into naked men on a whim. Just FYI."

Serhan looked to Tobias for clarity, but the English wolf just shook his head, as if to say, *hueys are just like that.*

"Very well then, Tobias," the alpha resumed. "What is it you want?"

"Shelter." His throat bobbed as he swallowed down his nerves. "Only for a few nights, until we can plan our next move. Weapons, if you have any."

Serhan rubbed his chin as two of his pack in their mortal forms arrived to offer him a pair of pants. "Weapons? Depends on what you seek." A pointed look at Markus also spoke to me. There'd be no silver among any pack-provided weapons, that was for sure. "As for shelter, you must tell me from what, or is it, from who?"

"The Ravens," Tobias replied. "They're after us. All of us."

"Not me really," Amy piped up.

Tobias's eyes shifted for just a moment before focusing back on the alpha. "Except for her."

The alpha eyed a place on the floor, nudging it with his bare feet. "You are a very curious wolf, Tobias Somfield. Loved by a hood whom you do not spurn, but defend. Traveling the world, away from your pack, in one of the largest cities of the world. Hiding from vampires. What is it that drives you? What is it that causes you to act out against your wolf?"

"The Ravens killed my mate." His lips quivered, even as he struggled to hold back a tear. "They killed my Kara, as well as my brother and my father. They denied me my pack. They denied me my legacy."

"Denied you your pack?" I couldn't stop the question from forming on my lips.

Tobias could have ignored me, but he didn't. He fixed on me, his conflicted gaze almost an apology. "I wasn't disowned from my pack because I challenged the alpha. I was forced from my pack because I was the alpha, and another challenged me. I lost."

Amy beamed, blind to the fact that, in our world, what Tobias had just admitted could get him killed. Not by a hood, though that would have certainly happened if he had gone moon mad. By any other wolf. *Weeding out of the weak and the wretched,* I remembered Cody explaining to me once when I asked him of the old-world practice. *An alpha can mess up, he can screw up pretty damned bad. But if he gets to the point where his pack rejects him, there is no place for him in this world.*

I held Tobias's gaze only a moment longer before turning on Serhan, awaiting his reaction. To my surprise, the Pera Pack's alpha grinned and put a hand on my wolf's shoulder.

"You are like us now," he said. "*Hayalet kurtları,* ghost wolves."

Tobias's eyes widened. "You are…"

"The castoffs of a long-forgotten alpha," Serhan interrupted. "This is why we hide from other supernaturals. If another pack or a hood learned of us, as the descendant of a ghost wolf, that knowledge could be deadly."

Markus's hand massaged his wounds. As he worked his hand around it, the glint of metal caught the dim light in the chamber. Silver: he dressed his wounds with his own weapon. It would heal him faster, as it would with any hood, but it would also make his blood temporarily toxic to any wolf. I had to wonder which he had intended.

"The black hoods control this region," my cousin said, stepping forward. He might have been the most reasonable member of my mother's clan, but he was still a righteous hood, a fact reinforced by his next words. "They know nothing of you. If you shelter us and help us get what we need, I swear that will stay the same."

Serhan allowed an amused grin to plaster over his face. "And the world as I know it remains unchanged."

TWENTY-SEVEN

"I'm guessing there were parts of that I didn't understand. Ouch, shit."

I grabbed Amy just in time to keep her from falling. Or, really, from falling again.

"Jesus, watch where you're stepping."

"Sorry, it's just so goddamned dark down here. How are you not falling down like I am?"

With three blinks, I tested out the landscape. If anything, the environment had brightened, almost as if we had reached the edge of a sphere of light. A few more steps confirmed it, as the mouth of the path in front of us, sloping upward, appeared like a halo.

"Your eyes just suck." I ignored the laugh she made under her breath. "Honestly, I think there's some of that I don't understand either."

Like why the pack's stall in the Grand Bazaar displayed a Writ of Authority, like they expected a hood to show up at any moment for inspection. Or why Tobias kept the fact that he was a toppled alpha from me.

Or how he knew I was in love with him even before I did, and why fate kept giving my heart away to wolves I would never be with.

Tobias walked at the head of the procession like an honored

diplomat. Markus, Amy, and I trailed several yards back, surrounded by werewolves of both forms, like the spoils of war to be paraded for Caesar. When we finally arrived at the end of the tunnel after an hour's slow walk, I could have sworn we'd covered miles. We could have been anywhere under the city now, even on the other side of the Bosporus. The door ahead looked modern, a precursor to the shocking sight beyond it.

"You seem surprised, hood."

Serhan leaned casually against a refrigerator, nursing a bottle of yellow soda. I looked back over my shoulder and discovered the door connecting to the tunnels had been disguised as a pantry in an otherwise mundane kitchen. Other wolves passed further into the house without regard to my wide-eyed amazement. Windows on either side of the room let me know that the sun outside had begun to set.

"It's a house," I said, sounding as simple as I did dumb.

"You didn't think we *lived* in the underground, did you?" The alpha sneered. "Surely you didn't think we'd bring strangers into our packlands on a first visit."

It was a clever subterfuge, and even though the sting of their lack of trust shouldn't have surprised or offended me, I found it still did. "I'm not exactly up on the habits of urban wolves, so forgive the gap in my judgment."

Before Serhan could snap back at me, I felt heat at my back.

"We need to talk."

Tobias's hand wrapped around my arm, just above the elbow, as he led me out of the kitchen, through a hall, and into a bathroom. The space was hardly large enough for him, let alone the both of us.

Werewolves had a superb sense of hearing in their animal forms, but it wasn't much hindered in their huey form. When Tobias reached behind me to open the water faucet to its full capacity, what could follow but something he wouldn't want anyone else to hear?

"What's our next move?"

Planning? He brought me in here to talk about… planning? Fine. I could do the emotionless soldier thing. Hell, I excelled at it.

"We send Markus out to do recon," I said. "The Ravens only know there's another red hood in town, but they don't know which one or what he looks like. He can sniff around without attracting attention. Once we know what the fallout from last night is…"

"I'm not talking about that." With a touch far more delicate than I realized was possible, the werewolf fingered a lock of my hair that had fallen from the braid in the tussle with the pack, sweeping it aside. "I'm sorry I had to say that you loved me. I needed Serhan and his pack to think there was some deep-seated reason you were helping me. No wolf would believe a hood would help a wolf avenge a mate simply because she thought it was the right thing to do."

Disappointment burned in my cheeks. Tobias had lied. Or, at least, he'd thought he'd been lying. "You were on the spot. It was the first thing you came up with. I can play along with it. Don't worry. I'll try not to make it too awkward. But what about what you said?" I asked, thinking back to his words in the underground. "Was is it a lie, you being an alpha?"

His bottom jaw worked before he answered. "It shouldn't be a surprise; you already figured out it was in my bloodline."

"Why didn't you just rekindle?"

"What, you mean start a new pack?" The werewolf's eyes

sparkled with amusement. "A wolf creates a new pack from a place of strength, not by the consequence of his weakness. Besides, it takes a strong wolf to survive that process. My brother and father had disappeared, and I already knew my father was dead. I wasn't in the place to handle that kind of emotional challenge at the time. The only thing I was doing was trying to free Kara before I went moon mad."

My chin dipped. "I know how you felt. I didn't want to be a hood at all after Cody…"

The memories tugged in my veins, and the familiar ache resurfaced. For the first time in two years, however, the pain was just an echo. For the first time, the reverberation of it didn't box me in. And knowing that, I could finally let it out.

"Between my mother's demand that I be what she wanted, and Cody's expectation that I be the opposite, I realized I didn't want to be either of those things. Now, I'm not, and I can't believe how much that loss means to me. Not to mention it set off this whole trail of events that's led to us being on the run, separated from Inga and Igor, and Caleb getting caught by the Ravens. If I'd just said *yes* when Cody asked me, or been the obedient daughter my mother wanted, we'd never be here."

"But then you never would have come to Chicago. I'd be dead along with Kara. Plus, you just wouldn't be my Geri." Chills dashed up my spine as his fingers laced through my hair. "We're going to get him out, I promise. Him, and all the slayers who want to escape."

"All the slayers who *want* to escape?" My weight shifted as Tobias dropped his hand. "You think there are some that don't?"

"You still think they're all pretending to like their situation," he said. "But is it really such a stretch of the imagination to suppose some of them do? You fell in love with a wolf. Why would a slayer deciding to be part of a vampire's harem be so different?"

Confusion clouded my thoughts. "But we're still going to kill them, right? The Ravens?"

"Of course."

"Then why would we leave behind slayers to make them stronger?" I asked. "If we cut off their supply to supernatural blood, even if we didn't find a way to kill them in battle, they'd eventually die from that alone."

His eyes shifted, as though he could see through the closed door to the wolf pack beyond. "They'll just find a new supply. For all we know, the Pera Pack might be like some emergency rations or special reserve for them."

Anxiety punched me in the gut. "Then our mission just became a lot more complex. We rescue the redhead who helped me escape, and any other she wants to bring. And Caleb, of course."

"If *he* wants to come."

Fire shot up my spine. "You don't honestly think Caleb wants to stay, do you? Come on, Vlad killed his family."

Tobias's head swiveled back. "What he said to you when you saw him... Maybe he was telling you that he felt he could protect the slayers in the harem better from the inside. Or maybe... I don't want to hurt you, Geri, but maybe he was telling you the truth."

What could I have said to that? That part of me wished it had been true? That if Caleb's heart could be so easily converted, I'd probably dodged a bullet? Hell, for all I knew, slayers were polyamorous to begin with. A harem might be Caleb's ideal situation. But something in my gut told me that wasn't the case. *The redhead was pregnant. That room had no other males, and a vampire couldn't be the father.*

"Where are the men?"

Tobias blinked thrice. "What?"

"Somebody fathered Alexandra's baby. It couldn't be Vlad or any of the other Ravens." The wheels of my mind spun. "There have to be male slayers somewhere in the compound."

The werewolf balanced his scruffy chin on a balled-up fist. "That doesn't change the pressing issue. If we are able to free them, then what? We've never made plans for something like this. 'Kill the Ravens' was pretty straightforward and didn't require any back-end tasks."

"We really need Inga and Igor on this part, don't we?"

"Wouldn't hurt." His massive chest compressed as he pushed out a breath. "I bloody hate being dependent on other people for things. Okay, fine, how do we reconnect with the good vampires?"

"I'm not sure. For the moment, I think we just have to make a plan without them."

A knock at the door made us both jump, followed by a string of Turkish I was certain had a few choice phrases.

Tobias reached behind me, his body pressing mine into the sink. His lips pressed against my ear. "Thank you, by the way."

I tried to ignore the way his nearness pureed my insides. "For what?"

"For being here," he said. "Until I had to think on the spot about why you came along, it never occurred to me that you're doing it entirely for other people."

I shook my head. "They almost destroyed the slayers. They're after wolves. It's only a matter of time before they come for the hoods. I'm doing this for all of us. Mostly, though, I'm doing it for Kara."

The name echoed across his face. "For Kara?"

"If I had listened to you when you first came to me, we might have been able to free her. She might still be alive. I know that, Tobias. I know that her blood is as much on my hands as it is the Ravens'."

His hand dropped from the faucet, cutting off the sound of the water.

"She'd have liked you."

"She did like me, I think. At least, for the short time we had together."

A moment later, both his hands laced behind me. Tobias and I were already touching, but somehow, he found a way to pull me closer. I blinked my confusion as he lowered his lips to mine.

Seconds before they touched, another fierce round of knocking jolted us.

Tobias was out the door before my eyes could open.

TWENTY-EIGHT

Wolves and hoods were never meant to break bread, let alone bake it side by side.

Perhaps because I was relinquished, or because the Pera Pack had come to see me as Tobias's pet, the wolves in the expansive home tried their best just to ignore me. Except for Ayşe, who had overcome her initial distrust to use me as an anthropological data set. Her fascination with hoods made me feel like I was being interviewed for what would turn out to be a tell-all book.

Markus, however, had a completely different experience.

"They all look at me like, at any moment, I'm going to wield my silver into a machete and take their heads. I swear that one with the two little kids wants to rip me up and feed me to her pups."

I sighed as I put away the last of the freshly-washed tea cups on a shelf over the sink. Guilt had driven me to become obsessed with relieving the burden of their household chores. "Think of it from their perspective. You're the monster from every one of the bedtime stories they've heard. Not to mention, you're a behemoth. *And* a foreigner. Basically, the only thing you've got going for you is that Serhan is curious about you."

"Honestly, I'd prefer he was a little less curious about me."

I dropped the damp towel over a rack to dry. "What is that supposed to mean?"

"I feel like he's cataloging me, like he's studying me for posterity. I think you and I are the first hoods this pack has ever seen. And since your abilities are offline, he's using me to figure out the best defensive strategy."

I hadn't sensed quite that vibe coming off the alpha. Not that I could say with any certainty anymore. "If I were an alpha, or even if I was a matron, I would do the same thing. I wouldn't hold it against him. In fact, I admire him for it."

"You would." Markus snatched a cup—and my ire—from the shelf and poured himself another portion from the constantly-brewed pot on the stove. "You want to hear my report or not?"

I motioned to the nearby table. In the week since we'd fled our rental house near the Bazaar, we'd had the same routine. The pack went about their normal business. Most of the adults, and even a few of the older teenagers, had jobs. The mothers of young wolves used the night to take their pups out. Anywhere else, little kids running around on city streets would have drawn judgment, but not in Istanbul. Anytime of the day, the population trafficked all the avenues, alleys, and byways, almost as if each citizen had a shift to report to for that distinct purpose. If a pack had to live in an urban center to stay off hood radar, Istanbul may have been one of the best places for them to blend into abnormal huey traffic patterns.

Markus alternated between spying on the Raven compound and looking for life at our old rental. He hadn't seen either Inga or Igor, though I told him that wasn't unexpected. I was certain they'd been trying to call us, and since the only one of us with a phone was Markus (who refused to call them, since it would tip off my mother about his having been discovered), they must have suspected the Eminönü house had been compromised. I suspected by now they'd also ditched their burner phones and phone numbers for new ones.

After getting myself a matching cup of tea, I took a seat at the table. "Give it to me."

"That's what he said."

"Markus, I know you're my cousin. Don't take this the wrong way, but I hate you."

"There's something going on at their compound," he said, getting serious. "Lots of things being taken away. The fact that they're coming in after dark tells me it's something they're concerned about overseeing personally."

"And the slayers?" I stared into my tea, its waters a whirlpool.

Markus shook his head. "Other than the one you said was named Alexandra, no sign of them. *She's* outside frequently, either alone or with that other one who took you from Galata."

"They must trust her then," I concluded. "Odd, since she was the one who blasted Timur with a solarium that let me get away."

"Yeah, about that..." My cousin rubbed the back of his neck. "Are you sure it was a solarium, and not, like, a flare gun or something? I'm not as much of an expert as Igor and Inga are. I mean, obviously, right? But I've never found any stories of a vampire who was able to survive one of those things."

I hadn't thought about it before, but now that he'd mentioned it, it did seem odd. "Maybe they can change the intensity somehow?"

"What, like on *Star Trek*?" Markus mocked holding up a communicator to his mouth. "Slayers, set solaria on stun. I repeat: stun only."

"Fine then, ass. What's your idea?"

"That the vampire wasn't really hit. They can move fast, Geri. Wicked fast. Your huey eyes might have thought you saw that guy take the brunt of the solarium, but he might have ducked out of its path long enough for it to miss him. But, getting back to Alexandra... She has a pattern."

My eyes widened.

"Every night, about an hour after sunset, she's driven a few blocks from the house and takes a walk at a park on the water. There's a dock there. She walks out to the end of it and spends ten or fifteen minutes just sitting, meditating or something. Then, she gets up, walks back to the car, and goes back into the compound."

"Any escorts?"

Markus leaned back. "Just one. Not that guy, Timur, and not Vlad, based on your description of him. It must be one of the lackeys."

My hands gripped the tea cup as resolve filled me. "I have to talk to her."

"Are you insane?" Markus belted out a laugh. "Out in public, where anyone can see you? And here your mother always said you were the best hood when it came to sneaking around that she'd ever trained."

The reminder of my mother sent a shiver through me, one that left a fleck of doubt at the back of my brain about my ability to pull off this plan. "Camouflage is all about not being noticed, not *not* being seen. Conservative women here wear full veils. Even Ayşe does when she's on the street at night. I'm sure she'd let me borrow it. I'll be just one of many hueys on that dock. The vamps won't even know I'm there."

"If that's what you want to do, let's do it. Or do you need another day to plan out the details?"

"I'm already operating on borrowed time here." My eyes drifted to a calendar hung on the wall over the tiny kitchen table. Even though the labels of days, weeks, and months were in a foreign tongue, members of the pack had circled full moon nights. Half of the time Tobias could be away from the pack without consequences had already fled to the historical record. Moon madness could begin to peek around the edges of his behavior at any point. So far, there'd been no sign of it. Perhaps staying with wolves slowed the descent, but our luck wouldn't hold out forever. Neither, for that fact, would Caleb.

"We go tonight. Which means… I better get some sleep."

"I can't believe you're sleeping in the same room as Tobias."

I couldn't ignore the hint of jealousy in my cousin's voice. He'd made no secret of the fact that, as far as wolves went, my best lupine friend would be a pretty sight to wake up to every morning.

Heat flared in my cheeks, but I turned to hide it. "We slept in the same room together in Chicago for almost a year. It's no big deal."

"That was before he outed how you feel about him to an entire foreign pack."

I lowered my voice. Just because I didn't think any of the pack were near us in the house didn't mean they still couldn't hear us if we didn't take care. "It was a lie, a story to explain why I would act unlike other hoods."

"A lie?" I didn't think I'd ever seen Markus wear a wider grin. "You keep telling yourself that. You look at him now the same way you used to look at Cody Ryland."

Any semblance of amusement melted from my face as I turned to the sink to rinse out my cup. "And look how that turned out."

My cousin's words replayed in my mind like the cries of an annoying crow, building a border to sleep. I lay next to Tobias on the bed, staring at the back of his head as cycles of breath moved his body in a gracious arc: rise, fall, rise, fall. We'd been permitted a room usually reserved for newly mated couples—a fact that only made our presence in it all that much odder. Amy had been given the option of setting up a pallet on the floor, but decided instead for a spot in the pup room.

I questioned her motives.

Markus slept under a makeshift canopy on the roof; both he and the wolves thought it best.

Late in the morning, sleep used me as its plaything. The pack's commune had no air conditioning; wolves had methods of coping with excessive heat ingrained in their bodies. No such luck for ex-hood hueys. Early afternoon licked at my chest, at my neck. The only options for cooling off were either to go jump in the shower, or to lose the few articles of clothing I had on.

It's no big deal, my hood brain said. *Wolves don't think about nudity the way non-wolves do. You know this. Remember that time Rick caught you and Cody out in the woods and you had nothing on your top half but your bra? The two of them thought it was no big deal. If your boyfriend didn't get all crazy about it when the two of you actually* had *been fooling around, Tobias won't even notice now.*

But you will, the female part of my brain countered. *Now that you know you love him, you want to make things* more *awkward? He's a widower, for goodness' sake! Keep your shirt on and just sweat it out.*

Ten minutes more, with the perspiration pooling in the hollow of my neck as I lay on my back, staring at the ceiling, and I could take no more. I sat up and began to peel the drenched cami from my body, only to pause, the bottom half of the shirt covering my face, when the weight of his eyes settled on me.

"It's hot," I muttered. "If it makes you uncomfortable, I can keep it…"

When Tobias rolled over and his hand pulled down my shirt, a tiny part of me shriveled, chastised for the audacity. When he draped his hand over my waist, hooked my hips, and pulled my body flush to his, spooning me, that same tiny part of me stuck its tongue out and blew raspberries.

His lips hovered over my ear. "The key to overcoming heat…" His mouth trailed down my neck like a vampire sizing up a juicy vein. "…is *not* to fight it. It only makes you that much more flustered."

"Flustered?" The word came out as a laugh. "What a British thing to say."

"It wasn't a lie, was it?"

I didn't have to ask him to clarify. Despite the sudden shift in the air between us, I knew what he was asking. "No, it wasn't."

"I knew. I can feel you, Geri. It never stopped, just softened a bit. These last few days, though, it's back, full force." He laughed against the back of my neck. "You really are one fucked-up hood, aren't you?"

In the miasma of his psyche, flecks of every emotion I felt swirled, but the dark ones pulled at him heavier. So wrapped up in the wash of what came over me, it took me a moment to reflect on what he said and truly hear it. Only then did I realize the truth.

"I can feel you." I turned over on my back so I could look him in the eyes. "Like I used to. Like I could before my mother stripped me of my powers."

"About time you figured that out." Tobias ran a hand through hair moist with perspiration. "Anything else occur to you?"

"Yes, actually." I leaned over him, putting a hand to his cheek. "I'm in love with you."

My lips had barely come down on his when the door crashed open, and something that seemed truly impossible walked in the door.

One of the slayers I recognized from Vlad's harem, Konstantina, holding Amy by the hair.

The man beside me disappeared, a wave of fur and tooth and fury taking form, all while I wrapped my hands around the handle of a blade I knew I would never wield against a slayer.

Amy dropped to the ground, calling out as Konstantina's foot prodded her further into the room.

"Did you really think we couldn't track you down?" the dark-haired vixen asked, stepping over the crumpled mass of my friend weeping on the ground. "Did you really think you could hide from us?"

Tobias lunged forward, but a wolf wasn't as strong in the day.

With a lash of the slayer's arm through the air, the wolf went flying. His body surrendered to the ground, motionless.

"You bitch!"

My foe grinned at my outlandishness. "Caleb will find it so *interesting* that I caught you in the arms of a wolf. Almost makes me want to drag you back, just so you can see the reaction of the man who cried from guilt after we made love last night, all because he felt like he had betrayed *you*."

Realization unfurled in my stomach. If she wasn't here for me, who was she here for?

"The werewolf, Kline," the slayer said, as though she could work out the question burning through my mind. "Though on second thought, he'll be much more compliant if we have you to dangle over him."

At a snap of her fingers, two thugs ran in. That the Ravens had hueys on call during the day was something I'd foolishly never considered. Before I could believe what was happening, a hog-tied Tobias whimpered and yelped, and their eyes turned toward me.

Ravens were one thing, but I refused to take out hueys, and harming a slayer would be like cutting up a bald eagle. Trapped in a corner, there was no solution for escape that wouldn't leave the carpet soaked with blood.

The blade crashed to the floor, the sound echoing against a backdrop of pandemonium in the rest of the house. This was no random smash and grab; this was a coordinated campaign, one to instill terror and seed confusion.

The slayer beamed at me with approval as her two thugs stilled. "Surrender, then?"

"I never surrender. I just know when to cause a distraction."

All three perpetrators' eyes bulged moments before they swung around, just in time to catch Markus's silver whizzing through the air. The lemon-sized pellets knocked the two huey's skulls, rendering them unconscious. The slayer, however, could move as fast as a vampire, and did so. Markus fell back into the hall from the force of her impact as she rushed past him.

Taking Tobias along with her.

TWENTY-NINE

Markus blew a rebellious lock of hair out of his face even as he shifted his weight, trying to gain comfort against the pull of his restraints. "Wolves always blame hoods whenever something goes bad."

"In this case, I'm not sure we're entirely innocent."

His hefting sigh took his eyes to the ground and his chin to his chest. "Geri, I have to warn you, I think you're going native."

"Meaning?"

"Meaning," Markus growled, "you're siding with wolves. Wolves, Geri! The very creatures we're born to defend against? To keep in line and buffer from humanity?"

Superiority was hard to cultivate while tied to a kitchen chair, but I did my best. "The only side I'm taking is the truth's. This pack has somehow managed to stay off our radar for at least forty years, and who knows how long before that. Then, within a few weeks of allowing hoods into their midst, their home is invaded by some Stockholm syndrome-suffering slayer. If I didn't know better, I'd swear they'd enthralled her."

"Slayers can't be enthralled. It's impossible." Markus looked up with eyes brightened by realization. "I read an entry in an old manuscript once, though, that said they're actually stronger in the daytime. Seeing as one threw a massive wolf over her shoulder and ran at warp speed with it, I think we can consider that confirmed. They got in through the tunnels too. Did you know that? Tunnels, I'm quite sure they didn't know about, seeing as they would have stumbled onto the Pera Pack before now, if they had. Bet that was another thing your boyfriend blabbed."

"Tobias?" *Raspberry.* "Don't be stupid."

"I was talking about Caleb." My cousin's eyes became vicious slits. "Wait, did you just call a werewolf your boyfriend? Oh my god, you *have* gone native. You're in love with a werewolf. *Again.* Your mother was right; there's something wrong with you on a very deep level. Your wiring is all kooky."

"Well, you know my mother. She's always right." Pulling at my restraints did nothing but frustrate me. Why try, then? If a righteous hood like Markus couldn't find a way, I didn't know how a relinquished hood like me stood a chance. "Did you say *wiring*?"

"Yeah, wiring," Markus repeated. "W-I-R-*ing*. Why, does that surprise you?"

"Nothing my mother says disparaging about me surprises me. Only, I think I know why neither one of us can get through these restraints now."

"Yeah, why is that?"

I cringed as I pulled again, recognizing at last why the hairs on my arms were all standing straight up. "Because it's insulated, electrified wire."

Markus chewed on that a moment. "Well, shit. Isolated wolves, but they still know our weakness. Sons of bitches."

"Not exactly an insult for a wolf. More a statement of fact, actually."

"You're not funny, Geri."

When the door opened, we both closed our mouths and faced forward, eyes blank. Hood training always assumed the superiority of our kind, but it allowed that certain circumstances might favor temporary capture. *Arrogance lubricates the tongue and rusts the blade. Your opponent will never allow you inside his head, but if he feels you are defeated, you're no longer a threat. Sometimes, letting them believe you've been bested leaves them at their worst.*

After the raid, when the pack was in chaos, it had become all too easy for them to turn their ire from the Ravens (like we *told* them) to the "true outsiders" in their midst. As hoods, blame fell upon us like snow on a field. Markus had wanted to fight; he easily could have extracted us from the home. But how many dead wolves would that leave? Even one was too many. Plus, if I had any hope of rescuing both Caleb and Tobias, I was going to need help, even more than Markus could give. At my urging, he had stood down. The pack had wasted no time in securing us.

Ayşe's grim features painted a new mask on her otherwise cheery face. The shewolf entered from the tunnel just beyond the kitchen door, flanked by two other female wolves whose faces I'd come to know from afar, but whose names I had not yet learned.

"Serhan was taken."

Weird, I thought. Wolves were a patriarchal society. Was it because this pack was also of a Muslim persuasion that women were being sent to interrogate another?

"Amy?"

Ayşe's face flickered. Perhaps she hadn't expected my concerns to lie with anyone but myself. "Safe."

"Where?"

"Another house. Other side of Istanbul."

"Thank you."

The shewolf's eyes widened. "You thank me for this?"

"You're protecting my friend. Of course, I'm thanking you."

She needed to keep the upper hand, which meant not acknowledging my gratitude. "Why did the Ravens take Serhan?"

"Because he's an alpha," I explained. "A vampire only lives for about five hundred years after he's changed, but the Ravens have discovered that the blood of other supernaturals lets them keep going past that. The blood of an unmated alpha or beta has that power. That's why."

The wolf didn't miss the conflict between my statement and who had been taken. "But Tobias is mated. Why take him?"

"Yeah, Geri," Markus piped up. "Tobias is mated. Illuminate us on how you expected that all to work out."

I let the emotion drain from my eyes. "I don't know. Maybe they didn't know either. Maybe they took him when they had a chance, to worry about the details later."

Through pinched features, she eyeballed me. "Lie."

I should have listened to Tobias and studied some Turkish. I wasn't sure if, in her broken English, she was calling me out, or giving me a demand. "Ayşe, please... If I tell you why they really have him, it would put you in more danger than you are already in."

Her shoulders eased. "Do you really love Tobias?"

"Yes."

"Ah, that." The shewolf's finger wagged, and with it, I felt the room lighten. When Ayşe spoke again, it wasn't with the heavily accented drawl I'd grown accustomed to, but with words flowing like honey. "That is the truth. Do you know why I ask you, Gerwalta Kline? Do you know how I trust now that you are telling the truth, and that you are not like other hoods?"

"Geri?" Markus stared at me, but with his head turned towards the wolves. "What's going on?"

"What's going on, Markus, is that I now understand why this pack was in hiding," I said. "They're an anathema."

Ayşe's face curdled. "I do not care for that term."

"And I don't like to be called relinquished," I said. "But that's what I am. I know what it is to be rejected by your own kind, the way a pack whose alpha line is female would be. *Serhan* was never the alpha, was he?"

Ayşe shook her head. "My beta. An uppity one at that."

Both Ayşe and I winced as Markus's chair screeched across the floor. Even if it only moved him an inch or two, he was going to give it his darnedest. "So *you're* the alpha? And somehow, you speak excellent English to boot."

"Of course, I speak excellent English!" Ayşe snapped. "I attended one of the best English-speaking universities in the country. *We are not typical werewolves, Mr. Kline. Once the others of our kind rejected us, we were no longer bound by their traditions. Nor did we fall under your jurisdictions."

"No, I get that," I said. "I just finished my BS in biochemistry."

"Really?" Ayşe's face brightened. "I just got my master's in organic chem."

She delved in the evil arts.

"If I can interrupt your girl bonding…" Markus interjected. "Your beta is gone, and our… *Tobias* is gone. Along with our slayer, so we really need to get out of here and rescue them while we still know where they are."

"Slayer?" Ayşe rose from her chair and turned a lazy circle. "There are no slayers. They're all dead."

"That's what we used to think too. But last year, I met one."

"Who she dated," Markus added.

"And who she just broke up with." I shot him daggers before turning back to Ayşe. "I'm sorry this happened. I'm sorry they found you. Believe me, I am. But now that they know about you, now that you're living right under their noses, they're not going to leave you alone. We have to deal with them, and if we're going to have any chance of that happening, we need to get the slayers out as well."

Ayşe's lips pursed. "We know the Ravens only by reputation. We have no idea where they are."

Now that Markus had begun to see the path to our liberation, his mouth became a lot more productive. "We do. In fact, I've been casing their place for the last week. But what my cousin seems to be forgetting is that the Ravens' compound is like Fort Knox."

Ayşe laced her arms over her chest. "Fort Knox?"

"It's a saying we have in America," Markus clarified. "Meaning, it's highly secured. Armed guards, multiple gates, and all manner of video, infrared surveillance, motion detectors… Not to mention it's full of vampires, and slayers who may or may not be loyal to them."

"And this slayer who you 'dated…'" The alpha used finger quotes. "He is a mole? Someone who will help us from the inside?"

Awkwardness skewed my features. "Not exactly. In fact, he might have bought into their cult. I'm not sure. But what I do know for sure is that the Ravens are now holding two people who are very dear to me, and there aren't many people in this world I care about. One way or another, I'm going to find a way to get Tobias and Caleb back and free the slayers, or die trying."

She digested this with steady, thoughtful repose. "Was Tobias assisting you in this quest?"

"The Ravens killed his mate, his father, and his brother. I was assisting *him*."

"He was right. You are unlike other hoods." The she-alpha stopped before me and reached out to pet my braid. "It makes me wonder…"

In quick words of her foreign tongue, the alpha sent her two backup dancers away, though I was certain not so far that they couldn't bound right into the room if they were needed. When it was just the three of us, she crouched in front of me.

"Let's say I did release you," she said, tapping my knee. "Can you guarantee that you will return my beta to me safely?"

It felt like I was shaking my head in a vat of molasses, so heavy was the weight of the deed. "I can only promise I'll do my best to free him."

Suspicion spooled out into a string of diminishing width. "The problem remains, how do we get into such a fortified compound?"

We.

"I'm not worried about getting in. I already know how to do that part. I'm worried about getting out. I did it once, but it was only because a slayer helped me."

"And your cousin, you ungrateful, little urchin!" Markus rebuked.

I ignored his whining. "I was hoping to talk to that slayer tonight. Markus discovered that she takes a trip each evening to one of the parks near the Ravens' place."

"That must be Bebek Park."

Markus nodded. "Yeah, that's the one. It's—Hey, you said you didn't know where they were."

"I don't," Ayşe affirmed, a mischievous smile on her face. "But as I said, rumors. Speculation. My pack has lived concealed in this city for over five hundred years. We know every corner, even if we choose not to visit them. We also know its weaknesses. Istanbul's weakness is the same as Constantinople's, as was the same of Byzantium: it is surrounded by water."

"And the Ravens' compound is right on the strait," I said, as anticipation began to tingle all around me.

Ayşe stood, a grin spreading across her face. "They'll expect us to come to the gates. They'll never be looking for an attack from the sea. Slayers fear water, and they don't think anyone but a slayer could ever be a threat to them. Once you're on the inside, we must work quickly."

"And the escape?" I asked.

"The same way we came. There is a huey who brings the products we sell at the Bazaar from Izmir. His boat will be far enough off the coast so as not to be suspicious. When we have everyone ready, a single flare will have him at the vampires' seawall within sixty seconds. Now, Little Red, tell me how it is you're planning to get in?"

"That's simple enough," I said. "Escorted by Vlad through the front door."

THIRTY

Not a single shopkeeper denied Ayşe's request, and few even questioned it. Traditional wardrobe in my size? Done. Silver bracelets—just to loan out for the night of course? Granted. A bit of these wires and those electrical components, and some of this perfume and a little of that makeup? They would send her a bill when they got around to it, *if* they ever got around to it.

Markus held up one of the silver bangles, turning it in his hand and capturing a video on his newly-acquired cell phone.

Ayşe tightened one of the stitches just below my hip bone and paused. "What are you doing?"

"If you want me to change this back to what it looks like now after we're done with it, I'm going to need to remember what it looks like. I'm a hood, not a jeweler. It's going to be tough enough as it is."

The alpha shook her head. "I still think it will give her away."

"It won't," I assured her. "A hood always has silver on her somewhere. Vlad must know something about hoods, as old as he is. He won't think twice about it."

"But she's relinquished," the alpha argued.

"She'd still wear it for…senti*metal* reasons."

Even possibly sending me to my death, he finds ways to joke.

"She got away with having her dagger with her last time, but I'm

246

not risking that again. If something goes south, I want to be able to find her. You hear that, Geri? Something bad happens, I want you to rip off this silver coin—" He held up the fake in his hands. "—and swallow it. If I don't get you out of this alive, your mom is going to order my execution."

Markus set down the phone and placed the bangle in his flat palm. In moments, the circle melted inward, becoming a pool of liquid metal. Into the molten goo, he dropped one of the little doodads the electrician had been able to scrounge up for him, before commanding the silver into the shape of a token styled like one of the reproduction Ottoman coins that decorated harem costumes sold in the Bazaar. A costume, for reasons I still couldn't comprehend, I was wearing.

"I feel like a reject from the touring company of *Aladdin*. Ouch!"

"Hold still!" Ayşe, crouched at my side, clicked her tongue. "If I don't get this side sewed properly, you're as likely to lose your pants as well as your head tonight."

"Believe me, Geri, of all the ways to lose your pants, in the process of outrunning vampires is not one." Markus held up the completed belt, a string of coins and bells that he snapped around my hips before standing back to admire. "You know, if Cody had ever seen you in this outfit, you might have never lost him to that slut."

"Her name is Lisa, and she's not a slut." The belt rotated on the tips of my fingers as I hid the odd silver coin with the embedded tracking chip in the back. "And, seriously, you want to bring up Cody right now?"

"Cody?" Ayşe tied off the stitch and took to her feet. "Tobias's alpha?"

"The same," I confirmed.

"So you were—or possibly *are*—involved romantically with *two* werewolves." The alpha turned to Markus. "Is this normal for hoods where you come from? In this part of the world, they'd rather kiss a goat than shake hands with a wolf."

"I don't think it was his *hand* she was shaking."

"Markus!"

"What?"

"Cody and I are *not* involved. In fact, based on our last encounter, he may hate my goats. I mean, *guts*." My arms akimbo, I turned once, giving my two companions the full scope. "So, how do I look?"

Markus balanced his chin on a balled-up fist. "Like an extra from the touring company of *Aladdin*."

When Timur's gaze fell on me under Galata Tower, he couldn't hide the grin.

"If you're trying to blend into the native population, you should know that, even in Ottoman times, costumes of this style were worn only by whores." The vampire sidled up to me, his eyes kept on a crowd that seemed to expect me to break out into some kind of performance at any moment. "Not to say it doesn't suit you."

An elderly couple approached, speaking a language I didn't understand. They seemed to be asking to take a picture with me. I happily obliged. "You're not surprised to see me."

"We have both your boyfriend and a wolf with whom you were curiously found in the throes of passion. Of course, I am not surprised."

"We were *not* in the throes of passion!" No sooner had I snapped than I mended. "When I visited before, Vlad made me an offer. After further consideration, I'd like to discuss that possibility with him."

"Is this then a demonstration of that American phrase, *dress for the job you want*?" He shooed away the two tourists with the camera, who were busily trying to shove a folded bill into my hand. "That offer was made before you escaped and killed two of our staff."

Don't back down. Don't allow his rejection. "Which should prove all the more why I'd be a treasured addition. Plus, there is the fact that I was a hood. The daughter of a red matron, even."

The vampire's curiosity piqued. "Why would that be useful to us, precisely?"

"See this mark?" I rolled my neck to the side, showing off my scars. "That was done to me two years ago by one of Cynthia Wu's children after he'd been punished with sunlight. My blood completely healed him in a few minutes."

Timur stood firm, his feet planted at shoulders' width and his arms crossed. "Impossible. News of something that miraculous would have reached us."

"News never got out. Right after that, I ripped his head off his body. Now, do you think you might have a use for me?"

Gone was the space between us, despite how foolish it must have been to move so quickly with so many tourists watching us. As though Timur himself realized his folly, his eyes scanned the perimeter.

"If what you say is true—" With his back to the crowd, my back to the tower, long, hungry fangs descended and deformed his words. "—do you know how much danger that would put your people in? Why would you make something like that known?"

"Because your boss has outmaneuvered me twice and taken away my people. I'm not easily overcome, Timur. I figure the only choice I have against someone like that is to either go down fighting against them, or rise up fighting *for* them."

Those fangs could be the death of me, but that grin would be the end of him. Timur raised a hand to eye level and flexed his fingers, as though inviting someone over. Temptation to look filled me, but I knew better than to break eye contact. Instead, I relied on my ears, telling me that again a car had just come to a stop at a nearby curb, ready to whisk me away.

THIRTY-ONE

Each day, the city became more mysterious, even as the streets became more familiar. Within a few minutes, I understood we weren't heading the same direction as we had the first time. Had the Ravens moved after my escape? Were there multiple fortresses around the city? Did I just fall into a trap, and Timur was doing nothing more than taking me to a more convenient place to drink me and dump my body?

"He wants to show you something first."

I blinked my confusion. "What?"

No chaperones or chauffeurs this time. Instead of a massive tank of an SUV, the vampire had bundled me into a pavement-hugging sports car with only two seats. At a red light, Timur pointed ahead. Even from this low-to-the-ground vantage, I could see the ancient walls rise just a few blocks ahead.

"Vlad wishes for you to accompany him on a private tour of the palace. He said it would be *illuminating.*"

"Is that some kind of solarium joke?"

Timur shrugged. "Vlad is not in the nature of making jokes. No Raven is. I understand you've spent time with our sister."

Nerves alighted and wormed their way into my gut. "Inga."

The light turned green; the car pulled into the intersection.

"Then you understand."

"A harem costume?" Vlad's lips pressed against the back of my hand, testing my resolve. "How fortuitous. I believe you can see the future, Miss Kline."

If I could wield silver, the coins on my belt would purchase your head being cleaved from your body, bastard. But what good would that do? The other Ravens would still have Caleb, Tobias, and the others.

"We see only the present," I said. "It is only within our power to determine how far into the future our adversaries are permitted to see."

Vampires had no pulse, so I couldn't be sure how a flush could overcome Vlad. Had I not known better, I'd have said it was lust coloring his cheeks. After a few unintelligible words to Timur, an exchange was made. The soldier left, and the prince led me by the hand, strolling beside me.

"Have you visited Topkapı yet, Miss Kline?"

"I'm willing to bet you've been spying on me long enough to know the answer." Before us appeared a set of magnificent doors, with grandeur on a scale that made the castles I'd seen in Germany come off as fixer-uppers. "This barbican looks medieval."

His eyes brightened. "You know about architecture?"

"I know about castles and fortresses." I pointed to the turrets on either side rising above the stone archway gate. "This was either built as a nostalgic throwback in the nineteenth century, or during the Middle Ages, at a time when whoever lived here suspected they might actually be invaded."

Vlad gave a slight nod as the doors, which had swung open by powers unseen, closed behind us. "They were wise, the Ottomans. It took me years to understand. Years to appreciate, to *accept*. Then, even longer to learn their ways. Eventually, my wisdom exceeded their own."

"You do have the benefit of a much longer life span," I noted. "One that is getting longer all the time, I hear, thanks to all the wolves you've killed."

"All in the name of progress."

I bit down so hard, the taste of blood teased my tongue. Hopefully, he couldn't sense it. *Play along.* "Where are we going?"

"The slayers whom I guard have grown up in my care. They know this world. You, however, are what my girls would call *yabanci*. A foreigner. An outsider. If you are to decide to join my harem, I wish you to know its origins."

"I know the basics," I insisted. "Many women, one all-powerful man who gets to have them all to himself whenever he wants. Sex slaves."

"*That* is the ignorant orientalist view of what the Ottomans— of what *I* have established. Call one of my *haseki* a sex slave and she'd laugh. Or kill you. They are quite lethal, as beautiful as they are. I believe you received a small demonstration this afternoon from Konstantina. No, the true purpose of a harem isn't sexual indulgence, Miss Kline. It's legacy."

"To create heirs, right? But a slayer can't be turned into a vampire, and you can't impregnate them, so how does that work?"

"I suppose this is one of the areas where my harem varies from the one that once thrived—" He pointed to a group of buildings, two stories high and as wide across as half a football field. "—in these very buildings. The slayers nurture not my biological progeny, but those reborn of the Dracule. *That* is their purpose: to sustain my life, so that my own purpose may endure as Sultan."

At this, Vlad paused, looking into the sky and spreading his lips wide. Gleams of a waning gibbous moon illuminated fangs that seemed to grow longer from the effect. "Did you know that werewolves once protected this very part of the palace? History says it was eunuchs who guarded the sultan's family. I am sure there were *some*. But who showed the greatest loyalty, and who the sultan entrusted with his inner sanctum, were the mated werewolves who were incapable of being with any woman other than their mates. That, too, is my revenge. I deny them that luxury."

I struggled to push out sound through a mouth gone dry. "*That's* why you're undoing mating bonds? As some sort of revenge against a sultan who died five hundred years ago?"

"Rarely are my reasons so simplistic. Your Caleb told me what you thought, that unmated royal wolves provide the best sustenance for my clutch to endure. There is some truth to that, though it was not the impetus for my serum to be developed. What I wished to do— what I *am* doing—is to destroy the werewolves from within. True, I could send my clutch to pick them off one by one. But there are thousands of them around the world. So much time and expense and coordination, when none of that is necessary. You see, Miss Kline, what we discovered is that destroying the mating bonds of the alphas leads to the deterioration of the pack as a whole. Alpha's prerogative becomes impossible. The fealty which keeps them true devolves. I have the luxury of forever, thanks to my slayers. I can wait for the process to play out over several generations."

"But without werewolves, what is the purpose of a hood?"

One of his eyebrows raised precariously. "An interesting query, isn't it? In your case specifically, perhaps one which I may help answer. You have so much to offer: an interest in genetics, familiarity with all forms of supernaturals, and an instinct for hunting down werewolves. In turn, I can offer you every comfort, every luxury you would ever desire." As he slow-walked us back to the main courtyard, he reached out his hand to me. "Join my harem, Gerwalta Kline."

"Your world would never offer me one thing."

"And what is that?"

My hand traced down the curve of my hip, taking his eyes for the ride. "What of my own legacy? What of wanting my own family?"

"I didn't take you for the motherly sort." Vlad licked his lips. "I have the resources required for that, of course. If I didn't, my crop of slayers never would have endured beyond the first generation."

"You know my proclivities. I am the namesake of The Betrayer." I leaned into him, twirling one of his dark curls around my finger. "Promise me my choice of wolf instead."

"If that's what you desire." His hands finally detached from his side to wind around my hips, pulling me close. "Do we have an accord?"

"Not yet." I pulled back. "Caleb told me this palace is a museum, and that there's quite a few Ottoman treasures here."

"Does my *haseki* desire diamonds? Art? Golden teapots?"

"A hood has no use for any of those." I leaned in, ghosting my lips over his. "Show me the weapons."

Desire curled in his eyes. "As you wish."

We walked in silence back across a stone path. A guard stationed at the door held an impressive weapon of the modern era, but gave no heed when he spotted us.

"Do you have every person in this place under your thrall?"

"There are less taxing ways of ensuring their acquiescence," Vlad said. "They are on my payroll."

"And they aren't worried they'll get into trouble?"

"What part of 'I am the sultan' did you not understand, Miss Kline?"

The room we entered, longer than wide and filled with display cases, came to life with a flick of a switch. My mother would have cried. I was on edge myself. The pieces of the collection were not only impressive, they were works of art: khanjars with jade hilts, kards embedded in granite, scimitars as long as my body… Arrows arranged in a quiver of tanned leather, gilded at the edges with copper… Iron helmets engraved with scrollwork so complex and elegant, its place on the battlefield could only be to make the enemy understand the vast wealth of the foe they faced.

And in one display case, though not the fanciest or most ornate, was a smaller sword, slightly curved, embedded in a wooden hilt that called to me. A typed slip of paper held in place by two pushpins was in several languages, the English of which read, *Kilij, 17th c., Balkans. Older,* a voice in my head said. *Much older.*

My hands flattened against the glass. "Beautiful."

Vlad couldn't hide his surprise. "Of all the treasures in this room, *this* is the one that you're drawn to?"

It was, even though far more exceptional pieces surrounded it. "It…" I cut myself off just in the nick of time, just before saying *it calls to me*. Because it couldn't. I was relinquished, more huey than hood, and not in any way, shape, or form on speaking terms with silver. It was impossible.

But I'd sensed Tobias, hadn't I?

What was happening to me?

Vlad leaned in closer, as though he could get between me and the glass. "Does it please?"

"Yes." I raised my weapon hand, wishing I could make this glass dissolve and take that sword by the handle. I hungered to feel the hilt pressed to my flesh.

When the vampire snapped his fingers beside me, I managed to draw my attention away just in time to see the guard who had previously been standing just outside the room scurry in. Vlad said a few words; the guard blushed and made excuses. A few more words from the vampire, this time spoken around fangs, and the guard dropped his argument and rushed away. Moments later, he returned, a set of keys in his hand. I watched, mouth agape, as the very sword I'd been drooling over moments ago was removed and rushed from the room.

"Done. It is being loaded into my car as we speak. The weapons curator will also be happy to entertain any questions you have regarding the sword and its history whenever you care to make an appointment with him."

"Loaded into your…" Evil dead or not, that was absurd. "You

can't just remove a four-hundred-year-old sword from a museum!"

"I already have." Two blinks, and the vampire was no longer feet away; he was standing before me, his hands in my hair. "I will compensate the museum for the financial burden. That, or offer a similar piece from my private collection. I hope this gift sufficiently demonstrates the dedication I have for my *haseki*—my *favorites*—Gerwalta. If you give yourself to me, I give myself, and so much more, back to you."

I didn't know why I felt the need to argue a present I was never actually going to receive with a man whose moral compass pointed towards a different pole than mine. "That sword must be worth thousands, maybe even tens of thousands of dollars."

"Your worth is far greater, and ten times more rare." His head tilted, as though he were mapping my side profile. "You have named your terms, and I have accepted. Are we in agreement, then?"

"I don't remember you presenting your terms."

"Mine is singular: loyalty. Not only to me, but to the whole clutch. If you are discovered to betray us, you will die. If we ask of your body, you must give it."

"Didn't you just chastise me for saying the women of your harem are sex slaves?"

He laughed at my ignorance. "We require only your blood. Anything more is at your own discretion, just as long as your lovers are friendly to the Ravens. My ladies mingle with the males of their kind at their leisure."

Which meant there were male slayers still alive. The question was where? If the females had ready access, somewhere in the compound or very nearby, I'd imagine.

For the third time, he offered his hand in the style of a suitor asking a belle for a dance. "Agreed?"

Do it, the voice inside me said. *You're going to kill him anyways, and you'll buy the others more time to infiltrate the house if you keep playing along.*

Putting my hand in his, I gave one quick nod. Then, my world flew out of control.

My mouth fractured, a silent scream cut from my throat, as his fangs pierced my neck. The pain flashed through my body, every nerve reacting to the attack. Then, numbness, almost as if, instead of the vampire's bite, I'd been injected with morphine. The ache ebbed away, replaced with a subtle chill and sense of euphoria.

Intoxication took me hostage as the prince drew back, his eyes wide and his lips crimson with my blood.

"Im…possible."

Equilibrium was such a challenge, I dared not try anything as complex as speech. Instead, I just looked at him, goofy and aloof.

"Someone lied to you." Vlad ran a hand over my hair, brushing back the stray hairs free of my ever-present braid. "They lied to you—lied to all of us. And now I know why."

"What did you… Why am I…"

The high-pitched trill coming from inside Vlad's coat pocket overlaid my incoherent mumbles. Amused, Vlad grinned as he pushed a finger to my lips while holding the phone to his ear with his other hand.

"Perfect timing, Timur. I believe I have just succeeded in getting Miss Kline to—Oh, really? Oh, very interesting. Yes, of course, bring around the car."

He slipped the phone back into his pocket. The way his expression shifted in the intervening moments sobered me. Curiosity curdled, leaving behind only resentment.

"The funny thing about this, in hindsight, is what I've just managed to do, I did without you having to canoodle me. Perhaps you're more like your mother than I supposed."

"Sorry?" Fingertips pushed into my temple finally steadied the room. "I don't have any noodles. I like dumplings, though. Why... Why am I so dizzy?"

"The disorientation is temporary, and will ease with rest," Vlad said as he took me by the hand. "Rest, I fear, you won't be getting for a while."

And with that, I stopped trying to keep a hold of both gravity and reality. I slipped into my own daydream, unaware of the nightmare that awaited me.

THIRTY-TWO

Pain shot through me as Vlad slammed my face into the wall beside the fireplace in his massive home, rocketing me awake. My eyes shot open. Hungry, desperate lungs ate up air. With a twist of his wrist, I collapsed to the floor, panting, kissing carpet.

"An hour ago, I was prepared to offer you use of the mating suite for you and your lover. Now, I have to ask myself, how tight should I make your chains?" A kick in the side brought blood to my mouth. "And should they be silver?"

Because a werewolf would try to free me if they weren't? If he succeeded in killing Tobias, I doubted any would even let out a sigh at my death. Certainly not the Pera Pack, who must be blaming Markus and me for their discovery. Certainly not the Paradise Pack, whose alpha had sent me packing.

With a twist of my arm behind my back, Vlad pulled out my curdled cry and straddled my waist. The agony shot through me, from my wrist to my shoulder blades, and the strain bit into my resolve. I turned, catching sight of the sword he'd gifted to me sitting on a nearby table, the belt of coins discarded beside it. If only I could get to it…

"Just because I can't kill you without killing myself doesn't mean I can't cause you inexorable levels of pain. Act out against me, and this will be the baseline of your suffering."

"Wait, what? Why can't you kill…" Did I really want to finish that question?

The prince's hands flattened against the floor on either side of my head. He lowered his upper body, pressing his cheek to mine. "The bite I took: you said it felt different. Didn't you realize why?"

"Because I'm relinquished?" It was the only thing that came to mind when I compared Vlad's attack with that of Xin's child.

"Oh, you're something all right, but relinquished isn't what I'd call it. It's because what you felt was a maker's bite. My blood now flows through your veins, Gerwalta. You are of me."

The dim hall blurred in my vision, but I didn't need my eyes to see the truth. "That's how you keep the slayers from revolting. You've taken them hostage. You've made them Dracule."

"True that we cannot turn a slayer, but Igor discovered long ago a maker's bite will immunize a vampire from his victim's solarium. Sadly, though, it only works with the females." I could feel his smile stretch out next to my face. "As I said, I learned from the Ottomans well. Mehmed tried to infect me, to drive his ideology and his politics into my veins, to *internalize* my slavery, and make me my own captor. And that is what makes my *hasekis* so compliant: my blood is in their veins."

"You've given all the slayers in your harem the maker's bite. If they killed you, they'd die too."

"You really are quite the smart one, aren't you?" Vlad stood, finally ending the onslaught of pain. I struggled to push myself up on all fours. "Though sadly, their solarium can still knock us out for a few hours. Also, that still doesn't keep them from escaping. That doesn't assure their loyalty. Have you figured out that part of it, hood? Have you?"

No, I hadn't. I searched my memory, recalling the salon where I'd seen all the female slayers lounging, Caleb the only male in their midst.

The only male.

"By threatening the men." Agony ebbed as I rolled to my knees, struggling to my feet. "But how? How could you keep them from killing you?"

"Every supernatural creature has its weakness, doesn't it? Vampires: sunlight. Werewolves: silver. Hoods: electricity. And slayers?"

Vlad's arms wrapped around me just seconds before the scenery became a blur. Moving so fast played havoc with my lungs, leaving me a coughing mess when we came to a stop in his back garden, lights dancing like pixies over the Bosporus.

"Water." The vampire grinned as he beheld the vast resources surrounding his home. "A slayer forced to stand in water is powerless to conjure their damned solaria. Oh, yes, I learned. The way to keep power in check isn't with chains around the wrists, but with chains around the heart."

Igor's explanation of why he'd rented the run-down house in Eminönü bubbled up in my memory. *In the old part of the city, there's hundreds of them. Every grand home or even apartment block in Byzantine or Ottoman times had one, and a number of them still survive in one form or another today.*

"There's a cistern under the house."

"And I flood it just enough to keep their power—and their hopes— dampened. The moment one of the women acts out against me or tries to flee, the males pay the price. Alexandra could tell you from personal experience. I killed her husband only a month ago when *she* tried to escape."

My eyes flew shut, but the vision still danced on the back of my eyelids. "Caleb?"

"Your Caleb resisted the charms of my beauties far longer than I supposed he could, given how long you denied *him*. Let me guess: every time you got close to consummating, your body rejected the experience?"

I refused to dignify the question with an answer, or acknowledge even to myself that the reminder Caleb had slept with one of the slayers hurt. Instead, I huffed, glaring at him like my eyes could rip off his head.

The vampire planted his hands on his knees and bent over, laughing at my quivering frame. "That was pretty much the way of it, wasn't it? And the way you're staring at me, like you're shocked that I knew that, tells me that you *don't* know what's so special about you."

Fury fueled my strength, rage drove out the pain. The shaking stopped, and though I moved slow, I rose to my feet.

"I know what's so special about me."

Straight back, flashing eyes, firm voice…

"I am Gerwalta, namesake of The Betrayer, and I will be the one to ensure *you* never hurt another living soul, even if it does kill me in the process."

The vampire nodded, amusement brightening his features. "A nice sentiment, but all bluster, I'm afraid. You see, you don't have any power. You're nothing but a relinquished hood."

The cloaked figure in the tree at the edge of the yard crouched, the silver in his hand dancing.

"I have the best power of all: allies."

Blood sprayed across my face as Markus's weapon found its mark. Crimson rivulets drained down the vampire's mouth as he keeled over. Markus pounced, another ball of liquid silver at the ready, even as his eyes scanned me for injuries.

"No broken bones," I reported, even though I suspected at least a few ribs were cracked. "I'll heal. Ayşe?"

"She's sweeping the perimeter, taking out any guards who would see us escaping from the seawall." Markus turned to the house. "Tell me where we're going."

I pointed to the second story, even as we ran towards the doors. A silver spear through the neck could only sideline Vlad for as long as it took him to pull it from his throat and heal. Given the power of my blood on a vampire from my last encounter, I didn't suspect that would take too long.

"The women are there. The men are in the basement. I suspect that's where the wolves are too. There's at least one other Raven on the property, probably along with a handful of other vamps of later generations."

"So you go up and I go down?"

"No, we both go up. This house is expansive, and we need someone who knows it."

Markus eyeballed the two headless corpses outside the entrance to the harem. "If I had known beheading them was so easy, I'd have done that with Vlad. Nice sword by the way." He balanced my new weapon in one hand, examining it before handing it back to me. All his silver had gone into piercing Vlad. Literally. "Where'd you get it?"

Not a story I wanted to go into right now. "Just saw it downstairs and thought to grab it as we came through." I searched through the pockets of one of the victims of Markus's attack. "These vamps were young. I don't think a Raven would have been as easy."

Light spilling from a newly-opened door blinded us. I threw my free arm up, creating a band of shadow over my eyes. The measure against so many cocked and loaded solaria proved useless, as did the sword I grasped.

"We're here to save you, but we need Alexandra's help."

With a wall of ebbing luminosity behind her, the redhead stepped forward.

"Is this why I saved you?" she barked. "Just so you could get us all killed? What kind of fool are—"

"A hood!" I shouted. "A hood who knows that, as long as the Ravens survive, we're all in danger."

Another of the slayers, a dark-haired one with brilliant blue eyes, cackled. After a few blinks, my eyeballs toasting like marshmallows, I realized I knew her. This was the slayer who had taken Tobias.

"Idiot! Even time could not defeat them. What makes you think a *wolfsretter* stands any chance?"

"Because I'm not a *wolfsretter*. I'm something much more dangerous: a woman in love with someone they've taken. I will not be stopped. Not by reason, and not by regret."

Alexandra let her solarium extinguish, along with the fury in her features. "After Caleb did what he'd been put here to do, the Ravens took him below with the others."

I shook my head and let my sword fall to the side. "He's not the one I love."

At that, most of the others dropped their defenses as well.

"If not him—" Alexandra inched forward, confusion marring her features. "—then who?"

"His name is Tobias Somfield. He's a wolf."

The room repolarized, as all eyes went from me and Markus, to Alexandra herself. The redhead's eyes dropped to the ground as her hand rounded the child within her, cradling it in her grasp.

Her brilliant blue eyes sparkled with tears when she looked up. "You know of our limitation?"

I nodded, even though Markus managed a muffled "no" in the background.

"We'll figure out how to kill them all later," I said. "Today, our goal is freedom. There's a boat, just a few hundred meters off the seawall behind the house, waiting for us."

Alexandra gave a curt nod before turning to a woman with mocha skin and coal-black eyes. "You must be swift, Rashidi."

The slayer drew back, like she'd been singled out for ridicule. "There are too many guards at the gates."

"I'm not suggesting to lead them through the gates."

Rashidi went ashen. "Surely you're not suggesting we attempt to escape by diving into the strait. We'd be powerless in the water, you know that."

"The only power you will lack in the water is the power to destroy a vampire. If you are brave, and if you are steadfast, you will not lose the power to save yourselves."

Markus stepped between the two women. "Swim far away from the landing, straight out, staying as close together as you can."

My cousin drew one of the two flare guns we'd brought from inside his hood. "After fifteen minutes, if we're still not there, you fire this. They'll come pick you up. Don't wait for us. If we see the flare, we'll know you've gone. We'll find another way."

Rashidi glared confusedly at the hood before her. "Why are you helping us?"

"Because it is the right thing to do." Markus closed her hand with his own around the flare gun. "Which, frankly, isn't enough for me. But I know Geri. She's not going to get out of here unless all of you are safe, and I can't get out of here unless the same's true for her."

THIRTY-THREE

Every creak of the stairs signaled our defeat.

Alexandra noted my nerves. "The home is old, and it was shaken harshly by the last great earthquake. Don't worry, I will know if one of the staff approaches. We can sense vampires the way you sense wolves."

Probably not the way I *sense wolves,* I thought.

A keypad outside a white door beeped as the slayer punched in the code, a feat that Markus found suspect.

"Does everyone have access to the dungeon?" he asked as he swished a ball of liquid silver around in his hand. At least that obnoxious harem costume belt had come to some practical use. Otherwise, my cousin might have insisted on requisitioning my new favorite weapon. "Doesn't seem very secure."

"It's a cistern, not a dungeon," Alexandra replied. She held up a hand at shoulder level, sparking a solarium to light the stairway below. Three feet under a modern lattice, the walls morphed suddenly from smooth concrete to rough plaster. "Each man is secured with chains. We do not have the keys to those. The access is necessary for… visits."

The presence of a baby bump on the slayer told me what kind of visits.

"And the wolves?" I asked, fretful of the visions my imagination was conjuring. "Are they down this way too?"

Alexandra shook her head and took another step. "Not anymore." She swallowed, and I didn't miss the crack in her voice. "I suppose they decided that the wolves needed to be kept somewhere the slayers couldn't access."

The moment we splashed into knee-deep water, her solarium coughed out. Luckily, the buzzing, dull lights stringed up the hall were powerful enough to see.

"Are there any more Ravens in Istanbul other than Timur and Vlad?"

"Not right now. They travel in pairs, and rarely are the others here," Alexandra answered. "When they are, it's only for a few hours, just long enough to receive a treatment."

Remembering how Inga had been "treated" by Caleb's blood, I didn't need to question that part. "So we only have to worry about where Timur is, then. Maybe we'll be lucky enough to avoid him."

"Timur is already down here, lying in wait."

Sloshing water created ripples as Markus stepped around me to catch up to Alexandra. "Why didn't you say so sooner?"

The redhead paused to blink at him in confusion. "Were you expecting this to go smoothly?"

Markus's cheeks went crimson. "Why should anything be easy at this point?"

Suddenly, a low-level buzz tickled my hairline, and a lurch of my insides pulled in the direction to the right, to a space that seemed to be just more of the ancient foundation. Only, the direction in which I was drawn wasn't the one Alexandra was leading us to.

I pushed my hand flat against the wall. "It's him."

Markus came alongside me, weaving the strands of silver around his arm like a chain and pressing his palm flat against the plaster. "How can you feel that? You're relinquished."

I ignored his question, and posed one of my own. "How do we get in?" I eyeballed my sword, wondering, if I sliced into the wall and managed to break through, would its weakening bring down the whole house atop us?

"Get in where?" Alexandra asked. "The slayers are in a room up ahead."

As far as I could see up and down the corridor, there were no breaks in the wall, which arched overhead like an excavated cave. "There's a chamber on the other side of this wall. The wolves are in there. I can feel them. I can feel…" His name—his presence—almost broke me. "Tobias."

Markus joined me. "There's no way you could possibly sense the wolves."

"Tell me I'm wrong, then."

"You're not, but it's impossible—"

We both yelped when Alexandra's fingers laced through our hair and yanked us along.

"You swore to save the slayers!" she whispered. "They come first. After that, your wolves."

Tobias. My heart reached for him, latched on to him, and yearned for physics to break its own laws and let him pass through the wall to me. With every ounce of my being, I focused on getting my message to him. *I am here. I will save you. Just be strong.*

But Alexandra was right, and if she were to be believed, there was a Raven in wait ahead. I twisted from her hold as Markus did the same.

"The slayers first," I agreed. "But how do we kill Timur? We don't have any wood."

"Markus will take off his head." Alexandra turned, guiding us forward. "Without wood, it's the only way to kill a vampire."

Markus trudged on. "Or if we can get you out of the water, you can burn his ass with a solarium."

"Out of water, he can simply smoke and escape. Water weakens both vampire and slayer. They can't evaporate, but we cannot summon solaria. Besides, Geri and I can't kill him."

I gulped, hoping my cousin would chalk up Alexandra's declaration to the fact that I was relinquished and, therefore, unequal to the task.

No such luck.

"And why would that be?"

"Because Vlad has infected her," Alexandra said. "As he has done with all the female slayers. If we kill a Dracule, we kill ourselves."

"Whoa, wait." Markus's hands went out to the side. He came to a halt and turned on us. "Are you saying that a vampire's bite makes them immune from harm from their victim?"

Alexandra shook her head. "Only a maker's bite, only from the Dracule, and only in a female slayer. Or, it seems, a hood."

Realization dawned on me. "That's how you were able to hit Timur with a solarium and he didn't die?"

Alexandra's brow furrowed. "This is a topic I will gladly expound upon, at a later time when we are not all dead or imprisoned."

"I have got to write that down, and Geri, we're going to have some major tests to run. Okay, if I'm going to kill him, you should probably let me get in the front and I should—"

But Markus never got to say what he was going to do. One moment he had pulled out ahead of us, the silver under his command warping into a hanger sword, and the next, he was on his back in the water, his head submerged, and a vampire atop his frame. His weapon flew backward, splashing my face as it plunged beneath the muddied surface.

Even if they couldn't smoke, water had no apparent effect on a vampire's strength.

Alexandra tried to advance, but I pulled her back.

"You go," I said. "Save your people. I'll take care of him."

"But how will I cut the chains?"

The weapon in my hand vibrated, as though reminding me she was still here.

She. Swords didn't have genders, but something about this one felt particularly… feminine.

I pushed the hilt into Alexandra's hand. "She'll cut through them."

The slayer examined me, then the sword. "But this sword is so…"

"*She* will cut through *them.*"

This time, Alexandra didn't argue. One more glance at Markus struggling to break free of the Raven's hold, and the slayer nodded and turned on her heel, calling over her shoulder as she did,

"Remember, you are Dracule. Kill him, kill yourself."

I reached down into the water, tracking in my mind the arc I'd watched the hanger sword fly. Its handle practically leapt into my hand, and I shot up, getting a quick feel for the weight of the short sword in my grasp. A relinquished hood didn't have the power of a righteous one, but if I didn't do something, my cousin was going to die. Alone or not, I had to act.

Ayşe, we could really use you down here.

"You'll let my cousin up now."

His muscles, his strength, his abilities: nothing helped Markus to free himself. The vampire was too strong.

"This hood is an intruder," Timur purred, not threatened or even concerned in the slightest. "I couldn't possibly let him live. And since you can't kill me, I—"

As the blade bit into his flesh, the cloth of his shirt severed and blood rolled down his elbow. Timur shrank backward, his hand clasping over rent flesh. I put myself between him and Markus, fretting at the sound of my cousin trying to clear his lungs.

"I can come pretty close to killing you without actually doing the deed."

"Pretty little *wolfsretter*." Even as the blood flowed down Timur's arm and dripped into the water, the wound began to knit itself together. "A shame that you're born of a supernatural line already. You would have made such a glorious Raven. You have an innate taste for blood."

"You're really going to love this then."

The water slowed me, but my arms remembered motions

ingrained from years of training. I lunged, forward and to the right, using the momentum to drive a strike into the vampire's shoulder. Instead of taking the blow, Timur utilized his speed, unhindered by the deluge, to clear him from my path. That was fine; it was further away from Markus.

"Your blow was a fluke." Timur shifted again, advancing several feet up the corridor, toward the direction Alexandra had run. "Unfortunately, playtime is over. I have work to do. Just because we're going to kill the slayers doesn't mean we can't salvage their blood first."

Kill the slayers? Caleb! "I'll die before I let you hurt them."

"That's not completely off the table," Timur returned.

The hairs on the back of my neck tingled, and all at once, I knew we weren't alone.

"Hey, Markus? You good back there?"

"Yup. What do you need?"

I held his weapon up. "Something good for shooting down a Raven."

"I can do that."

The vampire turned, but I'd already hurled the hanger sword with all my might in his direction. Under my cousin's influence, the metal liquified, bending and twisting in midair. Within seconds, what had been a sword grew long, cylindrical. The arrow caught Timur in the back, right under his left shoulder blade.

When he pivoted to us again, a drop of blood dripped from the arrow tip that stuck out of his chest. "Did you really think your Tinkertoy was going to stop me?"

"Not at all." Markus grinned. "But it distracted you long enough for *her* to get here."

When a werewolf's growl rumbled through the air, the exhilaration had me on cloud nine. The Pera Pack alpha leapt, clearing over me and Markus as we crouched down.

For one terrifying moment, I saw it: fear. It sunk into the cracks of Timur's arrogance, seeping into his veins. Long, ebony fangs took the vampire at the throat, cutting off his screams. Soon, his body disappeared beneath the water, only his hands and flailing feet breaking the surface. Red waves washed from the tumult, painting a crimson sheen over the water. When his severed head floated to the surface, the tension left my body.

Ayşe shifted back to her huey form. "How did you do that?"

"I'm not sure. I didn't think I'd be able to throw hard enough for the arrow to go all the way through his body."

The shewolf shook her head. "No, not that. I mean, how did you call to me?"

I blinked away the confusion, even as we reached the end of the hall where Alexandra was cutting the chains off the last of the male slayers. "Yeah, well, all kinds of crazy shit going on tonight, I guess."

Inside the room, a dozen men in varying states of health and wearing only T-shirts and Bermuda shorts stared at me, the red-cloaked hood beside me, and the green-eyed woman with wild black hair who was more than a little nude. Those shorts alone had me wanting to kill Timur all over again. Unkempt facial hair hid their expressions, but two things became clear right away: they were young, and they were overall healthy. I looked around, expecting to find a dungeon straight out of a Hollywood movie, but it looked more like a partially flooded Ikea showroom. Clinical, spa-like even.

The slayer must have read the confusion in my face. "The water level can be controlled. It's only raised when the doors open and someone comes down here."

"Then why don't they just use their solaria to melt the chains?" Markus asked.

"Because they were never awakened."

I peered around the group of men, looking for the owner of the voice I knew so well. A moment later, he emerged. With bags under his eyes and his shirt stained with blood, there was still no doubt, this was my slayer. I crossed to him and threw my arms around him.

"Caleb." His name drew guilt to my tongue. "I'm so sorry. I don't know what happened. I… Are you okay?"

"I am now." His hands threaded my hair, pulling my head to his shoulder. "I was so scared I'd killed you. God, I wanted to tell you when you showed up in the harem, but I knew if I showed them how much I really loved you, they'd know I'd been playing them."

"Killed me?" I looked up into his eyes. "What do you mean, killed me?"

"When we were leaving Hagia Sophia, the night the Ravens took me. The second I cleared the exit, I saw them. I pulled my solarium from the church, but I didn't know you were running after me. It hit you. I saw you disappear. I saw you burn into dust."

"Burn into dust? I didn't burn into…"

No. No way, it was impossible.

"I didn't give myself to the flame," I said. "I didn't let the fire take me. *I* took *it*."

His face scrunched up in confusion. "Give yourself to the flame? What does that mean?"

"We'll have to talk about it later." Wrapping my hand around his, I pulled him from the room. "I have to save Tobias. He's still here somewhere."

"I'll help."

A red cape dashed into my peripheral vision. "Geri! Come on!"

Caleb pushed me behind him. "Who in the hell are you?"

Markus guffawed. "Calm down, Helsing, I'm one of the good guys."

"There are more vampires approaching." At the top of the stairs, Alexandra pushed the last of her clan through the door. "And Vlad is still nearby, but I don't know where. He must be smoke. They're always harder to sense when they're smoke. We have to get to the boat. He can't chase us over water, but my people have never had to face vampires in battle. We've lost the skill."

Caleb took Alexandra by the hand. "Just follow my instructions. Geri, if you're going to get the wolves out, you don't have much time."

I nodded. "Then we better get going."

THIRTY-FOUR

I ignored the thrill that ran through me. It sparked too many questions, and confusion would only slow me down. Later, I'd concern myself with how I could feel the tug of dawn kindling in my veins, though even without too much effort, I'd begun to understand what had happened to me that night at Hagia Sophia. I just didn't know *how* it had happened.

Alexandra sparked a ball of sunlight on her outstretched hand, at the ready in case one of the vampires infesting the front of the house reached the back before the slayers were clear. "The sun rises in a few minutes. We'll be safe outside, but in the house, we're still at Vlad's mercy."

"But Vlad is outside, injured," Markus said.

Ayşe shook her head. "Trust me, he's not. He's in the house."

Looking for us, no doubt. "Thank you, Alexandra. Caleb?"

"Yes?" He took my hand in his. I pushed down the need to rebuff his feelings; apparently, he'd thought our argument at Hagia Sophia had been no more than a passing lover's quarrel.

"The others have been imprisoned for who knows how long," I said. "They may be weak. Help them. A boat is coming as soon as we fire the flare. Please, don't let anyone drown."

"But I won't leave—"

My cousin cut him off. "I'll make sure she gets out, lover boy. Just do what she says, there isn't time for debating."

The slayer hesitated only a second, until the features of his face shifted into resolve. Caleb leaned in, kissing me hard, as though for the first time. Or perhaps the last.

"Hurry," he said. "We need to talk."

"I will."

The first time I was in the house, I'd dismissed the silver and gold that interplayed in Vlad's décor as emblems of vanity, trophies of a vampire who considered himself a sultan. But hadn't he himself said his actions were rarely for a single purpose? A silver grate may be just vanity, but it could also hold back a wolf trying to escape.

I pointed at the fireplace, to the shining grate. "Markus, can you reclaim the silver?"

"Gladly."

My cousin extended his arms, beckoning the metal. It obeyed readily, liquifying, flowing through the air to wrap itself around his chest, his belt. As soon as he'd finished the task, I turned to Ayşe.

"I can go first."

The alpha shook her head. "No, Serhan might attack you, not knowing we are working together. And if your wolf attacks *him*, we'll have too much chaos on our hands. Let me go first."

As Markus had said to Caleb only moments before, there wasn't time for debate. I nodded and stepped aside. The shewolf shifted, flesh giving way to fur and tooth to fang. The lithe creature disappeared down a hole easily big enough to pass a small sofa through.

Markus waved me on. "Someone needs to stay up here to pull you all up. There's no way your huey arms could handle the load."

My back straightened. "I'm not a huey."

"Relinquished isn't much better."

I put my finger on one of the gleaming sheets melded to his forearm. "I'm not relinquished either." The metal under Markus's influence refused to obey my command, but it still vibrated in response to my call. "Though apparently I need to figure out the whole commanding silver thing."

Markus gazed at me, wide-eyed. "How is that—"

"Possible?" I said, cutting him off. I put my sword on the ground in front of the grate as I turned to shimmy the bottom half of my body down. "We'll have to worry about that later. Take those cords from the curtain, use them for rope. Throw me my sword as soon as I'm in and clear."

"Will do."

With only the light that came from the portal above, my eyes took a few moments to adjust to the dim space. As the dark took on definition, I caught sight of Ayşe licking Serhan's ear. In his wolf, the Pera packling's frame heaved, his breaths congested. Around one of his ankles, a silver clasp had burned his flesh completely away, exposing bone. My sword made quick work of the chain. Markus would have to coax the metal from his wound once we cleared the room.

And there, on the far side of the room… was Tobias.

I ran over to where he sat, on the ground, inspecting him for the worst. Like Serhan, a silver manacle cuffed the werewolf, connecting to a chain that kept him from moving too far. Bubbled skin seemed to be the worst of his damage, and as I ran a finger under the metal band, I figured out why. Tobias's hair, oily and grimy, at first concealed the self-injury. Several handfuls of hair had been ripped from his head, which he must have used to create as good a barrier as he could manage between his skin and the silver.

The naked man crossed his arms and leaned back against the brick wall of the chamber. "Took you long enough."

Was he serious? Now? He was going to give me lip *now*? After I made sure he was safe, he was going to be in so much trouble.

I yelled up to Markus. "Pass down the curtain cord, Serhan's in really bad shape." Then, crouching down to Tobias, I ran my hands over the manacle and tried to get the silver to heed my command. It obeyed, thank god, losing definition and melting away. "I'm *so* sorry that I had to put together a coalition to invade the Ravens' stronghold, and that you were inconvenienced. I hope you didn't—"

But before I could say just what I hoped he didn't, Tobias drew me into his lap, threw his arms around me, and pressed his lips to mine.

His lips… so tender, so firm, so demanding. He waxed and waned the pressure, pulling me closer. If I hadn't broken the moment by mumbling into his mouth, he might not have ever let me go.

"You can't even let me kiss you without being contrary, can you?"

Serhan yipped from above as he cleared the tunnel, probably from the shock of having the metal leached from his blood. Ayşe turned, tilting her lupine head in confusion at discovering our intimate position.

She wasn't the only one confused, though. "How?"

The wolf turned sheepish, averting his eyes, looking everywhere except at me. "It doesn't matter."

The Pera Pack alpha barked before taking her turn to escape. Tobias held up a finger, the international sign for "one second, please."

"It does *too* matter." My hand flew to my mouth. "Oh, my god. They gave it to you, didn't they?"

"It's not just because of the serum." He didn't try to quell my fears. "There's been something between us for a while. We both knew it. We both felt it. We've been connected for… God, maybe since we met."

"But you're mated!" I said again. "It's impossible. You can't…"

"I can. I *do*." He finally looked at me again, but instead of remorse, daring filled his gaze. "Believe me, I've tried not to. But since we kissed the first time, I can't deny what I feel."

"Since twenty seconds ago?"

His hand ran through his patchwork hair. "Shite, you don't remember the night in Paradise, do you? You never talked about it, so I assumed you were too embarrassed. And believe me, I've had nights of guilt, thinking I'm somehow being unfaithful to Kara by loving you. I've tried to stop. But I can't. I love you, Geri. Whether or not it should be possible, it's true. And I didn't need the serum to realize it. I only needed the fear that I'd lost you."

"The night in Paradise?" Memories cast themselves on the back of my eyelids. *The full moon. He took on his human, even then. He kissed me.* "You were human on a full moon. You… Cody exiled you."

"No, he didn't. I asked to be released. I wanted the chance to be an alpha again. I wanted to free myself, free *you*, from Paradise."

"But who is your beta?"

But it wasn't Tobias who answered. It was Vlad. "Now *that* is the most interesting part of this all."

We turned to find him standing at the exit, his body solidifying from a cloud of smoke.

"Markus, run!" I shouted, even as Tobias shifted me behind him.

"Try to lay a hand on her, vampire, and I will rip you to shreds."

Vlad chuckled. "I have no intention of harming a single hair on her pretty little head. Offer me a thousand unmated alpha wolves, each holding a bar of solid gold, and they still wouldn't be as valuable to me as she is."

Tobias stood straighter. "That makes two of us."

The vampire ignored the statement, and set about pacing through the room. "Earlier tonight, when I tasted your blood, your secret revealed itself, Miss Kline. How you and your whole cursed race kept something like this hidden for so long is beyond me, but now I realize: you weren't hiding it at all. You don't know. If you had, you never would have let me bite you. You would have killed yourself first."

"I'm still wondering if that wasn't the right thing to do in hindsight." I eyeballed my sword where I'd dropped it when Tobias embraced me, halfway between us and the only means of exit.

"I have become a legend among men, but creatures like you? You are the legend I longed to find," Vlad continued as though I'd said nothing. "I honestly didn't think one could ever come to be, given how strict your hood matrons are on the mating and breeding of their bloodlines. *Hood begets hood,* isn't that a favorite idiom of theirs?"

"And cryptic vampire begets cryptic vampire," Tobias mumbled. "You've already killed too many people I love, demon. You got something you need to tell Geri, do it now. I'll be ripping out your throat in about twenty seconds."

Vlad halted, leaning forward as he spoke, like he was trying to provoke a dog tied on a leash. "They never killed the baby."

The sharp turn threw me for a loop. "What in the hell are you talking about?"

"*Die Verräterin,*" Vlad said. "The Betrayer: so called because she broke the most sacred of hood laws and mated a wolf, bearing his child. Oh, I don't doubt that Gerwalta Faust and her wolf *did* fry on silver spits, but it seems even the heartless harpy matrons could still be melted by the coquettish curls of a tiny, helpless little cub mongrel. It lived, and *you*, Gerwalta Kline, are not only The Betrayer's namesake, you are her direct descendant." He paused, his eyes kept locked into mine. "Isn't that true, Father?"

THIRTY-FIVE

Igor seemed more shadow than solid, or maybe it was the aspect of light that was changing. Above, dawn tickled the horizon. If only Tobias and I could get by and out of the house, the sun would assure our escape.

"Geri, Tobias, are you unharmed?"

"Oh, Father, they are my guests! They have been well treated, I promise. Now, do not change the subject!" Vlad rebuked. "You were always one who believed confession was good for the soul. Confess now. Confess the truth about this hood that you've helped keep hidden."

"This has to stop, Vlad." Igor labored to keep his expression even. "Hunting down other creatures, extending your mortality on the blood and bones of the innocent."

"You're one to talk." Vlad pointed back over his shoulder. "How long before you drain her for your own gain?"

I shuddered. "Igor, what is he talking about?"

"Didn't you hear me, hood?" Vlad bemoaned. "You are a direct descendant of The Betrayer. Hood, yes, but also descended from wolves. It has come down to you over a dozen generations. And my father…" He paused, shooting daggers at the man. "…kept it hidden for his own benefit. How else could a vampire live five hundred years beyond his vampire mortality?"

Tobias gasped. "But that would make you a thousand years old."

"A feat only possible with the rarest of supernatural blood," Vlad confirmed. "Slayer blood is rich, but burns away quickly. Even the blood of an unmated alpha or beta might give us another hundred or so years. But the blood of an *asenaic*? The legends say it can let a vampire live forever."

The knuckles of Igor's hand popped as he made fists. "*Nothing* lives forever, and I've only extended my life until I found a way to end yours."

"And Inga's?" Vlad asked.

Some degree of certainty ebbed from the elder vampire's expression. "I could not bear the weight of my many years alone."

"You wouldn't have had to, if you had shared your knowledge with me instead," Vlad hissed. "So, Gerwalta Kline, you see now why I could not let you go. You are the way I will live forever."

But my mind was still stuck at a point in the conversation from sixty seconds ago. "There's no way my mother is descended from wolves."

Igor's head dipped. "You're right; she's not."

"But if she's not, then—" Impossible. *Im-poss-i-ble.* "My dad?"

"I suspect that's why he was turned away from his own clan," Igor said. "And why he loves your mother when nobody else would, having done what she's done to her own daughter. He's mated to her. *Bonded*, like a wolf."

"And that's also why—" Vlad interrupted, "—I'll be going after him next."

No, not another life.

I lunged, the sword flying into my grip as I angled it for Vlad's chest. The vampire smoked, and I flew forward, landing in the belly of the hole.

"Quick," Igor said, pushing me up through the hearth above. "Into the sunlight."

"But Tobias!"

"You're more important! And I can't—"

A cacophony of snarls, growls, and cries filled the chamber below, rebounding on the stone of the hearth overhead. I pulled myself out and dropped the sword on the floor before lying down on my stomach and reaching back into the hole.

"Tobias!"

His wolf appeared below. He leapt, claws digging into the earthen sides of the tunnel. For one brilliant moment, the amber pools of his eyes met mine, and then, the tunnel gave way.

I barely moved in time to save myself as the stone edifice of the fireplace surrendered to gravity, collapsing in.

"Tobias!"

Markus appeared from nowhere, dragging me back, his words a jumble.

"…now!… Boat… flare… no time!"

THIRTY-SIX

Inga threw the blanket over my shoulders. "They might have survived."

I slurped a sip of my tea, slow and deliberate and as loudly as possible. "I'm sure Igor and Vlad survived just fine. A vampire doesn't need air to live. Wolves do."

Markus, his hood subsumed back into nothingness, shimmied below deck. "There's no word from Ayşe or Serhan. Either they swam off in another direction, or they tried to go out through the street and were overcome." He took a seat beside me and turned to Inga. "How did you finally find us?"

Inga looked away. "Brünhild."

That finally snapped me out of my haze. "Are you telling me she knew where the Ravens' house was all this time?"

The vampire shook her head. "We looked everywhere for some clue of you. *Everywhere.* Finally, last night, when we still couldn't find you after a week, we called your mother. Igor felt... *I* felt that she deserved to know you were missing. *She* knew where we could find you. She told us where to go."

"Your mother has access to the data I pulled off the dagger," Markus said, running a hand through his hair. "She must have looked at the history of where you'd been and figured it out."

But the reminder of Inga and my mother's history triggered a memory of something the vampire had once said. "Was the fact that I'm part-wolf why you suggested to her that I should be killed?"

Inga blanched. "Geri, you were a child. I didn't know—"

"WAS IT?"

Neither shame nor my glare would let her deny any longer. "I knew the danger of your pedigree being discovered by the Ravens was too great. I worried that Vlad would find you, that he'd seize you and succeed in his quest for immortality. It wasn't *you* I suggested she kill, but the chance that the propensity of your kind to breed with wolves would allow you to become some kind of vampire superfood."

Inga grabbed a newspaper from a seat nearby and blocked the sunlight that streamed in as Caleb opened the door. As soon as he closed it, she lowered it, awaiting his report.

"Only one unaccounted for," the slayer said. "A slayer named Haim."

His name means life, I thought, tasting the bitter irony. *And now he's dead.*

Caleb continued, "All in all, a successful rescue. The captain also says he just got a message from Ayşe over the radio. They had sent a member of the pack along with Amy to protect her, just in case. She gave us that wolf's phone number. He'll escort her safely to wherever we want to meet her, though she also strongly suggested we get out of Istanbul before nightfall."

"It is essential that we do, for both our safety, and those of the slayers." Inga's dalliance with emotions ended as she turned to Markus, all business. "I can arrange a private plane for this afternoon. You said you knew a place we could take refuge. Where?"

My cousin shifted in place. "Schloss Wolfsretter, in Germany. It's far from any vampire clutches, deep in the Black Forest."

"Seriously?" I evil-eyed the hood across from me. "You think the matrons would agree to let the home of our archives, our high council, and our training facility be overrun by slayers?"

Markus coughed a laugh. "I'm not planning on asking for permission. We'll worry about their reaction once they have it. Until then, it's the right thing to do. Besides, it will be us soon, won't it? Neither one of us is stupid, Geri. Vlad was already running a de facto slayer-breeding program. Now that he knows the power of a wolf-hood hybrid, a—what was the word he used?"

"*Asenaic*," Inga supplied.

"Right, an *asenaic*," Markus resumed. "It's just the logical thing for him to do. He's going to take hoods, and he's going to make them breed with wolves, and then he's going to use the babies as Capri Suns."

I shook my head. "You're wrong."

"What?" Markus's face distorted, his brow furrowed. "Come on, seriously? It's like a recipe, he's just going to follow it."

"No, he's not." I stood, making my way to the door. "He won't have to. You don't seriously think I'm the only one, do you? After a dozen generations coming down from Gerwalta Faust and—" A curt smile bit across my face. "He doesn't even have a name in our history, does he? Gerwalta's mate? We just call him 'the wolf,' as though that's all he was. I guess immortalizing him as an animal lets us forget his humanity."

I would end that somehow. I'd reach back across time, and restore my ancestor's name and his dignity.

I shook my head. "I can't have been the only one. We're going to Schloss Wolfsretter? Fine, then we'll make good use of our time there. We'll turn the archives inside out. We'll dig through them until we discover the truth. And then, we'll work our way forward. We'll find them. We'll find them before he does."

My cousin had the good sense not to oppose me. "Absolutely."

The captain didn't know what we were or why we'd been fleeing from a mansion on the Bosporus at five in the morning. He just wanted to know that he'd be paid for his trouble. Inga made sure the lira flowed like the waters around us.

The summer sun warmed my skin as we passed under the bridge, and Alexandra, raising a hand to block the sunlight, stepped up beside me on the deck.

"You mustn't lose hope. We survived for decades after the world thought we were dead. He can survive a short time until we find a way to free him."

"I saw a fireplace come down on his head, Alex," I spat back. "Tobias was a wolf, but he was still mortal."

"I have seen the brave survive fates worse than death." The slayer wove an arm around me. "Forget your eyes, what does your heart tell you?"

"That I should stop falling in love with wolves." I thought of Cody, thousands of miles away, of his pretty wife, and their chubby little baby. "I'm sorry, I don't mean to be bitter. It's probably best not to talk to me right now."

She nodded, pulling back her hold. "When it is the right time, I will be here. And for what it's worth, so will Caleb."

Caleb. In all my grief, I'd never paused to think of his. "He might not be when he finds out I'm in love with another man."

"You put so little faith in others. It does not surprise me, when you've had so much practice not putting it in yourself."

I gripped the rail, shifting my weight as the boat bounced over the wake of a passing freighter. "I've never lacked faith in myself."

"Not in your ability as a hood, but in your ability to love and to act in the way love demands of you, I think that's not true." Her hand tapped my shoulder as she turned to go. "Stop trying to be what other people have told you you are. Start being who you *really are*."

Who I really was. But who was I?

I was a woman who had loved and lost twice. I was a hood who had been relinquished by her own mother, and somehow—though I still didn't know how—had found her way back to her birthright on her own. I was the namesake and scion of The Betrayer, who, in turn, had been betrayed and lied to by her own blood.

I was Gerwalta Kline: *asenaic*, mate to Tobias Somfield in my heart if not by deed, and I would win back my wolf and have my vengeance.

The red orb of the east burgeoned in its fullness, chasing away the last remnants of the night, and I accepted the road it lit before me.

And then, I threw back my head, and I howled.

Kendrai Meeks was deported from the American Midwest after graduating college, and held against her will since in California. She *really* hates sarcasm. She first published in 2011, and has since put out books in romance and science fiction. In 2017, she decided to return to her first love, urban fantasy. She is the founder of the Bay Area Allied Indie Authors group. She has also been a featured speaker on a number of conference and industry panels on topics ranging from Fanfiction, to Audiobooks, to Serialized Fiction. She is a world music devotee and loves to travel (just hates to fly – a conflict, for certain). She enjoys twisting the extant into the exceptional, often basing her work on historical themes or legendary folk tales and mythology.

Acknowledgments

To the pre-readers: who devote time with kindness, and suffer through enough typos to fill a book. Literally and literarily.

To Laura, who literally worked to the point of illness to edit this well into the night.

To my colleagues in the Pubnado Entertainment Group - a fine batch of indie authors. We are more than friends, we are family.

To the other members of the indie community who continue to guide and console. They know their names.

And now, a preview the Red Chronicles #4, *Rebellious…*

The sky cried openly, even if I could not.

More fall leaves rusted away by the day. I sat and stared out my third-floor window, as the eroding canvas of trees laid a carpet over the span of the village to the west, to a point where the earth swelled up from the valley floor. Beyond that, a mountain, one which seemed out of place with its stark cliff towering over the land below. Schloss Wolfsretter looked like building blocks arranged by a child at this distance: a rectangle, a cone, a few squares. In my mind's eye, however, I could see its marble entry way, the stone-floored council chambers with its antique throne and tapestries reveling of the glories of the House of Red past. I could envision myself running across the chess board of its inner bailey. Tasting hazelnut soup on my tongue and hearing the wind twist its lithe fingers up the cliff when I fell asleep at night, cloistered in the Grand Matron's residence at the top of the tower.

A few years ago, teenaged me had despised that place, saw it as a center for indoctrination that bred hate for the man I loved. Now, my heart ached for it, knowing that I might never walk its halls again. A werewolf hadn't set foot inside in half a century, as far as I knew. What sane wolf would? The ghosts of their ancestors may still haunt the corridors and passageways. If they were unlucky, they may join them.

The street beyond the walls of my mother's private villa away from the compound, RotHaus, glistened under the street lamp, a spotlight that stood achingly empty. Wishing to see Tobias's form fill in the shadow and stride toward my door was foolish on so many levels, not the least of which was that he had no idea this house existed. Even if he'd managed to escape the Ravens, how would he find me?

But he hadn't escaped. How did I know? I didn't. But in the quiet moments between waking and dreams, I felt his presence in a way that couldn't be explained by logic, sensed his desperation and loneliness. He was alive, but I didn't know why or for how much longer.

Amy walked up from behind, putting a hand on my shoulder. "They're going to say yes. They have to."

She'd confused my wistful street-staring for worry over the fate of the slayers. I couldn't blame her for it; it was where my thought *should* be. A month ago, we'd rescued the last members of a supernatural species thought to be extinct, from imprisonment by the very creatures they were meant to balance. If not for the Istanbul wolf pack, we'd never have made it out with our lives. Here, we were hardly safer than if we stood in the middle of the street, protected only so much as the Ravens feared venturing so closely to the center of the hood world. Our only hope was to get the Council of Matrons to accept the slayers as refugees.

Which should have been as easy as asking, but anything involving a single matron never was, let alone a dozen of them. Markus was the only righteous hood among us, the only one who could appeal to the council. But to do that, he needed an official invite. One we expected to come soon after he relayed a message to my mother that he'd returned from Turkey. One that never came.

"No, they don't." I wasn't being pessimistic; I was making a projection based on years of keen observation. "Hoods are very insular. Outside of dealing with wolves as much as they need to, they keep to themselves. It's like a cult."

Amy cocked a hip. "Then why send Markus to ask? Why don't we just keep running? All we're doing by sitting here is giving those vampire creeps a chance to catch up to us at as leisurely a pace as they want."

When I'd told my cousin I thought we were wasting time approaching the council, it wasn't simply because I felt defeated (which I did) or tired (which I was) or indifferent about what the hell they would decide to do (which I was earnestly trying to convince myself was true.) In the absence of slayers, there had been occasional appeals for help when a vampire got too big in his fangs for comfort, but only when another of his kind didn't solve the problem first. Now that the slayers were back, not extinct, and in need of consolation and protection? Great, but they wouldn't consider it their problem.

"We're here because this is our best hope of finding the slayers shelter," I said. "They need sanctuary, aid, resources. The women know how to use their power, but the men don't. Half of them can't even walk up the stairs without getting winded. They need rehabilitation, rest, and the money we were able to pool together is running out."

Amy, however, thrived on positivity. How could she not? She found a new boyfriend with the changing of the month, each time hopeful *he* was "the one" until the *homme du jour* proved a disappointment. That never ended the cycle though, one powered and buoyed by the fact that Amy always had faith in one time being *the* time.

The blonde crossed her arms over her chest. "Well, even if they do say no, so what? If the hoods won't help, we'll just find someone who will."

"Like who?" I pulled my brown hair, a rambled mess without definition, out of my face as I looked up. "The vampires certainly aren't going to do anything. Even if most of them are decent, none of them are going to take on the Ravens."

"The wolves then."

I scoffed. "Yeah, right, the wolves. Like that's going to happen, them going against the Matron Council and their Machiavellian edicts."

Amy sat down beside me. "We help ourselves, then."

"*We?*" I fixed my friend with a withering stare. "Amy, you're not a part of this. You're not a hood, not a wolf, and you certainly aren't a slayer. Your best bet would be getting the hell away from us and setting yourself up off the grid for a while. Unless you want to discuss the process for becoming a vampire, I'd watch how we use the term 'we.' This is a supe crisis, and you're just a tourist."

The blonde's blood boiled, reddening her cheeks and sending her shooting from the room. A stray impulse told me to jump up and chase her, apologize for being rude. The wiser part of me knew what I said had been the truth.

Caleb slipped into the door, because apparently no one trusted me to be on my own for too long. Great, yet another person with whom I had a complicated relationship coming to comfort/lecture me. I turned back to the window, but this time, not because I was looking desperately for any sign of Markus, but because I couldn't bring myself to look at the slayer who had confessed his love for me, asked me to marry him, then got cozy in the harem before my 'no' grew cold.

"You shouldn't be so rough on her, you know." He slipped his hands in his pockets, looking back over his shoulder in Amy's wake. "She's loyal, brave, compassionate, all things I'd take over mystical silver-wielding or sunlight-throwing powers any day of the week. Even if she does have the worldly concerns of a 1990s Teen Flick Drama Queen."

"She shouldn't be wasting time..." I cut off my inner bitch. "If Amy stays with me, I'm going to get her killed."

"What makes you think that?"

"The Ravens already tried to kill her once, and that was before I knocked one of them off and stole all their gourmet meals."

I didn't have to be a bitch though. I'd apologize later. Again.

"Right. Okay. So, anyways, I've been sent in here to kick your ass."

I raised an eyebrow. "Meaning?"

"Meaning... It's time to stop moping. It's been a month since Istanbul, and sitting around being sad isn't helping."

I spun in my seat, making no secret of my anger. "We're not sitting around being sad. Our best shot at defeating the Ravens is with the backing of the Matron Council. Your people are undertrained, underfed, and under some illusion that I can give them what they need. I'm just a twenty-two-year-old woman from a tiny village in Michigan, Caleb. I'm not capable of being a healer, a therapist, a trainer, or a general."

"And... what? You think as soon as the Matron Council bestows its magnanimity on the slayers, you're just going to pass us along and wipe your hands clean?"

My fists clenched so hard, I'd not be surprised to find I'd drawn blood. "I don't owe the slayers anything. In fact, it's just the opposite. I should have spent the last month hunting down the Ravens and rescuing Tobias. Instead, I'm stuck in the Black Forest, playing house frau."

"Bullshit. You might spend your nights here, away from everyone, but you're barely sleeping during the day. Amy says you spend hours when everyone else is asleep training yourself ragged in the basement."

"Of course, I am. I'm going up against a six-hundred-year-old vampire with a god complex and his four closest buddies. You don't overcome someone like that by knitting socks. Or should I just rush into where my mate is being held prisoner and wing it?"

"What makes you think Tobias is still alive?"

Anger crackled in my bones, an impulse to find something silver and push it into a weapon threatening to consume me. "What makes you think he's dead?"

BOOKS BY KENDRAI MEEKS
RED WORLD SERIES

RED CHRONCILES *
~CONTEMPORARY URBAN FANTASY~
REQUITED (PREQUEL)*
RELUCTANT*
RELINQUISHED*
RAVENING*
REBELLIOUS*
RIGHTEOUS*

RED ORIGINS
~HISTORICAL FANTASY~
BEAUTY & THE BETRAYER
THE WOLF & THE WATCHER
RED & THE RESTORER

VAMPIRE SOVEREIGNS
~PARANORMAL ROMANCE~
VENICE DUSK

ENTER THE KINGDOM
~FUTURISTIC SCIENCE FICTION~
COURT OF DISCONTENT (PREQUEL)*
FREEBIRD
MISTRESS OF CINDERS
ISLE OF AFTER

*ALSO AVAILABLE IN AUDIO